"Open up," Bredalbane said, leaning closer to the intercom in the opening. "I feel sick and want to lie down for a while."

A voice from below drifted through the intercom. "Is Leslie with you?"

Bredalbane stiffened from another stab from the Death Merchant's auto-pistol. "No. He's still on guard. Everything is quiet. I'll be fine if I can lie down for fifteen or twenty minutes."

"All right," the voice replied. "Just so one of you remains up there."

There was a slight creaking sound, and slowly the surfaced slab started to open, beginning with the left side edge. Light came from below, increasing in proportion with the width of the opening.

Camellion was about to put a Bio-Inoculator dart into the back of Bredalbane's neck when the man attempted the impossible by trying to shout a warning.

All he managed to yell was, "It's a—"

In another second, Bredalbane was dead, pieces of his face flying against the stones from the impact of the 9mm hot load bullet that Camellion had sent through the base of his skull.

Camellion went in so low and so fast that he practically fell down the short flight of well-worn stone steps. He wasn't sure, but he thought he saw someone in the far corner to his left. He didn't have time for a second look. . . .

# THE DEATH MERCHANT SERIES:

#39 in the incredible adventures of the
# DEATH MERCHANT
## THE FOURTH REICH
### by Joseph Rosenberger

PINNACLE BOOKS        LOS ANGELES

DEATH MERCHANT #39: THE FOURTH REICH

*Copyright © 1980 by Joseph Rosenberger*

An original Pinnacle Books edition, published for the first time anywhere.

First printing, June 1980

ISBN: 0-523-40703-3

Cover illustration by Dean Cate

*Printed in the United States of America*

PINNACLE BOOKS, INC.
2029 Century Park East
Los Angeles, California 90067

*This book is dedicated to*
*Chris McLoughlin*
*of Atlanta, Georgia*
*and to*
*W. L. Fieldhouse*
*of Salem, Ohio*

I know perfectly well, just as well as those tremendously clever intellectuals, that in the scientific sense there is no such thing as race. But you, as a farmer, and cattle breeder, cannot get your breeding successfully achieved without the conception of race. And I, as a politician, need a conception which will enable the order which has hitherto existed on historic bases to be abolished and an entirely new and anti-historic idea enforced and given an intellectual basis. With the conception of race, National Socialism will carry its revolution abroad and recast the world.

> Adolf Hitler—in a conversation with Hermann Rauschning, president of the Danzig Senate.

The true demonology of the twentieth century is the conception of "race." In the name of "race," millions have been butchered. In the name of "race," millions more will be murdered.

> Richard J. Camellion

# Chapter One

A jumble of thoughts jigging in his mind, Richard Camellion studied the farmhouse, the barn and other outbuildings and the ruins of the ancient abbey. Made of
stone, all the buildings were shrouded in deep shadows, except when the half-moon struggled out from behind low-
racing stratus clouds—the front of what promised to be a
June thunderstorm.

Lying flat on his stomach and looking out through crow-
berry bushes, the Death Merchant felt safe with the patch
of wood behind him. The larch and spruce trees afforded
excellent protection not only for himself but for Kingman
as well, and at 3:30 in the morning, it wasn't very likely
that anyone would come across Mel in the parked car. The
little coastal town of Leith was four and a half miles from
the farm, and its good citizens wouldn't be poking around
in the woods in the middle of the night.

Camellion's mouth became a tight line. *But it's more
than likely that if Boyd's farm is one of the outposts of the
Brotherhood in southern Scotland, and if Korsey is a prisoner there, guards will be posted and the area wired with
protective devices. From here on in, the going could get
rough.*

Whether or not Loren Korsey was actually being held a
prisoner at the farm was another matter. At 1:30 in the
afternoon of the previous day, Korsey had radioed to the
Safe house of the SIS, the Secret Intelligence Service—
the British CIA, in Edinburgh that he was scheduled
to meet Jackson Boyd at the man's farm, that he had
learned the arms and ammunition were stored "somewhere
beneath the ruins of the abbey," and that he would send
another report no later than midnight. The report had not
arrived. Backup SIS agents, who had used a Bumper Bee-
per transmitter to track Korsey to the farm, had reported

1

that Korsey had driven to the farm, but that he had never left the place.

Camellion had decided to move against the farm. Charles Phegley, the senior British SIS agent connected with the joint British/American operation, had been against the action, maintaining that Camellion was substituting assumptions for facts.

"We should wait for developments," Phegley had argued. "A wrong move at this time will alert the Brotherhood to our direct involvement."

The Death Merchant had almost laughed in the SIS agent's face. The Brotherhood of the 4th Reich was already aware that it was more than just under observation by some of the best intelligence agencies in the world—and for a very good reason! The Death Merchant, with the help of the *Bundesnachrichtendienst,* the Federal Intelligence Service of the Federal Republic of Germany, had not only killed the inventor of the Transmutationizer, a hellish device that could reduce a human being to a handful of ashes within a matter of minutes, but had also smashed the West German branch of the worldwide neo-Nazi organization.

Camellion had also pointed out to an angry Phegley that Loren Korsey was the only lead they had to the Brotherhood in Scotland; the only agent who had managed to penetrate the outer rim of the deadly movement.

"The faster we investigate the farm, the sooner we'll get to the truth," Camellion had told Phegley and the two other SIS agents. "It's not an 'assumption' that Korsey went to Jackson Boyd's farm, it's a fact. Fact two is that Korsey's car is still at the farm, hidden somewhere. Your own agents reported that the B-B transmitter is still working, but that the car is nowhere to be seen. To me that indicates that Korsey slipped up somewhere along the line. For all we know, he might even be dead."

Much to the annoyance of Phegley and the other British agents, Klaus Heinrich Hahn, one of the BND agents who had worked with the Death Merchant in West Germany, had agreed with Camellion. So had Felix Rheinecker, the second West German intelligence agent.

No lights burned in the single story farmhouse which Camellion judged to be 500 feet in front of him, to the west. Slowly he moved the Nite-Sight infrared viewer to the north, adjusted the f:1.6 lens and looked through the eyepiece. About 300 feet to the north of the farmhouse were the ruins of the abbey, the great stones of the single half-wrecked wall, hoary with age, many of the enormous blocks of limestone strangled in vines and thick with centuries of moss.

The abbey of the Black Friars had been sacked in 1559 and deserted since then. Over the years the hammer-beam roof of Fife oak had fallen in and slowly rotted away. Farmers had carted away many of the stones so that now only half of the south wall remained, the south wall, the foundations and the stone floor.

The Death Merchant lowered the Nite-Sight device, rolled over on his left side and took the Audio Counter-measures Service System from the canvas Gussett bag by his right hip.

*Korsey reported that arms and ammo are hidden beneath the ruins of the abbey. Unless they're buried, that means some kind of room. And I'll wager that's where they're holding Korsey—if they haven't already killed him! Damn, it's quiet. I can almost hear my toenails growing.*

Camellion screwed the ten-inch parabolic reflector to the end of the telescoping antenna, extended the antenna of the A.C.S.S. to its full length of eighteen inches, slipped the plug into his right ear, turned on the monitoring device and began the sweep, thinking of how the CIA office of Science & Technology must have labored to perfect the ultrasensitive acoustic verifier that could provide positive feedback identification of sound, plus verify any circuitry involved in the various kinds of alarm systems—microwave, infrared, capacitance proximity, etc. The A.C.S.S. was such a marvel of technology that one could not be misled by r.f. noises such as nearby broadcasting stations, neon starter switches, and other electrical interference. Broadbanded, the A.C.S.S. had full spectrum tuning, its feedback verification was such that the intrusion device could hear itself amplified; thus it formed a closed loop, the cycle repeating itself. Maximum range was 10.2 miles. Minimum range 110 feet.

The Death Merchant turned to the right and pointed the parabolic reflector due north. Instantly he heard the waves of the Firth of Forth breaking against the granite rocks of the rugged coastline a mile north of Leith. He then turned the reflector toward the farmhouse and tuned the range to 600 feet. He heard faint sounds, the sounds of heavy but steady breathing, and some snoring. Slowly he moved the

3

reflector over the outbuildings and at the same time calculated the various distances ahead of him. West of the woods was a small field of barley several hundred feet wide, the west side of the field was separated from the large farmyard by rough-hewn boards forming X's over knotty-knob posts.

Of the utmost importance to Camellion, as he continued to scan the area, was the absence of any hidden electronic alarms: Not once did the red light on the side panel of the A.C.S.S. blink a warning. Then, when the reflector was in line with the northwest corner of the abbey's south wall, Camellion detected the whispering. Carefully he listened. *Two men at least.*

He did some thinking. He could go in at an angle. Even so, he was still between 800 and 1,000 feet from where the men were talking. And suppose they moved while he was in the process of crossing the area? At least now he had proof that there was a high strangeness about the abbey ruins. Why else would guards be posted there? Actually there wasn't any problem. Either he could go to the ruins or he could go back to the car and drive back to Edinburgh with Mel Kingman.

*Well, let us pray!* He took the plug from his ear, removed the reflector, pushed down the antenna and returned the device and the reflector to their side of the Gussett bag. The Nite-Sight device followed.

The Death Merchant next checked the two Smith & Wesson M-59 autopistols resting in special shoulder holsters; each weapon was equipped with a silencer and contained 14 9mm Luger cartridges. The holsters, like the coveralls, were a dull black.

From a holster on his left hip, he pulled the Bio-Inoculator, the best dart gun in the world. Fired electrically by a mercury battery, the totally silent weapon contained twenty-two steel darts, each one coated with *Pavulon*, a variant of the South American plant toxin *Curare.*

The Death Merchant looked up at the sky. The clouds had thickened and soon the moon would be but a memory. In spite of the danger confronting him, Camellion had a comfortable feeling about what he was going to do. For a change, Momma Nature was on his side: the line of clouds would hide the moon for the next hour—*more than enough time.* And since he would be doing the job alone, he wouldn't have anyone else to worry about. Kingman? *He's*

4

*a natural-born killer and a ten-carat survivor. He could take care of himself in the middle of south Chicago!*

Alone—the perfect way to operate. In spite of all the preposterious rubbish about the human species being gregarious, an individual was born alone and died alone—*and if he has the sense God gives to retarded frogs, he'll realize that he lives alone.*

The moon disappeared behind the clouds and, with the Bio-Inoculator in his left hand, Camellion left the wood and started out across the barley field, moving in a northwest direction and automatically employing the *Ninja* art of stealth . . . keeping a low profile, making sure of where you put your feet, so that your weight will not cause twigs to snap, and doing it all with lightning speed.

There was some degree of danger, always the chance that one of the enemy might be scanning his way through a night sight infrared viewer. Not very probable, but very possible.

He crossed the barley field, got down by the wooden fence, listened for a moment, then gingerly tested the top plank—*as solid as one of the molars in the upper jaw of a hound dog.*

He eased himself over the fence, taking care that none of his equipment rattled or made any kind of noise. The trick now was to make sure that movements were absolutely silent. If his feet swished through the dew-wet foxtail grass, or he stumbled over a half-buried rock, the show would go off the road in one hell of a hurry.

He pulled the left Smith & Wesson from its shoulder holster, switched off the safety and crept forward in as low a posture as possible. Five minutes later, he reached his immediate destination: a dwarf willow 150 feet from the northwest corner of the abbey wall. His eyes had adjusted to the darkness and he worked quickly in assembling the three components of the A.C.S.S. He turned on the monitor, tuned the range to 150 feet and began the scan at the east end of the abbey wall. Only normal background sound. Not until the reflector was pointed toward the west end of the stone wall did he hear the muted conversation between the two guards, even catching a word now and then— "rain"—"tomorrow"—"we'll"—"I."

The Death Merchant smiled. *Rain or shine or come the end of the world, neither of you will see the dawn.*

He quickly disassembled the A.C.S.S., returned the parts

5

of the device to the bag and clipped the underneath side of the bag to a ring on his coveralls. He had moved the A.C.S.S. back and forth and was almost positive that the two men were six to eight feet from the west end of the wall.

Again he moved forward at an angle, all his senses on extra alert. He reached the end of the wall, paused a moment and listened intently. He grinned again. He could hear the voices of the two men—*they aren't far away. Six feet. Make it eight, since the wall is two feet thick. So let's get on with it.*

He stepped around the end of the wall, in that split second his eyes recording what lay before him—two men sitting on stones, one leaning back smoking a cigarette, the other hunched forward. What appeared to be automatic rifles were leaning against the wall.

Before the two men could absorb what was happening, Camellion put two darts from the Bio-Inoculator into the chest of Lester Knox, the Scot who was smoking a cigarette, the steel needles stabbing into him with the force of .22 caliber Magnum bullets.

Ian Bredalbane, on the verge of panic, tried to jerk a revolver from his belt and stand up. His right hand was around the butt of the Webley and, spinning around, he was halfway to his feet when the muzzle of the silencer attached to the 9mm pistol in Camellion's right hand almost broke off three of his front teeth.

"Freeze, or I'll blow your head all the way to Edinburgh," Camellion hissed. "Take out that gun with the thumb and forefinger of your left hand and place it on the ground. I said place it. Don't drop it."

In the half-darkness, Camellion could see fear on Bredalbane's bearded face—and astonishment at being confronted by an attacker wearing a life-like rubber mask that looked like Adolf Hitler!

His mouth half open, Bredalbane used his thumb and index finger to take the Webley from his belt. Camellion stepped back very quickly and watched him place the revolver on the stone floor. Just as swiftly Camellion moved behind the man and placed the muzzle of the 9mm pistol against the base of his skull.

"Where's the entrance to the room below and how do we get in?" Camellion demanded. "Don't lie and don't stall. Talk or die. The choice is yours."

6

"In that pile of stones," Bredalbane said nervously, his accent a typical Scottish "burr". He glanced in the direction of the large stone that, set together, resembled a gigantic cube, twelve feet high and twelve feet on all sides.

"Go on, laddie."

"You take a small stone from the wall on the other side," Bredalbane said. "An intercom is in the opening. You speak into the intercom and identify yourself. The door is opened from below."

"How many men are down there?"

"Two."

"Where is Loren Korsey?"

"I—I don't know anyone by that name."

But Bredalbane had paused slightly before answering. To Camellion that hesitation, plus the inflection of his voice, indicated that he was lying.

"What is your name?"

"Ian Bredalbane."

"And the dead man?"

"Lester Knox. Why?"

"You had better give your right name when you speak into the intercom," warned Camellion. "If it's the wrong name and that door doesn't open, you'll end up with your backbone shot out. And just in case they want to know what you want, tell them you're sick. Tell them anything. But that door had better open. If it doesn't, your life will close. Now move!"

With the Death Merchant right behind him, Bredalbane walked over to the "cube," went around to the center on the north side and, urged on by a jab from Camellion's M-59 Smith & Wesson, pulled out a stone that was at eye level. The stone was slightly larger than a brick.

Giving the Scot a savage reminder with another poke of the pistol, Camellion was quick to notice that the "door" was a slab of stone slightly smaller than the average door.

"Open up," Bredalbane said, leaning closer to the intercom in the opening. "I feel sick and want to lie down for a while."

A voice from below drifted through the intercom. "Is Leslie with you?"

Bredalbane stiffened from another stab from the Death Merchant's autopistol. "No. He's still on guard. Everything is quiet. I'll be fine if I can lie down for fifteen or twenty minutes."

7

"All right," the voice replied. "Just so one of you remains up there."

There was a slight creaking sound, and slowly the surface slab started to open, beginning with the left-side edge. Light came from below, increasing in proportion with the width of the opening.

Camellion was about to put a Bio-Inoculator dart into the back of Bredalbane's neck when the man attempted the impossible by trying to shout a warning.

All he managed to yell was, "It's a——"

In another second, Bredalbane was dead, pieces of his face flying against the stones from the impact of the 9mm "hot load" bullet that Camellion had sent through the base of his skull. The hollow nosed slug smacked against the wall, flattened out and, with a low whine, zinged upward as Camellion darted through the opening and the thick slab, three-fourths of the way open, began to close.

Camellion went in so low and so fast that he practically fell down the short flight of well-worn stone steps. It was fortunate for him that he had executed such a maneuver. Several machine guns roared and streams of projectiles passed over his head, some coming within inches of his scalp. The swarm of steel-jacketed death rocketed out the doorway and headed for the clouds.

It was years of training and years of experience in the field that saved Camellion's life. Trying to control his furious momentum, he caught a glimpse of two Primus propane lanterns hanging from the ceiling, and four startled faces. Three of the men were standing by a table. The fourth, his hand on the lever that controlled the door, was by the rear wall. The Death Merchant wasn't sure, but he thought he saw another figure in the far corner to his left. He didn't have time for a second look.

William Carwood and Malcolm Telford tried to sight in on Camellion with pistols. John MacDonald attempted to line up his Wz63 sub-gun on the darting figure. Angus Badennoch was trying to do the same thing with his Vz61 Skorpion machine pistol when Camellion, coming to the bottom of the steps, jerked himself to the right and opened fire with both the Bio-Inoculator and the 9-mm autoloader.

Two B-I darts struck MacDonald in the chest. MacDonald groaned, looked astonished and fell back, the Polish Wz63 vomiting a dozen 9mm slugs, most of which struck the stone ceiling.

Badennoch caught a 9mm Luger bullet high in the chest. The second high velocity slug gave him a second navel, several inches above the one God had given him. The final darkness draped over his brain before he even started to sag.

Billy Carwood succeeded in getting off one shot from his Bernardelli autopistol, the .380 ACP bullet tugging at the left side of Camellion's collar. Snorting like a bull, Carwood again tried to pull the trigger. But the silencer of the Death Merchant's Smith & Wesson popped faintly and so did Carwood's skull, when the 9mm bullet bored through the frontal bone and burst into his brain.

By now, Malcolm Telford had managed to close the door—for all the good it did him. He fired one shot from his Star pistol, the .45 slug missing Camellion by a foot. It was the last act Telford would ever perform. Camellion, darting inward and weaving as he made the rush, killed the Scot with a Luger slug that struck him in the left side of the chest and punched him to the wall. The next 9mm slug took a path through his left eye and splattered the rear wall with chips of bone and gray-white brain matter. With blood flowing out of the empty socket, Telford dropped to the floor.

"DON'T SHOOT! DON'T SHOOT! I'M KORSEY!" a voice cried weakly from the left rear corner.

Camellion lowered neither the Bio-Inoculator or the 9mm auto until he was close enough to see that the man was Loren Korsey, who was naked to the waist and tied to a heavy chair with ropes bound around his wrists and ankles. It was instantly evident to Camellion that the man had been the victim of an inhuman beating. His face was swollen, his right eye blackened and closed, his lips puffed. Ugly red-blue cigarette burns were hidious flowers of torture on his hairy chest.

"Whoever you are, you were an idiot to come here," mumbled Korsey. "We'll never get out of here alive. All that gunfire was heard at the house."

"We'll make it," Camellion said, "and if we don't, be thankful that you can only die once—*I'd hate to go through it twice!*" He pulled a razor-sharp Vindicator from its horizontal sheath across his stomach and started cutting the cords around Korsey's wrists and ankles.

"Did you tell them anything?" Camellion asked.

"Would I still be alive if I had?" snapped Korsey.

9

Camellion cut the last cord, shoved the Vindicator into its flat, black holster, and Korsey, a tall, rugged-looking man, got weakly to his feet. The Death Merchant was beginning to have a new respect for the man. Originally, his opinion of the man—whom he had never met until this morning—had been almost as low as the butt of a Wellington well-digger. The man was an "independent contractor," a per-assignment joker who worked for The Company. Camellion had never trusted such contract agents. Either they double-dealed and played both ends against the center, or fumbled like a third-string ballplayer entering the game for the first time. Apparently, Korsey was the exception.

Camellion picked up the Polish machine gun that John MacDonald had used, opened the magazine pouch on the dead man's belt and pulled out several extra magazines. It was then that he noticed that the "stones" of the north wall were imitation. The entire wall was a phony.

Korsey, picking up the Czech Vz61 Skorpion that hadn't helped Badennoch, noticed Camellion's hard glance at the wall and said, "Machine guns, grenades and ammunition are stored behind the fake wall—all commie stuff, like these babies." He patted the Skorpion. "Say, how the hell did you manage to get down here? God, what a mask!"

"Never mind," Camellion said. "We've got to get out of here. You work the lever. I'll go to the top of the stairs and hold the fort. We'll run for it; there isn't any other way. There's a car waiting for us on the side road."

Korsey didn't comment. A sharp operator, he knew that the man in the Hitler mask was pure disaster looking for a place to happen. He went over to the lever and waited until Camellion was at the top of the stone steps.

"Hold it," Camellion said. "Wait until I put out the lights."

He pulled one of the 9mm autopistols, the silencer popped twice and the low-ceiling room was plunged into darkness.

Slugs didn't heat up the chilly air toward the doorway, once the door was open. The Death Merchant could hear dogs barking and see that lights were on in the house. Four beams from flashlights were moving back and forth and up and down in back of the house.

A moment later, Korsey was by the Death Merchant's side and looking at the lights.

10

"We could pick them off easy, but we'd only reveal ourselves," he whispered. "I can't run too fast. I hurt too damned bad."

"You'll ache a lot worse if they catch us, and so will I," Camellion said. "You take the inner side of the wall. I'll take the side facing the house and meet you at the end."

Keeping low, in the manner of grave robbers, they darted to the wall. The Death Merchant changed his mind about moving along the outside when he saw that the beams from the flashlights were a hundred feet closer.

"Get going," he ordered a groaning Korsey. "I'll hold them off here and you can take it up when you reach the other end."

"Good idea." Korsey started off, stopping on the way to pick up the two Yugoslav 64B assault rifles leaning against the abbey wall.

To the side of the wall, the Death Merchant put down the Polish Wz63 and pulled the two 9mm Smith & Wesson autopistols. Unlike the Wz63 machine gun, the two handguns would not show any flashes of flame when they were fired. The fire flashes would be concealed by the silencers.

Camellion dropped flat and thumbed off the safety levers of the two automatics—*about now, the eyes of the goons should be accustomed to the darkness.*

An instant later, several Polish KbKg assault rifles opened fire, two streams of 7.62mm steel-cored slugs stinging into the stones at the end of the wall, the violent meeting between metal and limestone showering Camellion's head and back with dust and fragments.

*Uh huh. Their eyes have adjusted to the darkness!*

Coming up fast for the kill, barking and snarling, were four Doberman Pinschers.

*Poor dogs! I hate to waste them. They're only doing what they have been trained to do.*

Camellion didn't have to kill the animals. Korsey, reaching the east end of the abbey wall, cut loose with one of the 64B assault rifles, the sharp cracking of the short bursts shattering the quiet of the early morning.

Three of the Dobermans died without as much as a whimper, cut to pieces from Korsey's stream of 7.62mm projectiles. The fourth Doberman yelped pitifully from a 7.62mm bullet, jumped a foot, fell and lay still as four Scots, who had been popped by Camellion's projectiles, were knocked to the ground.

11

Kenneth Boyd, the younger brother of Jackson Boyd, the owner of the farm, fell to the grass screaming like a woman being raped by a poker. He had taken a 9mm through the belly and was unlucky enough to still be half-conscious. Another Scot had been killed instantly by a bullet that had stopped his heart. The third man was very lucky. He had been hit in the groin and was dying. But he didn't know it. Shock had switched off his consciousness. The fourth man had been struck high in the right leg. He lay curled on his side, cursing his luck and the pain, dying and not knowing it. The slug had severed the femoral artery and he was bleeding to death.

Eight other men dropped and flattened out in the foot-high foxtail grass, Robert Kerr whispering fiercely to Jackson Boyd, "One of them is using a silencer, damn his black soul to hell."

"How are we going to explain this disaster to Dunbeath?" Boyd whispered hoarsely.

The Death Merchant didn't linger. Taking advantage of the lull—the only firing now was from Korsey who was finishing off the magazine by raking the grass—Camellion rolled behind the side of the wall, got to his feet, sprinted to the east end and said to Korsey, "You act like the nickels and dimes of your days were spent on the use of automatic rifles. I hope you're as good at dashing across a field."

"I have nothing to lose but my life," Korsey said resignedly. He handed the second Yugoslav A–R to Camellion. "Where do I meet you, in case I do succeed in crossing the field?"

Camellion cocked the 64B automatic rifle. "A point in the woods directly in line with this end of the wall. Have you ever made a run like this before now?" Camellion glanced again toward the west, then swung around to face Korsey.

A smile twisted across the Englishman's swollen mouth. "I think, old chap, our SIS training is equal to the combat courses given at the Pickle Factory's Farm," Korsey using the English term for the CIA's training installation.

"Move it," Camellion growled, annoyed at the hint of smugness in Korsey's voice. "Don't get your zigs mixed up with your zags, and crawl under the fence, not over it."

He watched the man move off at an angle slightly to the

north of the wall and turned again toward the north, a deep suspicion growing in his mind. He first looked down the north side of the ancient wall, then leaned around the end and fired a short, raking burst along the south side, hoping to convince the members of the Brotherhood that both he and Korsey were still at the end of the wall. He didn't think he would succeed and he was right.

A hurricane of slugs came tearing in his direction, the storm of lead striking the south side of the wall toward the end and once more throwing chips and dust into the Death Merchant's face. Several slugs ricocheted so close to his face that if they had been razor blades he would have received a close shave—in a sense, he had! Another spitzer-shaped 7.62mm burned through the thick knot of the black ragg-knit Norway cap, jerking it back on his head.

After getting off another 12-round burst toward the southwest and west, Camellion drew back, turned and looked toward the fence and the field. Because of the darkness he could not be sure, yet felt that he had caught a brief glimpse of a figure dropping down close to the fence. If so, the man had to be Loren Korsey.

The firing from the enemy had stopped. A man with less know-how in survival might have tried to draw their firing by triggering off a short burst. Camellion knew better. He knew he had wasted enough precious time. Pure instinct warned him that the assassins of the Brotherhood were probably crawling through the grass, in an attempt to close in at the end of the wall from either side.

He put down the almost empty automatic rifle and drew both Smith & Wesson automatics which he had earlier filled with full clips. Should he make a dash across the yard, there would be no one to return the enemy's fire, in which case he would never live to reach the fence and Korsey would get a backful of slugs before he could get to the wood. *I'll just have to gig those frogs another way!*

An autopistol in each hand, he took a deep breath, stood up and began to race in a weaving course that took him slightly to his left. Far behind him KbKg assault rifles roared and projectiles started to hiss and thud, thud, thud all around him, some burning into the grass around his legs, others streaking close to his body. Once again a hard point 7.62mm tore through what remained of the knot on top of the Norway cap. A second solid base bullet bored through the Gussett bag. The bag jerked against the clip and the ring holding it down, there were several loud clangs, and the $2,600 Nite-Sight viewer and the $21,650 Audio Countermeasures Service System were instantly reduced to junk.

By this time, Camellion was forty feet east of the end of the wall—far enough for what he had in mind. He turned to the right, dove down into the grass and wriggled around toward the west while slugs slammed in all around him, making the grass twitch and jerk. One bullet was of such proximity that its impact tossed bits of grass, sweet clover, and dirt into his face.

However, he had seen what he had wanted to see: the fire flashes from the muzzles of the automatic weapons—six or seven. He could not be sure.

Aiming mentally, he fired four shots from each Smith & Wesson; his reward was a loud cry of pain. Very quickly he lowered the autopistols and began to wriggle back to a new position.

A fourth of a minute passed. He heard a loud scream a hundred or so feet to his left. Several more seconds and there was another cry and a wailing, "I'm h–hit!"

For an instant, Camellion was startled. What did he have—magic bullets? *And Korsey doesn't have a silencer!* The answer hit him with the force of an iron fist—*as plain as the nose on a warthog's face! It's that screwball Kingman! He's left the car and is in the action. He's using the silenced Heckler & Koch SMG.*

Camellion continued to slither back through the grass. But he stopped and hugged the ground the instant several enemy assault rifles up front began raking the area with wide, sweeping bursts—further proof that Kingman was firing from the wood. The Brotherhood was firing blindly, in an effort to find the silent gunner.

Wondering if Korsey had managed to reach the fence and cross the field, the Death Merchant got to his feet and raced the rest of the way to the fence. His lungs demanding oxygen, he dropped to the grass a few seconds ahead of another blast of bullets which passed over his body, some of them thudding into the posts and the crosspieces of the fence.

He rolled over on his back and slid underneath the fence, at the center where the two crossed boards formed the broad "x," and crawled to the north, to the first fence-post. Turning, he raised his head and looked west. There

14

was only silence and the darkness. Distant thunder rumbled in the northwest.

With the hope that Kingman wouldn't make a mistake and shoot him, Camellion took half a dozen deep breaths, shoved the Smith and Wesson autopistols into their shoulder holsters and secured the straps over the weapons. Then he jumped up and started the run-for-life across the barley field. He sprinted left, darted to the right, all the while racing at abrupt angles that made it impossible for anyone to zero in on him.

Not a single shot was fired behind him.

A streak of black-clad lightning, he reached the edge of the wood and almost crashed into the tall weeds, grass, and tangled shrubbery. Panting, he snuggled down into some kind of thick leafed bush with purple and pink flowers, turned to the west and figured he was fifty to seventy-five feet to the right—the north—of the abbey wall's east end.

He pulled one of the 9mm autopistols and waited. Kingman and Korsey couldn't have missed him running across the field. He would let them come to him.

Presently, he heard the undergrowth rustling, a short distance to the left.

"Camellion! Where in hell are you?"

The low, husky voice elonged to Melvin Kingman.

"Over here," Camellion answered. "Did Korsey make it across the field all right."

"Yeah, he's OK, but he wouldn't be if I hadn't been there with the H and K," said Kingman. On his hands and knees, he reached the Death Merchant and Camellion saw him grin. "And neither would you, so don't start clacking your tongue about my disobeying orders."

"Where's the H and K? I suppose Korsey has it and is watching across the field?"

"You got it, but I don't think they'll try to come across," laughed Kingman. "I know I wasted three of them. I think four.

Camellion listened to the thunder. Closer now. But it didn't matter. They'd reach the car before the sky opened up.

With the lights of the Subaru wagon still turned off, Kingman turned the blue and white vehicle onto the dirt road, switched on the lights and stepped on the gas, the expression on his face stern. Neither he nor Camellion had

15

expected the electrifying news that Korsey had just imparted to them. Jackson Boyd, never dreaming that Korsey would ever escape from the farm, had bragged of the lastest accomplishment of the world-wide Brotherhood. Several weeks earlier, neo-Nazi agents had stolen enough uranium from a nuclear power plant in France to build an atomic bomb that, when detonated, would have twice the power of the one dropped on Hiroshima toward the close of World War II. The A-bomb was to be assembled on one of the Greek islands in the Aegean Sea, then smuggled into Cairo, Egypt, where it would be detonated by remote control. The Brotherhood calculated that the terrible blast would be blamed on the Israelis and that world opinion would turn against tiny Israel.

To compound the brutal plot, phase two of the plan involved using three American-born Cubans in an attempt to assassinate the President of the United States. Whether or not the attempt succeeded was not important. Either way, the Brotherhood intended to make patsies of the three Cubans. If the American Secret Service didn't kill them, the Brotherhood would. If American gunmen, working for the Brotherhood, couldn't kill the Cubans before they were hauled off to jail, that wouldn't make any difference either. The hero of the three Cubans was Fidel Castro, and they thought they were being recruited into the Cuban intelligence service. It was precisely this information that the Secret Service would pull out of them—with drugs if necessary. The blame for the attempted murder—or murders—of the President would fall on the shoulders of Castro. And on the Russians!

They rode in silence, Kingman driving fast but carefully, Loren Korsey hunched down next to him, Camellion in back, taking off the black coveralls. By the time Kingman was toward the end of the dirt road and preparing to turn off onto the concrete highway that would take them the short distance back to Edinburgh, the Death Merchant was stuffing the coveralls and the rest of the equipment, including the disassembled Heckler & Koch submachine gun, into a special compartment underneath the rear seat. He braced himself as Kingman turned. After the turn was completed, he reached into the compartment and took out a black hat with a small brim, a Roman collar, and the type of pleated black bib worn by priests and ministers. He put on the hat,

16

placed the bib and collar on the newspaper and pushed down the back of the seat, closing the compartment. There was still danger. The police force of Leith was so inexperienced (with real hard-core crime) that the small force couldn't have found an elephant in a large closet. Nevertheless, one had to be prepared. Even dumb bobbies could get lucky.

Kingman, crusing along at 60 mph, revealed that he was also thinking of the possibility of trouble, saying, "In case we should be stopped, you can always tell them we're taking Korsey to a hospital in Edinburgh. With his face swollen and you in that garb of an Anglican priest, the cops would believe it."

"They had better," Camellion said, slipping his arms into the sleeves of a dark suit coat that had been on a hanger by the window, "or they're dead." He buttoned the coat over the Smith and Wesson autopistol tucked in his belt and carefully arranged the newspaper over the second pistol next to him on the seat.

"No, we will not kill innocent Scottish policemen," Korsey said in a firm voice. "In the first place, I don't think the police will stop us. They don't patrol this highway. In case they should halt us, I'll handle the situation." He turned and glanced at Camellion, who sat with arms folded, his odd blue eyes cold and staring.

Mel Kingman lashed out at Korsey with typical bluntness. "You dumb Limey! If they search this car, we'll all end up in jail! What do you think you're going to do—hypnotize them?"

"Not at all," Korsey said, gingerly rubbing his right jaw. "I'll tell them the truth. I'll inform them that I'm in reality an SIS agent and give them a certain number in Whitehall, in London, to prove it. Sorry I had to fool you chaps by pretending to be a contract agent for your CIA."

Kingman's eyes shot to the rearview mirror in search of Camellion.

"How does that grab you? We've rescued a goddamned double!"

"He practically admitted as much to me back at the farm," Camellion said calmly. "And I don't think your remark was a slip of the tongue, was it, Korsey."

"Phegley would have told you once we reached the safe house," admitted Korsey. "You were both on a need-to-know basis. I wasn't a double. Your center in the States knew I was SIS. Neither of you should feel distressed. I too am on a need-to-know status."

"Oh, sure!" sneered Kingman.

"I think he means the fact that none of us were told about the theft of uranium in France," the Death Merchant said. "The French couldn't hide a secret like that. The Company and SIS have sources in too many high places."

"Very perceptive, Mr. Camellion," Korsey said.

A few raindrops pelted the windshield.

# Chapter Two

Fanatics often succeed in their efforts because of their total self-confidence and logic-tight compartmented dedication. Sir Hugh Kilsyth MacLean, the Lord of Dunbeath, was so brimming over with both that he felt more than qualified to write *GOD'S WORD PROVES THE VALIDITY OF RACIAL HYBRIDITY,* a book that would prove why the Aryan race should rightfully rule the world. The book would also prove that the people of Scotland were also Aryans.

At the beginning of history, Scotland was inhabited by a people called Picts. When Roman enemies occupied England, the Picts and wandering bands of Gaels from Ireland kept them from entering Scotland. Obvious! The Picts and the Gaels were branches of the Germanic tribes that had sailed across the Channel hundreds of years before the birth of Christ. The fact that there was not one iota of honest evidence for this thesis did not bother Sir Hugh. Had not Rome been destroyed by the Aryan Germans? Of course! According to the warped logic of Sir Hugh, this was "proof" that the Picts and the Gaels were branches of the Germanic tribes. Why, the terrible Picts were such warriors that the Romans built a huge barrier called Hadrian's Wall across the island to keep the fierce Picts out of England.

During the Roman occupation of England, St. Ninian and other missionaries introduced Christianity to Scotland—a silly, masochistic religion started by a Jew, according to Sir Hugh. After the Romans had left the island, four separate kingdoms grew up in Scotland: the Picts; a Gaelic tribe from Ireland called Scots, who gave the country its name; the Britons; and the Anglo-Saxons—and even a moron knew that the Britons and the Anglo-Saxons were German in origin. Later invasions of Norsemen and Danes combined with the early settlers and mixed and intermarried to form the Scottish people of the present.

For two years Sir Hugh had labored on his "masterpiece," and would have had it completed had it not been for the numerous interruptions and the various setbacks, the latest of which was the incredible bungling at the farm of that idiot, Jackson Boyd.

Sir Hugh regarded his youngest son steadily. He was very proud of John-Percy, who was as dedicated to the cause of world Nazism as his two brothers.

"I am sure in my own mind that the Korsey fellow was either an American or a British agent," Sir Hugh said firmly. "I should say he was a part of the force that destroyed Maybach One on Baron von Hammerstein-Equord's estate in Berlin, six weeks ago."

John-Percy, a huskily built man in his middle thirties, slowly nodded in agreement. "Boyd reported that only two men rescued Korsey," he said nervously. "Those two and Korsey almost wiped out the entire force at the farm. Father, we must consider this a disaster. I know that the paper in Dunbeath will be full of the tragedy. The London papers won't be flown in until tomorrow.

Deep in thought, Sir Hugh tapped the speaking tube of the dictaphone. "It was Boyd's fault. His lack of intelligent security is responsible. We shall punish him for his stupidity later. Our immediate problem is dealing with the people who have interferred with our Master Plan."

Dirck Van Memling, the fourth man sitting around the huge fireplace in the great hall of the MacLean ancestral home, said in a low, even voice, "Part of the problem must involve the probability that SIS and the CIA will——"

"Don't forget the West German BND," interrupted Gilbert Drummond, who acted as Lord MacLean's secretary and personal bodyguard.

"Very well, the BND," Van Memling said with annoyance, giving the tank-like Drummond a hard look. "The point, Lord MacLean, is that the various intelligence agencies involved will link you with the Brotherhood. Your support of Hitler during the last war is well known to Whitehall, and the old timers of Dunbeath still are not too fond of you and your family, even if you do control this area."

Sir Hugh turned his head slightly and smiled. "Don't you think I considered that possibility when I organized the Brotherhood of the Third Reich three years ago? There isn't any evidence to connect the MacLean family with the Brotherhood. None whatsoever."

"There is Jackson Boyd and his best friend, Robert Kerr," John-Percy said cynically. "It's true, he can't name any of us. He and Kerr only know that they are working for someone in Dunbeath." He turned and looked speculatively at his father. "It's reasonable to assume that they have considered us MacLeans. We own the mills and most of the land. Certainly that is more than ample for SIS to suspect us, Father."

"Only if Boyd or Kerr should reveal what they know," Sir Hugh said confidently. "They won't. They realize what would happen to them if they did. And there isn't too much danger that the British Secret Intelligence Service will put any kind of pressure on them. SIS doesn't dare. To do so would expose its hand to the world press. To be sure, more than half a dozen murders will rock the British Isles. However, our contingency plan to blame the killings on the IRA will be believed by the general public, if not SIS. The IRA is hated in England and not too well thought of in Scotland."

Van Memling, sitting in the same kind of chair as the three other men, one that was massive and well padded, made no attempt to curb the irritation in his voice. "British Intelligence will not believe that the IRA shot a group of farmers, just at random. I don't care how well Boyd and Kerr might convince the press and the local police, SIS will never believe such a concoction of lies." He stared at the flames flickering in the enormous fireplace. "It will be you, Sir Hugh—the Lord of the MacLean estates—whom the British will suspect, and don't expect SIS to use conventional methods in its investigations. Don't expect its agents to come here to your home to question you. No, my Scottish friend, its methods will be far more subtle."

"My dear Van Memling, the prime factor is that they will never be able to prove anything," Sir Hugh said. "Evidence! Proof! Those are the key elements, and they do not exist for British Intelligence." He suddenly tilted back his head, a pleased expression on his face. "Please be quiet, all of you. I have thought of something to include in my book."

Sir Hugh turned on the dictaphone. He lifted the tube on its flexible wire and began speaking into it.

John-Percy MacLean, sitting between his father and

21

Dirck Van Memling, glanced furtively at the Belgian whom he feared and disliked. A humorless man, Van Memling had thick gray hair, gray-green eyes and was in his late sixties, two or three years younger than Sir Hugh. Always dressed neatly in dark suits, he had permitted a slight paunch to invade his waistline, although he carried it well on his tall frame.

John-Percy didn't actually know who Van Memling was. He did know that the man was far more than a textile buyer. Van Memling came to Dunbeath Hall every three or four months. Ordinary textile buyers would not be guests at his father's home, nor would they verge on openly insulting Sir Hugh as Van Memling often did. The puzzling part was that Sir Hugh didn't seem to mind Van Memling's contemptuous comments, much to the chagrin of John-Percy and his two older brothers, as well as close associates of Sir Hugh who were members of the Brotherhood.

Two years earlier, John-Percy and his brothers had asked their father for some explanation regarding this domineering Belgian, all three expecting their father to lose the temper for which he was famous. Sir Hugh had remained calm.

"Don't concern yourselves with Mr. Van Memling," he had said. "He is a very important man and is absolutely necessary to our cause, to our revival of Nazism. Never question me again about him."

Nigel MacLean, the eldest son and the president of Mac-Lean Fabrics, Ltd., had quietly checked the shipments that Van Memling always ordered on his visits to the mills at Dunbeath. The bolts of woolens always went to the firm of Albert Plage & Sons in Brussels, one of the oldest and most respected wholesalers in Belgium.

Privately, the three sons suspected that it was Dirck Van Memling who was supplying the bulk of the money needed to carry on the underground activities of the Brotherhood. Sir Hugh was a wealthy man, but his entire fortune would not have kept the Brotherhood going for six months, not even with bribes. Why the A-bomb and assassination plot was costing 100-million pounds!

If Van Memling was supplying the money, where was he getting it?

Long ago, John-Percy had made up his mind that his father knew best. His predictions—like Hitler's—were uncanny. The Communists in the Soviet Union *were* making vast strides in their attempt to take over the world. NATO forces in Europe *couldn't* last two days against a Soviet invasion. The Middle East and Western oil supplies *were* encircled by Soviet Forces. The United States Government *had* proven itself to be a government of weak, unrealistic fools by giving away the Panama Canal to a dictator whom Fidel Castro counted as one of his best friends. Central America was being taken over by Communist revolutionaries. The Caribbean Sea was becoming the Red Sea. The United States *was* appeasing the Soviet Union.

John-Percy became interested in what his father was dictating. . . .

"There is no greater sin than trying to merge one's seed with the negro and abandon one's identity. God says, *'I had planted thee a noble vine, wholly a right seed: how then art thou turned into the degenerate plant of a strange vine unto me. For though thou wash thee with nitre, and take thee much soap, yet thine iniquity is marked before me.'* God laments, *'Mine heritage is unto me as a speckled bird.'* Again he speaks to white people, *'What hath my beloved to do in mine house, seeing she hath wrought lewdness with many, and the holy flesh is passed from thee, when thou doest evil, then thou rejoicest?'*

"Losing a child to death is painful enough, but when a parent loses his genetic seed through race-mixing, there is nothing that can ever change that seed into becoming racially pure. God says that mixed seed will never be renowned. That is, it will not be resurrected to enjoy eternity with the rest of the pure white race. Can there be any sin more damning than this?

"I shall prove that——"

"Enough of this nonsense! I don't have time to sit around here and listen to you dictate!" Van Memling's voice was sharp as he cut off Sir Hugh. He stopped staring at the fire and swung around quickly to face Sir Hugh, who was switching off the dictaphone, and John-Percy and Gilbert whose angry expressions revealed their true feelings.

"All of you seem to have forgotten the danger involved in assembling the bomb and smuggling it into Cairo," Van Memling said angrily. "There is equal danger in eliminating the American President."

Sir Hugh folded his hands in his lap and hunched down in the chair. "The uranium is no longer in France," he said, an edge of annoyance to his heavy voice. "It is on its way to the island, and I foresee no difficulties in assembling the bomb on schedule. I suggest you cease your senseless worrying."

"The killing of the American President will be far more difficult than getting the bomb into Egypt and exploding it from Greece," John-Percy said in a tight voice, shifting his weight in the chair. "The American President is well guarded, and even the experts in our employ, those Mafia gangsters, are finding it difficult to set up a cross-fire that will eliminate the Cubans after their mission is accomplished."

Added Gilbert Drummond in a voice that did not match his mammoth body, "The American President is always on the move, making his ridiculous re-election speeches. Or have you forgotten that the Americans will elect a new President this year?"

"I haven't forgotten!" Van Memling gave a sinister little laugh. "I can't say the same for any of you and your security methods. Jackson Boyd knows about the plan, does he not?"

John-Percy and Sir Hugh started to speak at the same time. John-Percy deferred to his father.

"It was a most unfortunate accident that Boyd learned of our master plan," explained Sir Hugh, who was nervous for the first time. He turned his eyes from Dirck Van Memling. "I told you how Boyd learned of the plan."

"Yes, you did—six months ago!" snapped Van Memling. "And your choice of a courier leaves much to be desired. Sending a man who couldn't hold his liquor is inexcusable. However, it does prove that Jackson Boyd is a man who can be trusted, at least up to a point."

"It was my brother Nigel who selected Jason MacMoran," John-Percy said defensively. "I admit his choice was a poor one. Yet I still maintain that neither Boyd nor Kerr will talk, no matter what kind of pressure is applied to them. They are loyal. I suggest we quit kicking a dead horse."

Remembering how the contents of the master plan had been leaked to Boyd by MacMoran, John-Percy felt guilty, and he looked away from Van Memling's piercing eyes. But he was right. MacMoran should never have been sent.

A MacLean Fabrics, Ltd. plane was to have flown Mac-Moran to London. From London he was to have flown to Paris where he would contact one of Van Memling's agents. The plane from Dunbeath was scheduled to stop at Edinburgh, to pick up another member of the Brotherhood who would also go to London, his final destination being Athens, Greece. What had happened was that, on the flight from Dunbeath to Edinburgh, MacMoran had nipped at a bottle of gin. By the time the plane had landed at Edinburgh, MacMoran was too drunk to continue. Fortunately, self-preservation forced itself to the surface of his gin-soaked mind and warned him that he should not continue and should get to safety. The only safe place in the area was Jackson Boyd's farm outside of Leith.

The disgusted pilot and the second man had flown on to London. MacMoran—lucky not to have been arrested for public drunkenness—had hired a taxi and gone to Boyd's farm. There, worried about how he would excuse his behavior to his contact in Dunbeath, he had proceeded to get drunker, take Boyd into his confidence and inform him of the plan to explode an A-bomb in Cairo and to assassinate the American President. The astonished Boyd had quickly informed his contact in Edinburgh. The Edinburgh station had instantly alerted Dunbeath.

A sleeping MacMoran had received a bullet in the head that same night!

Dirck Van Memling said in an accusatory tone, his voice rising in anger as he talked, "If that swine MacMoran had known for whom he was really working, no doubt he would have named you MacLeans to Boyd. Gentlemen, it was a masterpiece of bungling on your part. Now, this same Jackson Boyd and his best friend and one other man—what is his name?"

"Irwin Masterson," supplied Sir Hugh.

"These three men are the center of attention and being questioned at this very moment by the police, and since the IRA is supposed to have done the killing, IRA will have every right to question them also." His eyes jumped to Sir Hugh MacLean. "Yet you sit there and tell me that Boyd and Kerr will not crack! What assurance do we have that Masterson won't crack under the pressure and reveal that he and the other two, as well as the dead men, are members of the Brotherhood? Why, you pull anything out of the human mind with drugs!" Van Memling paused, then finished in bitter anger. "Amateurs! You're all amateurs!"

John-Percy reddened. Enraged at Van Memling's harsh words, Drummond drew back, fury in his eyes. Only Sir

Hugh remained calm, a thin, ironic smile on his pale lips.

"I think you will admit, Mr. Van Memling, that the Brotherhood has had its share of successes. As far as we can ascertain, none of the intelligence services are aware of the secrets we have stolen from NATO; and we have succeeded in assassinating thirteen people with the Transmutationizer. Seven of those were vital to our plans. The other six—all unimportant people—were killed merely to confuse the authorities of the nations in which they died."

"Naturally, your scheme was brilliant," sneered Van Memling, placing his hands on the large arms of the chair and leaning forward, movements that made it seem he was about to spring. "The end result was that you lost not only the Transmutationizer but its inventor as well. The Transmutationizer gave us the edge, but its secret died with Professor Koerber."

"The Transmutationizer is not necessary to the building and detonation of the bomb!" Sir Hugh shook a finger at Van Memling and faced him squarely, a steely toughness in his voice. "Stop being so pessimistic. While you are dwelling on our failures, consider our successes also. We have lost some battles, but certainly not the war. The Arabs are emotional and prone to violence. We know how they will react against the Jews when Cairo is vaporized."

"Only the Arabians have nuclear weapons," Van Memling said cautiously. "And Arabia is one nation where you haven't been able to place agents."

"It doesn't matter. The United States can't let Israel fall. American banks have too much money invested in that country. In an all-out war, the Americans will have to aid the Israelis. For that reason, I have decided that the bomb is more important than the killing of that fool in America."

Van Memling stiffened ever so slightly and peered closely at the Scottish nobleman. "What are you suggesting?"

"Simply that it may not be possible to coincide the assassination of the American President with out explosion of the bomb in Cairo. I don't want to divide our forces and efforts of concentration. Our full attention must be placed on the bomb and in outwitting the enemy close to us."

"For a change we're in agreement," Van Memling said. "I have always insisted that your scheme to kill the President of the United States was too dangerous and not worth the effort. One reason is the timing. Another is that the

Central Intelligence Agency has many contacts within the Mafia operating in the United States. However, I must insist on one thing: Security here in Scotland must be tightened."

"None of our records are in this area," Sir Hugh said quickly. "They're all on Skye, in the installation there."

"Get to the point, Van Memling," John-Percy said evenly.

"Jackson Boyd and Robert Kerr must be eliminated. I want those two killed as quickly as possible. We can't risk their revealing anything."

Sir Hugh shrugged. Whether Boyd and Kerr lived or died was of no importance to him.

"Do you actually believe killing them is necessary?" John-Percy asked, somewhat hesitantly.

"A corpse cannot talk, and it cannot be tortured," Van Memling said flatly.

# Chapter Three

To the loyal Scot, Edinburgh is not only the ancient capital and the second largest city in today's Scotland, but it is also the Valhalla and the civic essence of the brawny north counties of Great Britain. "Auld Reekie" the Scots call Edinburgh—and they will tell a visitor with pride that Auld Reekie is the seat of Scottish royalty and the very center of the chief events of the bloody drama of Scottish history.

Edinburgh is old, beautiful, and crammed with the ghosts of an unforgotten past. Only the most stolid visitor will fail to respond to the broad, handsome sweep of Princes Street and its gardens, beyond which is the thrilling vista of Castle Rock, dominated by the ramparts of Edinburgh Castle.

Like all cities, Edinburgh has sections that visitors never see. Morrison Street (which became Bread Street after it intersected Lothan Road) was in a rundown section of the city. At number 1434, toward the center of the block, there was a sign close to the sidewalk, in front of a two-story house. The sign was painted white and mounted on an iron pole. The black lettering read: *David Brunanburh. Treatment by Methods of Swedish Massage.*

The picket fence needed a coat of paint. So did the house. Yet a coat of paint would have made house and fence appear ostentatious. All the other houses were just as drab in the shabby neighborhood. A flagstone walk led to five steps. Beyond the steps was the front porch and the front door. The door opened to a hall, to the left of which was a reception area and the room where Brunanburh took care of the aches and pains of his patients. The big bearded, friendly man with the miracle hands (he was more adept at curing bursitis and fibrositis than some doctors) was also a ham radio operator. Everyone in the neighborhood knew that was why there was a hi-gain antenna stretched from a tall pole-pipe on the roof to an even

28

taller pole, with numerous guy wires, in the backyard. Brunanburh even had a short wave set in his massage room and a speaker in the reception area where his numerous patients could listen in on programs from the Voice of America.

In the hall, to the right, was the flight of stairs by which one reached the second floor. Here the British Secret Intelligence Service had its station—one enormous sound-proofed room that, four years earlier, had been four small bedrooms.

There were several filing cabinets against one wall; next to them was a table filled with short wave equipment. Against the opposite wall were four gray metal cabinets that contained tools of the trade: bugging equipment; plastic explosives and various types of detonators; cameras and weapons. In one corner was a four-burner hot plate, a cabinet filled with canned food, a sink, and a refrigerator. On another table against the wall, was a H-160 Sanno computer and a computerized weather station. On the floor, at one end of the table, was an electronic air cleaner. Several tables, a long, low vinyl couch and numerous vinyl easy chairs were scattered about on the linoleum floor.

Heavy rust-colored drapes covered the front and the rear windows. Three banks of fluorescent lights, three tubes in each fixture, hung suspended from the ceiling, while in the center of the ceiling an exhaust fan pulled cigarette smoke and other fumes from the room.

"Mr. Victor Hopmeir"—Richard J. Camellion—sat on the couch sipping at a cup of tea and eating dried figs. Next to him sat Klaus Hahn and Rudolf Gertenshalger, the two BND agents from West Germany.

Arnold Steel, the CIA liaison between Edinburgh and the American Embassy in London, sat hunched in an easy chair, studying his notes.

Ronald Lynch and Martin Shevlin, the two SIS agents, sat at one of the tables, Lynch toying with a deck of cards, Shevlin studying a map of northern Scotland and marking off distances with a divider.

Melvin Kingman sat at another table, cleaning a pair of Coonan .357 Magnum autoloaders.

"Mrs." Catherine "Kingman"—Catherine Griffin—the only woman in the big room, reclined in one of the easy chairs, her attention focused on the crossword puzzle she was working.

The ninth man in the room was Charles Phegley, the senior SIS agent. He stood by the hot plate, making a cup of tea. Tall, thin, narrow-shouldered and sharp-featured, the career SIS officer had worked with Americans on other occasions, but some of the members of this present group reminded him of the American films he had seen about gangsters in Chicago. Steel was a decent enough chap, cultured and scholarly; and the woman, who was posing as Richard Camellion's daughter, was sensible and highly educated, even is she didn't wear a bra and didn't mind that the nipples of her ample breasts were usually outlined against the often thin blouses she wore. She did have a natural beauty and an unaffected warm personality. Phegley often wondered why she had joined the "assassination agency," the phrase that SIS men used among themselves to describe the American Central Intelligence Agency.

Phegley thoughtfully placed two lumps of sugar in the cup and stole a glance at Richard Camellion and Melvin Kingman whom he considered extremely competent killers. To Phegley, the paradox was that both men were also extremely intelligent.

The muscular Kingman had a degree in electronic engineering, wrote science fiction paperback novels for American publishers in his spare time, and knew more about the British poets of the Romantic Period than an Oxford professor of literature. Half-drunk, which was frequent, he would quote entire passages of Byron's Childe Harold, or poems by Keats or Shelley, Blake or Coleridge.

He was also a chronic complainer. The suite of rooms he shared with Camellion—his "father"—and Catherine Griffin—his "wife"—at the Braid Hills Hotel was "too cramped." He even had the procacity to complain about the texture of the toilet paper in the water closet of the Morrison Street Station, maintaining its texture was too coarse.

And he was a racist who disliked American blacks, American Indians, and Mexican nationals. The only group he damned more was the American government, muttering often about ". . . liberal idiots who have reduced the average American to a second class citizen . . . a damned nation ruled by aliens and minority groups!"

Strangely enough—and unlike Phegley—he respected the

30

Jewish minority in America, saying, "They're the only people who have the guts and determination to get an education at all costs!" He respected the Israelis as well. "Sure, they're responsible for the American people paying four hundred percent more for gasoline, but man! Look how they've conned those fools in D.C."

The lanky, hard-muscled Camellion was even more of an enigma. He spoke any number of languages and knew more than just a smattering about any number of subjects, including philosophy, theology and other disciplines in the Humanities.

Stiring automatically, Phegley stared into the cup and thought of a discussion he had had with Camellion on, of all things, mystics and mysticism. Camellion had even included the psychoanalytic basis for such experiences—"This sort of preternormal experience would seem to be the redirection of the libido into the religious sentiment."

Equally as astonishing to Phegley was Richard Camellion's manner of speech and his choice of phraseology. At times, his rhetoric was that of a college professor. Other times, he used American slang and street vulgarisms.

Many of his remarks were puzzling—"I respect God too much to be religious." Death was his "little brother."

Phegley picked up the cup and walked toward the easy chair facing the couch. It was glaringly obvious that Richard Camellion was a supreme master in the art of disguise. Sitting there on the couch, he appeared to be an elegant man of almost 70, a stooped man with a thin straight nose, wavy silver hair, and a small, pale-lipped mouth.

The SIS officer wondered what Richard Camellion looked like, then recalled what Courtland Grojean had told him about the man: *Don't get the idea that he's paranoid. He's depressed a lot, which is in our favor. As your own British psychologists will tell you, partially depressed people are more realistic in their self-perceptions than are non-depressed people. Depressed people see their abilities more accurately. Camellion will get the job done. But he'll probably blow up Buckingham Palace doing it!*

Listening to Camellion and Klaus Hahn discuss firearms and sitting down in the easy chair, Phegley privately admitted that the sinister Grojean had not overemphasized Camellion's ability. He had almost single-handedly rescued Loren Korsey, in what Korsey had described as an "incredible action."

31

*Little wonder he called "Death" his "little brother"!* Phegley sipped the tea. Another realization jumped into his mind: *He's a man who seeks to control the lives of people around him. And he's an expert in killing. There is only one man in the world with all those qualifications—the Death Merchant.*

Phegley lowered the cup, placed it on the saucer he was holding in his lap and became attentive to what Camellion was saying.

"Despite all the things you've read and heard, law officers in the United States are not about to shift to the auto-pistol. The autoloader is still a small drop in a tremendous sea of double-action revolvers. Over here across the pond, it's just the opposite, with revolvers being as rare as horns on a mule. But you Europeans don't have the crime we have in the States."

"Yeah, I'll second that." Kingman shoved one of the Coonan .357 Magnums into a shoulder holster. "A 158-grain .38 Special has probably killed more men in the U.S. than any other cartridge besides the .22 rimfire."

Hahn glanced from Kingman to Camellion and thought for a moment.

Nice looking and a few years this side of 40, he had the appearance of a man who did a lot of exercising and who was always calm and very sure of himself.

Another natural-born killer! thought Phegley.

"You admit that America has a lot of violent crimes," Hahn said to Camellion. "Yet you are opposed to Washington taking handguns from American citizens. I find your view contradictory."

"It seems that way to you because you're a European and don't understand the situation," Camellion said. "We have judges in the U.S. turning loose stone killers, or else placing them for a year or two in lollipop factories. Some have been declared 'sane' in as little as six months and set free to murder again."

"Excuse me! What is this 'lollipop factories' you speak of?" asked the heavy-faced Rudolf Gertenshalger. Not yet 35 years old, he had bland features, wore his hair long, and usually took his cue from Hahn. His pale gray eyes were constantly on the move, constantly on guard.

"A mental institution," Camellion supplied. "Europeans in general don't realize that the anti-gun people in the U.S. are liberals who refuse to admit that crime is due to moral decay. They don't dare admit it. If they did, they would have to admit that it's their lenient policy toward crime and criminals that is partially responsible for the soaring crime-rate. An admission of truth would also deviate them from their left-wing purpose of disarming the American people. So they shift the blame for crime to guns and to people who own guns."

"You sound very positive." Hahn said.

"I sound that way because I am. You always have to blame some group. Hitler blamed the Jews. Lenin placed the blame on intellectuals and the middle class. The liberals, left-wingers, and just plain fools blame crime in the U.S. on people who own handguns. The facts prove otherwise. FBI statistics for 1977 show 19,120 deaths from murder and criminal manslaughter. Handguns were used in 48 percent of the cases. This figures out to be 9,178 handguns. But there are over 50-million privately owned handguns in circulation in the United States. On this basis, the guns used to kill in 1977 represent only 183/10,000ths of only one percent of that 50-million figure. Or, we can say that 99.999817 percent were not involved in any kind of crime. But the anti-gun people don't dare give out these figures, which clearly prove that handguns are not the cause of crime."

Hahn and Gertenshalger, realizing they were both verbally outgunned, didn't know what to say. Catherine Griffin did.

"Sacrificing freedom is never an answer to social ills," she said evenly, looking up from her crossword puzzle. "The anti-gunners would have us Americans give up the most effective means of self-defense and have us down on our knees praying that the police will arrive in time to save us from the violent criminal.

Ronald Lynch, the chain-smoking SIS agent, ventured his opinion, "It would seem to me that there should be another answer. Guns can only kill. That's their sole purpose, other than target practice."

"Another idiot heard from!" Kingman sighed. He pulled back the slide of the second Coonan .357, thumbed on the safety and shoved the weapon into a right shoulder holster.

Lynch reddened, put down the cards, and drew up straight in the chair. Martin Shevlin looked surprised, put down the dividers, and frowned angrily at Mel Kingman.

"Now see here, I don't have to take those insults,"

Lynch said sharply. "I have a right to my opinion. I demand an apology, you—you damned bloody assassin!"

"I didn't say you didn't have a right to your opinion, old boy." Kingman capped the oil can. "I just said you were an idiot, or you'd know that a pistol or revolver is the only weapon that makes the old and weak, the woman and the already injured capable of dealing out death to an attacker. The gun is remote control protection. It's easy to learn to shoot adequately. This makes the gun manageable. No other system of self-defense has ever approached this combination for effectiveness, nor has one ever approached the biggest factor of all in favor of the armed citizen who knows how to use a weapon—deterrent effect."

Kingman turned and looked at Lynch with hard eyes. "Go to prisons and rape-crisis centers right here in Great Britain. Talk to people who've experienced violence firsthand. The cons will tell you how they fear a handgun, and most women will tell you damn fast they wish they had had a gun when they were assaulted. Apology? Go to hell."

"Gentlemen! That is quite enough. We can't have this common type of bickering." Charles Phegley hoped no one noticed how his hands shook around the cup and saucer as he stood up and, with his eyes, warned an enraged Ronald Lynch, who had knotted his hands into fists and seemed to be on the verge of springing at Mel Kingman. Lynch, staring at Kingman, relaxed, turned to an embarrassed Shevlin and picked up the deck of cards.

Phegley, still standing, turned to Camellion, who had taken a box of dried figs from one of the inside pockets of his coat, draped over the couch's arm to his right, and was removing the cellophane from the box.

"I can't permit such rudeness, Mr. Hopmeir," Phegley said crisply. You must learn to control the people of your group. As for this incident, I feel that an apology on Mr. Kingman's part would be in order. I should not want to have to make a report of misbehavior to your superior."

The Death Merchant dug into the box, took out a fig and looked at Phegley who, with his graying beard, neatly trimmed, and finely chiseled features, almost reminded him of some El Greco walking on the edge of ecstasy.

"I agree with you. Lynch isn't an idiot anymore than Kingman is a damned bloody assassin. But I'm not about to tell anyone to apologize. Whether he does or doesn't is his decision."

34

It was Arnold Steele who saved Phegley from a situation that threatened to become even more demoralizing. "Mr. Shevlin, have you figured out those distances?" he asked in a matter of fact tone. "We have to know every inch of the highway before we can construct any logical frame of reference. Isn't that so, Mr. Hopmeir?"

"The time factor is not all that important," replied Camellion, looking at Phegley who had sat back down and was sipping tea. "If you're right about Sir Hugh MacLean, if he is connected with the Brotherhood, he will be expecting us."

"Boyd and Kerr and those two constables didn't blow themselves up in the car last night," Kingman said laconically. "I'd say somebody's been alerted."

Martin Shevlin put down the dividers. "We'll be taking the plane from Edinburgh to Inverness. That will be only a short hop. I estimate the driving distance from Inverness to Dunbeath to be slightly under two hundred miles, merely a good day's drive."

"We can only base our conclusions on the evidence," Phegley said sourly to Camellion. "Sir MacLean's love of Nazism goes all the way back to the days of Hitler. He was imprisoned during the war, and the government took over his mills and his chemical plant. As you Americans would say, he was a real screwball, which perhaps contributed to his wife's committing suicide in 1961."

"I think it is best that we make our decisions on the information Herr Korsey gave us before he was flown to London," Klaus Hahn said, taking a gold cigarette case from his pocket. Instead of opening the case, he turned toward Camellion. "He mentioned several times that when Boyd was bragging about the Brotherhood's plan, he referred to Dunbeath. Who else is in Dunbeath but Sir MacLean?"

Catherine Griffin folded the copy of the Edinburgh Times and placed it on the table. "Dunbeath's the only lead we have," she said hopefully.

"Sure it is, and we'll follow it through," Camellion said. "I'm only sorry that we couldn't question Boyd and Kerr before they got blown apart. Of course, we still have the two other survivors from the farm shoot-out, but I don't think they know anything of real value."

"Which explains why they weren't blown up in the second car," interjected Kingman. "They weren't important enough to be dangerous."

"Right on. Boyd and Kerr got the business because they possessed vital information." The Death Merchant's voice became bitter as he stared at Charles Phegley. "If you had let me handle the situation the way I wanted to, right now we'd know what that information was. I could have pulled the truth out of those Hitler-loving dirt-bags. I'd have given them the Texas Treatment. They'd have been only too happy to talk."

"This is not your American Wild West, Mr. Hopmeir," Phegley said sternly. "Here in Great Britain we do things differently."

"I'm well aware of that," Camellion said. "With all due respect to your Queen and country, it would seem that the British never want to detour when they can take the long way around."

"Please be more explicit," Phegley said icily.

"We're wasting our time going to Dunbeath if a check-out of Dunbeath Hall isn't on the schedule."

"There are laws," insisted Phegley. "As I have explained previously, we can't obtain a search warrant on mere suspicion."

"It's a good thing he didn't listen to you about Boyd's farm," Catherine Griffin said with barely concealed disapproval in her voice, "or Korsey would be in a nameless grave by now. What you fail to understand is that this new breed of Nazi is no different from the one that was in the Hitler Gang. They're planning to kill our President and slaughter a couple of million people in Cairo; yet SIS meticulously insists on playing by the legal rules."

Phegley, who loathed shrewd women, responded with an air of self-confidence, "The American Secret Service has been informed about the assassination attempt, and Sadat's Internal Security Bureau knows about the A-bomb. It isn't likely that the President will be killed."

Kingman chuckled sarcastically. "If those fruitcakes do make the attempt, I hope to God they don't use a handgun, or the anti-gun idiots will blame every poor gun-owner in the U.S. Hopefully they will make the attempt with water. That way the liberals can scream for a ban on water. No one would be allowed to bathe or go to the beach. Naturally all swimming pools would be closed."

The Death Merchant wasn't amused. "Knock it off, Mel.

36

You're not funny. After all, that turkey is our President, and no man who occupies the oval office deserves to be shot down or whatever."

Charles Phegley, his eyes on the Death Merchant, cleared his throat. "I'm sure that under the circumstances, your CIA and our Whitehall will come to an arrangement as to methods we can use against Sir Hugh McLean. We'll know at five this evening when we radio to London."

Rudolph Gertenshalger spoke up in heavily accented English. "We do have a layout of the grounds surrounding Dunbeath. We can assume that entire area is protected by numerous warning devices."

"That's the rub. There isn't any way we can sneak in." Having eaten the last fig, he crumpled the empty box and tossed it across the room at the wastebasket by the radio table. He missed. "The only way to go in is use a method that is direct—this predicated on the assumption that Sir MacLean will not permit us to search his ancestral pile of stones."

"He won't," Phegley. "It would be a waste of time to even ask him."

"I don't understand any of this," Klaus Hahn said. He shifted uncomfortably on the couch, cigarette smoke pouring from his mouth and nostrils as he spoke. "Herr Steele and Herr Phegley will remain here at the station. That leaves six of us. I hardly think Catherine will be going with us to Dunbeath Hall."

"I'm going as far as Dunbeath!" Catherine said, surprised. She looked from Hahn to Camellion. "Well, am I not?"

"You're not," Camellion said. "There's no use in keeping up the act, in pretending that you and Mel are husband and wife and that I'm your father whom you two are taking on a vacation. Dunbeath is MacLean's town. He doesn't know we're coming, but he knows someone is due to arrive. Any strangers will be viewed with extreme suspicion. Let's be practical: Dunbeath is not a resort town. For us to go up there and pretend to be Americans on a vacation would be ridiculous. And how would we explain the two Germans and the two SIS men. They just happen to be there, huh?"

Catherine laughed nervously. "I want to see the Scottish countryside up north. I suppose I'll have to settle for the sights of Edinburgh."

Ronald Lynch said gruffly, "That still leaves six of us. I

should think any assault by six men would be preordained to failure. Going at Dunbeath Hall isn't the same as sneaking onto Boyd's farm."

"Mr. Phegley, can you give me an estimation of how much power Sir MacLean has in the area?" Camellion asked.

"In the sense that his two mills employ ninety percent of the town, Sir MacLean is Dunbeath," Phegley said. "The population is only 6,800. The Constabulary numbers only eleven men."

Martin Shevlin interjected, "Two or three of the Constables should be on his payroll. They could keep tabs on the town for him."

"Technically, MacLean owns the entire town," Phegley went on. "Dunbeath is in one corner of his holdings which extend upward into the mountains. He has thousands of acres. I don't know how many. I didn't think it important to ask London for that information."

Kingman peered skeptically at Phegley and snapped on his cigarette lighter. "How can anyone technically own a town? Either he does or he doesn't. Hell, a woman can't be half-pregnant."

The senior SIS officer smiled. "Sir MacLean inherited all of the properties when he inherited his title. He's the largest *laird*—landowner—in the area. Yes, he actually owns the land, the same way you would own a piece of property in America. The people in Dunbeath, some of whom have had their houses since the days of their great-great-grandfathers, pay rent to Sir MacLean."

Kingman finished lighting his cigarette and blew out smoke.

"Then Sir MacLean literally owns the whole damned works?"

"The whole damned works. However, he wouldn't evict any of the families, not even if the head of the household was unemployed. He could, legally. But he wouldn't. If he did, he'd be breaking one of the most ancient of Scottish customs, a kind of unwritten law, the Right of Protection by which a *laird* who's a nobleman must protect the people on his land. It's a system that has worked well for over a thousand years, only now the 'serfs' don't have to fight any wars for the lord of the manor."

"It's a pity that Scottish immigrants didn't bring that Right of Protection with them to the United States," Catherine Griffin said half-jokingly. "The Scottish people have contrubuted a lot to America."

"Including the Ku Klux Klan." The Death Merchant grinned and folded his arms over his chest. In response to the startled looks, he added, "At least part of the name. "The way it came about was that a group of Confederate veterans were feeling their booze the day before Christmas, back in 1865. Feeling prankish——"

"The soldiers of your South, after the American Civil War, correct?" interrupted Ronald Lynch.

The Death Merchant nodded. "What the Southern veterans did was don white sheets and drape their horses in a bizarre burlesque of the ghosts of the Confederate dead. For another joke, the seven men took the name Kuklos, Greek for circle, added Klan from the Scottish clans from which they had descended, and rounded out the name to be Ku Klux Klan. They adopted the fiery cross, the call to arms of the old Scottish clans, and added a weird litany of mystic rigamarole, including the circle of fire that was to become a symbol of terror."

"I'll be damned," exclaimed Kingman. "So that's how the KKK began!"

"Yes and no. The Klan began as a fun group. The purpose was only to scare superstitious blacks, but not to hurt them physically. What happened is that as new members joined, the KKK became an effective method of intimidating newly freed slaves. Ex-Confederate General Nathan Bedford Forrest was the Klan's first Grand Wizard, and after the Klan grew to almost half a million members and started enforcing its will by beatings, burnings and murder, Forrest disbanded the organization. I think this was in 1869. But the Klan's been around ever since."

"Interesting, very interesting," commented Phegley.

"I would like an answer to Mr. Lynch's question," Arnold Steel changed the subject. "Six of you cannot possibly attack Dunbeath Hall."

"I'll buy that," seconded Mel Kingman. "I don't even think we'd be safe in Dunbeath. I know for well that six of us can't pull off an attack. Man, that's like telling a turkey to wave a red flag the day before Thanksgiving."

The Death Merchant smiled slightly. *I know for well! Kingman can't escape using the idioms of his boyhood in Kentucky. But he's damned good at his job.* Camellion's smile broadened as he recalled the preparations for the

39

flight from New York to London. The security-conscious Kingman had urged him to arrange to get seats on the left side of the jetliner. Intelligence people often choose a seat to the left because most people, being right-handed, tend to spend more time looking to the right. Therefore, people on the left aren't noticed as much as people on the right.

Camellion scratched the top of his head and twisted his mouth to one side of his face. "I think you're both half-right about Dunbeath Hall. Six men would be too many. But maybe three could pull it off. I'll have to think about it."

Even the usually phlegmatic Arnold Steele stared at the Death Merchant in disbelief while Kingman said in his blunt manner, "Either you're kidding or you're nuts. The facts are that we couldn't take Dunbeath Hall without a small army, not if Sir MacLean puts up any kind of resistance, and from what we know of the dingbat, he'll fight like hell."

"It's like Don Quixote said in *Man of LaMancha*," Camellion said slyly. " 'Facts are the enemy of truth.' There are all sorts of possibilities regarding Dunbeath Hall."

"Uh huh, you might be right," Kingman said mockingly. "As I read you, you're saying these are the opinions upon which I am going to base my facts! We're going around in circles and getting nowhere fast."

Camellion, ignoring Kingman's stare, focused his attention on Charles Phegley. "Mr. Phegley, do you have relief maps and Mercator Projection maps of the area around Dunbeath Hall, say a hundred mile square area, and on large scale with one inch to five miles? I should also like a manuscript map, showing every path and building, but I don't suppose the latter is possible."

Phegley uttered a short sardonical snort. "You know we haven't any of those maps here. This is just a watch station. What you suggest will have to come from the SIS Cartography Section in London. We can put in the request when we radio. It will take only a day or so to get them here." He wanted to ask Camellion why he wanted the maps, but his pride wouldn't let him.

"Mr. Hopmeir, are you serious about using only three men?" asked Martin Shevlin, his expression one of concern. "If you are, I suggest you're making a very grave tactical error."

40

The Death Merchant regarded Shevlin with indifference.

"I suggest we wait until we find out what The Company and SIS have decided. We'll pick it up from there. Sir Mac-Lean's not going anywhere."

Catherine Griffin looked at her wristwatch, "It's 4:35. That's only a wait of 25 minutes."

Kingman crushed out his cigarette and got up from the table.

"I'm going to fix myself a drink," he announced. "Anybody want anything?"

Everyone shook their heads and Kingman went to the refrigerator and took out a bottle of blackberry brandy. He had met Richard Camellion only six weeks ago in New York City and didn't know him all that well. He did suspect that Camellion wasn't joking about using only three men. Men of Camellion's caliber never joked about death. But why should he want a Mercator map which was used chiefly for navigators on water? *Hell, maybe he thinks Dunbeath is surrounded by a moat.*

He filled a water glass half full of brandy and wished he had a place to practice his ballet exercises, a method that worked just fine for keeping the reflexes in shape, a method that couldn't be beaten for practicing perfect timing and control. Of course the British would think he was queer if they saw him pirouetting or performing other intricate movements. *Well, what can you expect from people who go around saying 'shed-u-al' for schedule and 'cat-supp' for ketchup? Culture-happy people living in a goddamn dream world . . .*

Forty minutes later, everyone in the room was still recovering from the unexpected. Everyone but Richard Camellion . . . During the radio report—voice, by dual-conversion scrambling—Whitehall had informed Charles Phegley that he would no longer be the officer in charge of the operation, that, henceforth, all final decisions would be made by "Mr. Hopmeir."

Trying to maintain his composure, Phegley had verified the order, then had put in a request for the maps, saying that Mr. Hopmeir had requested they be sent with all possible speed.

London had replied that the maps would be on a plane that same day and would arrive at Edinburgh's main airport early the morning of the next day.

End of conversation. Phegley had switched off the short-wave set.

"All we have to do now is figure out an approach plan," Arnold Steele said. "And that is in your department, Mr. Hopmeir." He had taken off his coat and Camellion had been surprised to see that he was wearing a Ruger Model 207 .357 Magnum in a left-sided 4-D mini-shoulder holster.

"Yeah, it's time for the facts of life," said Kingman a little drunkenly, the slight slur in his speech surprising no one, since he was working on his second waterglass of brandy.

Eight pairs of eyes fixed themselves on the Death Merchant.

"We'll fly to Inverness on schedule, day after tomorrow," Camellion said. "From Inverness we'll drive. I won't be able to tell you how far until I see the maps."

"May I ask why not?" inquired Phegley stiffly.

"Because the last lap will be by boat . . ."

# Chapter Four

Proudly, the bow of *HMS Taurus* cut through the moderate waves of the North Sea. Armed with three-inch guns and nine 40mm antiaircraft guns, plus hedgehogs and depth charges, the escort vessel carried a complement of 152 men and was used primarily to patrol the fishing lanes between the United Kingdom and Iceland. She was fast, too. Up to 23 knots. Now, however, she was doing only 18 knots, her speed reduced by the 5-ton lighter, amphibious, resupply cargo vehicle she was towing behind her bow. The LARC, an over-the-beach amphibious wheeled vehicle used to deliver cargo from ship to shore, had to be towed, since the landing vessel was too large to fit the automatic davits of the *Taurus*.

"I don't mind telling you, I think this is one damned moronic mistake," Kingman said grimly. "The Queen's 115th Scottish Regiment is stationed near Dundee. We could have used a hundred of those jokers and bagpiped our way right up to the front door of Dunbeath Hall. Sir MacLean might be the local big-butt up there, but he's not so dumb as to take on the British Army."

Standing on the forward boat deck, below the front of the box-like bridge, he glanced half-angrily at Camellion who was standing to his left. Like the Death Merchant, he stood with his hands on the railing to brace himself against the slight roll.

"I know you don't mind telling me," Camellion said resignedly. "You've told me so often during the past four days that I'm beginning to think you're a recording."

"Yeah? Well, you'll hear it again if this deal flops."

"We could have used the hundred and fifteenth. Sir MacLean wouldn't have resisted. The man's not a fool. The thing is, if we barged in there with troops, the press would surely get in on the act. Suppose we didn't find any evidence linking him and his sons to the Brotherhood? Then

43

what? We'd look like fools and so would the British government."

"My contention is that we're risking our lives when we wouldn't have to," Kingman said roughly. "We're doing what you accused SIS of doing: taking the long way around. After all, the Secret Service will have extra men around the President. He's protected."

"You're forgetting the A-bomb. Should we do things your way and come up with nothing, without any evidence, you know what will happen. Whoever is assembling the bomb would simply go completely underground and we'd never find them, or the bomb. We couldn't expect help from the Greeks. Their intelligence service, such as it is, is riddled with Russian doubles and is only the toy of the crooked politicians."

" 'Crooked politicians' is superfluous," growled Kingman. "The word politician means graft and all that goes with it." He pulled the hood of his heavy cotton sweat jacket over his head, to protect his ears against the cold wind of the North Sea.

"Doing it this way, we'll have some chance," the Death Merchant said, consulting his wristwatch—14.00 hours, or two 'clock in the afternoon. The *HMS Taurus* was on schedule, and only forty nautical miles east of the Scottish coast. One hundred and thirty miles to the northwest lay the Orkney Islands, separated from the northeast coast of Scotland by the Pentland Firth. Due north, 146 N.M. to the north, were the Shetland Islands. The southwest coast of Sweden was 214 N.M. to the east.

"Some chance!" Kingman muttered in disgust. "In the first place, we can't be certain that the maps are accurate. From the beach, the distance across country to Dunbeath Hall is roughly forty miles. In the second place, we're going to hit the sand only eleven miles south of Dunbeath to the north and Berridale to the south. Most of the men in Berridale are fishermen. They'll pull out in their boats before dawn. It's not impossible that they could spot the LARC leaving this tub and heading for the beach. Or see the jeep rolling out when we're on the beach. I'm damned sure you've thought of that."

The Death Merchant uttered a little laugh. "I hardly think that any of the boats will turn around, and their crews rush back to shore to warn Sir MacLean and his cutthroats."

44

"We don't know that there aren't members among the fishmen!"

"There might very well be, but it's unlikely that the entire crew of any one boat might be. Suppose a member of the Brotherhood does see us and suspect something is wrong? He won't be able to tell the Captain and the other men of the crew. All he'll be able to do is suffer in silence. As for the shore, there's no moon tonight. We won't be seen from the shore, at least not by anyone on the fishing boats. Should they see the *Taurus,* so what? She's just another patrol boat in the North Sea."

The Death Merchant's words didn't convince Kingman, who had a rule about getting all the odds that could be gotten.

"We don't know what kind of widespread alarm system MacLean might have either. I don't mean hardware on his estate. I'm talking about human spotters. And there we'll be: going across country in a British jeepster. Man, I tell you, that's the pits."

Remaining silent, the Death Merchant looked up at the sky. There were only cirrus clouds, the strong winds of high altitude having blown them into long streaks of mares' tails. These clouds, from 20,000 to 30,000 feet, indicated a depression, or low, some 500 to 1,000 miles away. But the weather will be clear tonight and possibly all day tomorrow.

He suddenly turned to Kingman and regarded him with a mixture of amusement and interest. "You know, Mel, I'm somewhat surprised that a pro like yourself should worry so much, especially since you were an instructor at the detect, destroy and demolish facility at the Farm and have a lot of hard experience in covert activities.

Kingman finished lighting a cigarette, then dropped the lighter into his pocket. He exhaled smoke, turned to the Death Merchant and leaned sideways against the railing, bracing himself with his feet.

"Courtland Grojean had to have told you," he said with the air of a disciplinarian. "Only he could have released the P-files."

"Grojean gives me a bio on any man I work with. I can't trust a case officer or a contract-man who talks a good battle plan but who might turn chicken at the sound of the first shot."

"You have your methods of operation and I have mine,"

Kingman admitted. "I don't believe in taking unnecessary risks. It's against my training."

"But your training didn't prevent you from lending a hand at Boyd's farm." Camellion raised the high collar of the pile-lined brawny jacket and watched Kingman's hands and eyes. Both would always reveal a lot about a person.

Kingman nodded slowly. "I did what had to be done. You would have done the same. But I suppose I'm really bugged at having to take orders from a contract-man. I'm convinced that's what you are. You're too damned good to be a career officer."

"It doesn't matter," Camellion said, and glanced up at the sky again. "Getting this job done is all that matters. And that means finding out the names of the people who have the bomb, where they have it, and how they intend to smuggle it into Egypt."

"We're trying to catch the tail of a comet—and you know it!"

"Of course. Making the impossible possible is what makes this work so interesting. We do more in a year than most people do in a lifetime."

"Yeah, prepare for the worst but pray for the best and expect something in between!" Kingman fingered his mustache, smiled slightly and turned to face the bow.

Amused, the Death Merchant wondered what Kingman's reaction might be if—*I told him the full truth: that what we might or might not do doesn't matter, because the United States, along with the rest of civilization is doomed?*

The 6,000 year old era was coming to a close. It was all a matter of cycles. Time cycles repeat because human nature does not change. That is why wars occur at regular intervals. For the same reasons, civilizations rise and fall.

Already the United States was in the Indian Summer of its culture, a "summer" that would be of very short duration. The time was drawing near for mobocracy, to be followed by dictatorship, by Caesarism.

All the elements were present, but Americans would never recognize them—*of course, the human species is self-destructive. We can expect no less from Americans, who are emotional about petty things, addicted to hero worship, and are used to bosses and regimentation in their daily lives. Without realizing it, they permit themselves to be conditioned by governmental and corporate bureaucracies and indoctrinated by the standarized mass media. Gregari-*

*ous, they join clubs, councils, leagues, associations, lodges, fraternities and societies. They follow but seldom lead. They do not realize that there is no deadlier form of self-deception than forcing the worthy elements of a civilization to become the servants of the drones . . .*

There were other signs of the approaching fall of democracy. The savage class wars that would erupt between 1980 and 1985! A leader who was a naive idealist, who had convinced himself that only he knew what was good for the nation.

Equally as dangerous was the growing role of women that had led to many changes in public opinion. The desire for freedom had been replaced by a desire for security. As if freedom were compatible with security. *Security can best be maintained in a prison. Or a hospital.* There was the tendency to focus on the child; there was the youth worship syndrome, the desire to avoid risks at all costs, and the emotional personalization of issues and the high suspicion of individualism. *The same as in ancient Rome*, mused the Death Merchant.

Camellion stared north, watched the spray splash over the bow, listened to the water and the other noises of the vessels and speculated on the rays of light he had seen emanating from Martin Shevlin. The aura had been brown, tinged with black—*he's as good as dead* . . .

A loud voice, someone speaking through a bullhorn, interrupted his thoughts. "MR. HOPMEIR, YOU ARE WANTED IN THE RADIO ROOM. PLEASE COME IMMEDIATELY."

Camellion and Kingman turned around, looked up and saw a sailor leaning out from one of the forward bridge windows. Camellion acknowledged the call with a wave of his hand, then started toward the radio room.

02.00 Hours. The blunt, square front of the LARC rose from the water and the four large wheels rolled onto the beach, the sound of the 280 h.p. engine breaking the stillness of the night.

Its large rubber tires sinking into the sand, the LARC moved 20 feet forward, the driver lowered the front section, and the Death Merchant drove the jeep from the interior down the ramp. Next to him sat Martin Shevlin. In the rear were Melvin Kingman and Ronald Lynch. All four men were dressed in 5-color camouflage coveralls and carried a variety of weapons, including gas and demolition grenades. An extra can of petrol was strapped to the rear of the jeepster which resembled a German Kubelwagen more than the classic American model jeep.

Camellion pushed down on the gas and steered the jeep several hundred feet up the steep incline. Down at the beach, the sailor at the controls of the LARC backed the vehicle into the water, turned it around, revved up the engine and headed back to the *HMS Taurus*.

The Death Merchant stopped the jeep under several tall oak trees, switched on a penlight, looked at the compass mounted on the dash, then consulted the manuscript map in his lap.

"God help us!" said Kingman. "We're lost already!"

The Death Merchant grinned. "We're right on the mark. The ruins of Glenford-at-an-inn should be six miles to the west."

"You wouldn't know it from here," said Ronald Lynch, who was studying the coastal area through large Navy binoculars. In places, fog crept over the uneven moor, along the strange, brooding terrain that was grassy, yet virtually devoid of all else but gaunt ribs of rock, heather, and wind-tortured clumps of gorse or bracken.

The Death Merchant turned off the penlight, put on a pair of holographic "one-tube" night-sight goggles, shifted gears and pressed down on the gas. There would be a lot of rolling hills and meadows, but nothing that the jeep couldn't handle.

In contrast to the other men, he was at ease. Some people take a certain reassurance from being amid trees and fields, hedgerows and meadows. Remove these familiar things and many people feel a vague yet strangely persistent distress: they stand exposed and feel more vulnerable. But to Camellion a vantage point on a high tor that looked out upon the monotone of a moor, green yet hardly more hospitable than an open sea, induced a sense of isolation and singularity that even gregarious spirits need at times, a need for private moments of old dreams and lost years, for reflection and assessment.

The jeep bounced along, Camellion glancing now and then at the illuminated compass. Quickly the moor was behind them and they were on a slant in pitch darkness, with only the diamonds of stars for company. He crossed a field of heather, detoured around a wooden fence, and headed into another meadow, the tall grass, bathed in dew, slapping against the tires and the sides of the jeep.

Here and there limestone hills surrounded wide stretches of open land, like shells protecting precious pearls. Easily, Camellion drove the jeep around hills and over meadows, his right hand aching from all the shifting he was being forced to do. There was danger, not only from large rocks hidden by grass but from the area's blackfaced sheep that might be sleeping. During the daytime, the sheep would wander across roads with the boldness of sparrows. At night they slept where they pleased. More than once the engine noise of the jeep had disturbed sheep sleeping in the grass, and they had scattered. But there was always the danger that some moron in the flock might not get up and move out of the way in time.

After what seemed hours of bouncing along, they came to the ruins of Glenford-at-an-inn, a mossy stone pile so ancient that one section dated back 50 years before Christopher Columbus reached America.

Kingman, Lynch, and Shevlin, their eyes having adjusted to the moonless night, could see the ruins dimly. Camellion, however, had a much better view; to him the stones of the old fortress stood out as if cloaked in early twilight, the holographic goggles amplifying the near-infrared radiation 250,000 times.

The Death Merchant laughed. "There you are, Kingman. See how we're lost. So far the map is accurate. I'll bet a fifth of really good brandy that the rest of the map will be correct."

Kingman snorted and pulled a pint of peppermint schnapps from the outside pocket of his leg. "Ask a man the time of day and he tells you how to build a watch. Hell, we've still got 34 miles to go."

"We're on schedule," Ronald Lynch said, looking at his wristwatch. He stared at Kingman who had opened the bottle of booze and was about to tilt it to his lips. "Don't you think it's dangerous to drink, considering what might lie ahead?"

"Dangerous?" Kingman sounded amused. "Not to me it isn't. I like to be relaxed in a shoot-out. That's how all this is going to end."

"If we get there in one piece," Shevlin said.

"Time to take another bearing," Camellion said. He stopped the jeep not far from a long sloping hill, looked at the compass, took the penlight from his pocket, opened the map on his lap and studied it.

At length he said, "Another 2.6 kilometers and we'll be able to use a road. We'll go north on the road for 13.9 kilometers."

"We should be coming to a farm before long," Shevlin said.

"We will in a few more miles," Camellion told him. "We'll be going through the farmer's field. Just beyond his field we'll come to the road."

"How close to the house will we be?" Lynch inquired.

"Slightly more than half a mile," Camellion said. "They might hear us. There's no way we can be sure they won't."

Shevlin's tone was curt. "Who cares? They'll be sound asleep. Should they hear us they won't know who we are."

"I'd just as soon not have to kill an innocent farmer," Lynch said. "But I would if I had to."

The Death Merchant switched off the penlight and stuck it back in his breast pocket. He folded the map, glanced again at the compass and got the jeep under way. Expert driver that he was, he didn't lose any time in wasted motion. Nonetheless, a lot depended on pure luck. Even though the manuscript map might be accurate and list every landmark, it did not give the topography of every square foot of territory. There was always the possibility that a wheel might run into a hole and twist or break an axle. Or running over a large grass-hidden rock could do it.

With the grass and undergrowth slapping against the side of the jeep and the cool wind grabbing the faces of the four men, the black vehicle was soon making its way through the meadow.

"What's the next landmark?" Lynch called out.

"Inchahone's Point," Camellion said. "It's a large hill shaped like an inverted cone. We'll see it at the end of the thirteen kilometers."

To the south, to his left, Camellion spotted the neat, compact farmhouse, as dark as a witch's thoughts. Then the field ended and there was the road, nothing but a two-track dirt deal, but more than sufficient for Camellion's purpose. He slowed, turned onto the road and, increasing speed, headed north.

To the Death Merchant, the road ahead of the jeep was very clear. The night-sight goggles took care of that. To the other three men the eerie ride could be compared to driving in a pitch dark tunnel and never reaching the end.

At a rapid clip, the jeep passed the farmhouse in the distance and ate up the miles, covering the 13.9 kilometers in what seemed a surprisingly short time. Camellion looked at the speedometer and checked the mileage—how about that? We're right on the mark.

He stopped the jeep and announced, "This is it. Now we turn off and go northwest all the way. If the creek doesn't rise, we might get there in one piece."

"A creek!" exclaimed Shevlin. "We must cross a creek?"

Kingman laughed. Camellion said tolerantly, "No creek, old buddy. It's just an expression we Colonials use."

"Can you see Inchahone's Point?" Kingman stared around in the darkness, convinced that Camellion had made a serious mistake in judgement in thinking that four men could invade the grounds of Dunbeath Hall and get to Sir Hugh MacLean before anyone could stop them. In Kingman's opinion, all these preparations were a lot of damned nonsense. It was as broad as it was long. So they couldn't use the men of the 115th Scottish Regiment because that method might create a big stink in the media and because there wasn't any hard evidence that Sir MacLean was connected with the Brotherhood of the 4th Reich. Okay. If they succeeded in reaching Sir Hugh, Camellion would use his own direct-to-the-point methods in making the man talk. *He'll break every bone in that old crackpot's body. But if the old man dies, what then? What kind of protection will we have against Sir MacLean's men? That will leave John-Percy MacLean. Camellion will probably go to work on him first. But suppose neither one of them are at Dunbeath Hall? Just because they usually are doesn't mean they will be tonight. If they aren't, there will probably be a scandal anyhow. Except that we might not be around to know about it!*

At the briefing, Kingman and the two British agents had asked Camellion what they would do if Sir MacLean died and they found themselves with a corpse on their hands.

The Death Merchant had smiled enigmatically. He would tell them after they got there, he had said. *Now what kind of answer is that?*

"Yeah, Inchahone's Point is there, to my left," Camellion answered Kingman. "I can see it in the distance, about two miles away."

The wild ride continued. The Death Merchant took the jeep across empty, rocky flatlands, meadows thick with fox-tail grass and, on diverse occasions, fields that were still fertilized by methods that had been in use for hundreds of years: a concoction of water, ashes, lime and dung. He by-passed strands of black woods, the trees sometimes oak or hickory, ash or pine. In the daytime and under different circumstances the countryside would have been interesting, albeit even under the best of circumstances this part of Scotland was still raw country and always would be . . . all loneliness and solitude, for city folk a land to hurry through before darkness falls and dreads too primitive to acknowledge rasp one's nerves.

Gradually the ground became more rocky and the wind more chilly. The jeep was on an incline, one that was miles wide and miles long, a slope that was so gradual that in daylight the slant would hardly have been noticeable. The top of the grade was a thousand acre plateau, the elevation 930 above sea level. Dunbeath Hall was situated on the south side of the really small plateau.

The ride became rougher, the jeep rebounding with greater rapidity. Finally the movement of the vehicle became one bounce after another, the springs groaning, the tires squealing in protest. With effort, Camellion drove the jeep under a large brooding oak and shut off the engine.

"Men, from now on we walk," he said.

Kingman tossed out the empty bottle. "You feel a little sunshine and someone comes along and throws muddy water in your face. All right. Let's go pin the tail on the don-key."

# Chapter Five

Each man with his own thoughts, Camellion and Kingman, Shevlin and Lynch moved up the grade toward the top of the plateau. Other than a variety of autopistols, they were also armed with Ingram submachine guns equipped with Sionics silencers. The Death Merchant's special .44 Magnum Backpacker Auto Mags had been at the U.S. Embassy in London; the powerful weapons had been flown to the SIS Watch-station on Morrison Street, in Edinburgh, and he carried each AMP in a black shoulder holster. He also carried the Audio Countermeasures Service System. Mel Kingman had the Solenoid-Inductor Intensifier in a rigid flight pack on his back.

Camellion had estimated that, from where he had parked the jeep, Dunbeath Hall was 4.827 kilometers, or three miles, away. Getting there was another matter.

Whenever possible, they moved through the trees and hurried over open places, their caution mounting in proportion to the adrenalin that flowed. Every so often, Camellion looked at the luminous numbers of the pedometer he carried. The slope was such an inchmeal incline that without the pedometer, he wouldn't know when they had reached the flat surface of the top. It was on the top that they would find the silent alarms, if any. It was even possible that the side of the forest of white birch might be protected with ultrasonic motion detectors or infrared beam breakers. Not very likely because of the wild life in the woods; the alarms would be going off dozens of times a day, and night, too. It was a certainty that the manor would be covered by protective devices, each door and window, and, because Sir MacLean knew he was being investigated, extra guards would be on duty.

They realized they were getting close to the top when white birch trees began to predominate and the large rocks became less abundant. In an eerie stillness—nothing except the soft rustling of leaves in the wind—each footstep sounded like a drum. To a man, they were anxious to get to the top, close in on the manor, and do what must be done.

The Death Merchant halted the men when the pedometer showed that they had trekked slightly under two miles. All that lay between them and the manor was half a mile of woods. From this moment on, the utmost caution would have to be exercised.

"I take it the fun's about to start?" Kingman whispered. He unbuckled the strap of the flight pack, started to slide the rigid frame pack from his back and looked at Camellion, who was down on his right knee and taking the main unit of the A.C.S.S. from a shoulder bag.

"Quiet fun, I hope," Camellion drawled. "I don't have to tell you jokers that if and when trouble does start, kill everyone in sight, except Sir MacLean and his brat, John-Percy. You've gawked at their photographs long enough to know what those two ass-heads look like."

"I hope the diagram of the manor house is accurate," offered Shevlin in a thoughtful voice. "We could head for the old boy's bedroom and end up in the bloody kitchen or whatever." He laughed at his own attempt at humor, then added, "I should suppose the diagram is accurate. It was drawn to scale during World War II when Sir MacLean was arrested."

"We're even luckier that the diagram was in Whitehall's files," Lynch said. "I was surprised that they even found the damned thing. I suppose it was in Sir MacLean's file." He looked at the American agent who called himself Victor Hopmeir and thought that he looked truly weird in the night-sight goggles. The goggles were very large and, over the bridge of Camellion's nose, a slim tube protruded upward to the center of the forehead. The tube was the "guts" of the device.

Finished with attaching the parabolic reflector to the end of the antenna, the Death Merchant pulled up the antenna of the A.C.S.S. and turned on the device.

"I'm ready," he said to Kingman who was almost finished with the Solenoid-Inductor Intensifier, a square black box with an ON and OFF switch, a range knob and meter, and a volume knob that could be turned from LOW to MEDIUM to HIGH. The S-I-I was a device that could effectively block any beam or microwave protection device, accomplishing this "miracle" by "over-feeding" any enemy beam, thereby preventing the alarms from going off.

"That damned Steele is really a cold-blooded bag of bones," Kingman said and turned on the device which began to hum ever so faintly. "He reminded me three times of what this do-dadder cost and insisted that I protect it. And get this: He said we should save the A.C.S.S. and the goggles at all costs. He's more worried about the equipment than he is about us."

"Set the S-I-I to maximum," Camellion said, all business.

Kingman turned the dial all the way to the right. "That's it—67 feet. Do you think it will be enough? I guess it will."

Martin Shevlin didn't know what to make of Kingman, whom he considered as much a savage as Hopmeir. Yet Kingman considered Steele cold-blooded! Those Americans, such rowdy, violent people, like Wild West cowboys the first time at sea, chewing tobacco while the typhoon roared down upon them.

The Death Merchant removed the night-sight goggles from his head and handed them to Ronald Lynch. "They're set to maximum intensity. Don't fool with the small knob at the top of the tube. Take the point. Kingman and I will be on either side of you." He looked toward Shevlin but couldn't see the British agent, his eyes not having had time to recondition themselves to the complete darkness. "Shevlin, you stay at least five feet behind Lynch. We've got to stay close together in order for the S-I-I to function properly. Oh, Kingman. Shut off the S-I-I. Don't turn it on again unless I tell you to."

"I say, I don't believe I understand." Ronald Shevlin was very calm, the total professional. "Why can't one leave the S-I-I unit turned on constantly. We could then walk through with complete assurance that we would be protected. We can't. Obviously there is a reason why."

The question was a reasonable one. "When the unit is on more than ten minutes in a stretch, there's always the danger that the coil might overheat. It's best to turn it on only when it's needed."

"I see. Thank you," Shevlin said.

"Let's get with it," Camellion said briskly.

They moved toward the northwest, at an angle that, when they came to the north side of the woods, would place them a hundred feet to the east of Dunbeath Hall. Out of necessity they moved very slowly, Lynch staring ahead, and to the left and the right through the night-sight goggles, the Death Merchant's eyes glued to the panel of the Audio Countermeasures Service System.

The red light remained dark.

The trees were white birch, each trunk tall and straight, the leaves and branches forming a solid canopy that blotted out even the light of the stars. In the daytime, no ray of sunlight was likely to reach this dark, dank, lonely world of growing things where, in places, the trees were so close together that even a malnutrated person would have had to stand sideways, hold in his stomach and squeeze in between the trunks. In other places there was plenty of room and the men could pass through the trees without any difficulty.

Like four turtles they plodded along, moving along, their booted feet sinking into the deep grass and the undergrowth thick with leaves, plants, twigs and rotting branches. Here were numerous plants that could thrive only in cool, wet shade—and wet it truly was, the trees dripping with dew that would never completely dry during the day because the sun could not penetrate the leafy barrier overhead.

Camellion looked at the pedometer. "We've reached the halfway mark," he said.

Not once had the red signal light of the A.C.S.S. blinked. The four men moved on.

"I told you there wouldn't be any alarms in the woods," Kingman said in a low, indignant murmur. "Damn these low branches. There's enough water around here to take a bath in."

"Don't be overconfident, my American friend," warned Shevlin. "The other side of these woods might be ringed with alarms."

This time it was the Death Merchant who disagreed. "The other side of the woods will be clear. Tell you why. In good times, MacLean wouldn't need protection. Who'd bother his estate? Some poor farmer. And I doubt if he's had time to install new devices since we've been on to him.

After a short time they saw a glimmer of light in the distance—the lights by the front door of the manor house. Now, with a landmark to move by and with which to measure the distance, the four moved with renewed effort. The

56

Camellion chose a window toward the southwest corner. "Turn on the S-I-I," he said to Kingman, "and hold it close to the window. It won't take me long to cut the glass."

He quickly took the A.C.S.S. apart and returned the units of the device to the bag. From one of the inside compartments of another bag, he took a glass cutter, a roll of surgical tape and a pocket knife. Then he went to work on the window, the bottom section of which was a yard above the ground. With the glass cutter, he slowly cut a horizontal line 28 to 30 inches long, 8 inches above the lead sealer that held the glass to the frame. He made the second horizontal cut 25 inches above the first one. He next pulled a long strip of tape from the role, cut off an estimated 36 inch strip and very carefully pasted it perpendicularly in the center of the window, so that 3 inches of each end extended beyond each horizontal line.

"Damn it, can't you get the anvils out of your butt?" hissed Kingman. "We're totally exposed out here."

"Nivir feer, me bhoy. I'm a pahst mahsther at this," Camellion said, cutting off a second strip of surgical tape. This length of tape he placed to the left of the first piece.

"This is Scotland, not Ireland," snapped Kingman, "and you're not very funny Hopmeir."

"It wouldn't be very funny either if this window fell inward and the glass shattered. "One mistake on my part is all it takes.

He placed the third strip next to the second one. Three more strips followed, each to the right, the ends of each piece extending three inches past the two horizontal lines he had cut.

Now for the next two lines. He cut a long perpendicular line to the left, each end of this line intersecting the ends of the two horizontal lines. He cut the second perpendicular line to the right, and when he was finished, its ends, too, intersected the ends of the two horizontal lines.

Camellion put the glass cutter into the bag and took out a small hammer whose striking surface was made of rubber. With extreme caution, he began to tap along the four cuts, ever so gently, feeling pride in his work when he heard the glass separating from the window. Within several minutes the glass was completely free.

He pulled at the ends of the surgical tape that extended past the top horizontal cut, and after he had freed each end from the section of uncut glass, he very slowly pulled the

59

taped glass toward him and separated the ends of the tape from the bottom section of the glass. Carefully he lowered the cutout section of glass and placed it upright against the side of the house, whispering, "Be careful that you don't cut yourselves on the bottom."

"Isn't Sir MacLean's bedroom toward the center of the house?" Martin Shevlin asked. He pushed the firing lever of the Ingram to full automatic.

"Right and on the second floor," Camellion said. "There's an elevator at both ends of the house, but we'll use the main staircase. Be careful that you don't bump into anything.

"I've got the goggles; I'll go in first," Lynch said nervously. "Are you sure the alarm won't sound?"

"Positive," Camellion answered. "Hand me your chatter box and get inside."

Reluctantly, still doubting the effectiveness of the Solenoid Inductor Intensifier, Lynch handed Camellion the Ingram, then, with some effort, put his right leg through the opening. Getting inside the house was difficult. He had nothing to hold on to, and didn't dare touch the glass, fearing it would break. However, with Camellion and Shevlin steadying him on the outside and giving him a boost, he managed to get inside without too much difficulty.

"I'll go in next," Camellion said, and passed the Ingram submachine gun through the opening. "Mel, after I'm inside, hand me the S-I-I."

Once the four were inside and six feet beyond the window, the Death Merchant switched off the Solenoid-Inductor Intensifier and handed the instrument back to Kingman who placed it in the backpack.

Camellion took the night-sight goggles from Lynch, put them on and looked around the room which, to him at least, was no longer dark. There were couches and upholstered chairs, the style from a bygone era, from a generation that had been consigned to the history books.

The Death Merchant led the way. In single file they moved lengthways across the room to the door on the north side. A .44 Magnum Auto Mag in his right hand—a special Lee E. Jurras silencer attached to the barrel—Camellion pulled open the door and looked around the left side of the doorway.

A long hall. A night light burning at each end. Six doors and an open archway on the north side. Seven doors on the south side of the hall.

The Death Merchant chose the archway.

The next room was a display room for *objets d'art*. In glass-topped cases were delicate miniatures of Dresden porcelain. There was Chinese porcelain, as well as sculptures of silver, of bronze, and of ivory. Camellion paused for only a moment to admire the chess set under glsss. Each piece, seven inches tall, was carved from the best quality of Chinese jade.

There were modern sculptures, these resting on long tables. There was a striking Greek horse, cast in solid bronze and remarkable for its harmony of abstract form.

The Hindu goddess Uma, fifteen inches tall and cast of silver, leaned lightly on her right hand and delicately held her expressive left hand before her. Camellion recognized the sculpture as one of the finest realizations of the female form in Nepali silver. Though idealized, it was modeled with unusual naturalism and almost seemed to have been taken from life.

Beyond the display room was a square foyer, the beginning of a hallway at each end. On the south side was an open elevator, to the north a large, open doorway.

"If I remember the diagram correctly, we're coming to the main dining hall," Camellion whispered. "Beyond it is another foyer and the stairs."

They crept into the dining hall that was sixty feet long and forty feet wide, and paused to get their bearings. Two very long tables caught their attention, each one covered with a twilled woolen tablecloth that reached to the floor and was of a plaid tartan design, the red, green, orange and black colors and the width of the stripes the distinctive pattern of the MacLean clan. On the walls were shields, crossed broad swords, maces, battle axes, and tapestries depicting hunting scenes.

The Death Merchant and the men started down the length of the dining hall, going between the two tables. They were in the center of the room when, without warning, the lights of the three chandeliers came on. Reflex automatically caused the Death Merchant and the three other men to freeze, the sudden brightness almost blinding them.

Men poured from underneath the two tables, moving so

fast that the heavy table coverings were almost pulled off. The Death Merchant and his men knew they had walked directly into a cleverly set trap, and that there wasn't anything they could do about it. Surrounded on all sides, all they could do was take as many of the enemy with them before they went down.

The Death Merchant had time to think *Kingman was right!* and to explode the head of one man with a .44 AMP Magnum bullet before one of the attackers grabbed the rounded silencer, attached to the Auto Mag, with both hands and started to twist the big autoloader from his right hand. Another man grabbed the strap of his left shoulder bag and tried to pull him back while another neo-Nazi, coming in from behind, attempted to throw an arm around his neck. Camellion stopped the man with an *empi* smash, the point of his elbow crashing into the man's stomach. Camellion ducked a right cross, kicked in the groin the man who had aimed it and used a *Nukite* spear hand to stab in the neck the man who had twisted the Auto Mag from his hand. He aimed a left-legged spin kick at another man, but the Scot ducked to one side as still another man grabbed Camellion's leg. Several more grabbed him by the arms. Again someone pulled heavily on one of the shoulder bags and, much to his disgust, he felt himself going down.

A loud roar of a pistol! One of the Scots yelled and crashed back from the grand-slam impact of Kingman's .357 Magnum bullet. Then a fist flattened out against Kingman's jaw and several hands reached for the Coonan autoloader.

Then the Scots were all over Kingman and Shevlin and Lynch, who fought with all the fury of cornered wildcats. Very quickly, the Ingram submachine guns were twisted from the hands of Ronald Lynch and Martin Shevlin, but not before Lynch's chatterbox had popped and ripped open two men, splashing him and three of the attackers with blood and tiny pieces of ripped clothing.

Kingman, an expert in the West Java *Tjikalong* school of *Pentjaksilat,* tried a *hariman* ("tiger") kick that, if it had landed, would have stunned an ox. But as good as he was, he could not fight a dozen men at the same time. Neither could Lynch and Shevlin. Dozens of hands pulled them down. Fists crashed against their jaws. The side of a pistol slammed against Kingman's head.

The Death Merchant felt himself rolled over on his stomach, his arms jerked around to his neck, and handcuffs snapped on his wrists.

*Someone talked! They were waiting for us!*

Then the universe exploded and a hundred million supernovas crushed his consciousness . . .

# Chapter Six

Consciousness returned to the Death Merchant with jerks and false starts. Even after he was awake, he still had several moments in which he thought he was in the middle of a nightmare. Then he felt the throbbing pain in his skull, became aware that he was lying on his left side on a stone floor and that the steel of handcuffs were cutting into his wrists. His lower jaw and his right ribcage ached—*it's a nightmare all right. It was a setup and we walked right into it . . .*

"He and the others are conscious, sir," he heard a voice say.

"Prop him and the others against the wall," another voice said calmly. "I want them to know what fools they've been."

None too gently, hands grabbed the Death Merchant by the shoulders, yanked him up to a sitting position, dragged him across the floor, and shoved him back against a moss-covered wall. Other men did the same with Kingman, Shevlin, and Lynch, all of whom bore the marks of a beating. Shevlin's right eye was black and blue and swollen shut. Kingman's jaws were swollen. Lynch's lips were caked with blood, and his nose was twice normal size.

In the flickering light cast by two kerosene lanterns hanging from the low ceiling, Camellion and his three men saw that they were in one of the ancient dungeons of Dunbeath Hall. Rusty iron rings were set in the walls, rusty chains dangling from the rings. The half-open door was oak, a foot thick and bound with iron bands. The smell was dank and cold. In the dark corners, spiderwebs of hundreds of years had accumulated.

It was the men just inside the door, sitting relaxed on chairs, that commanded the Death Merchant's attention and elicited stares of hatred, fear, and curiosity from Kingman, Shevlin, and Lynch. At once they realized that all their weapons were gone and that their pockets had been searched.

Kingman, propped up against the wall next to Camellion, mumbled, 'I hate to say 'I told you so,' Hopmeir."

"Yeah, and I hate to hear you say it," Camellion said and stared up at the men sitting in front of him toward the door. He recognized the three MacLeans from their photographs: Sir Hugh, John-Percy, the youngest son, and Edward Tynes MacLean, the second eldest son. Camellion did not recognize the huge man sitting to the left of Sir Hugh. The man must have weighed 300 pounds and was all muscle. As for the four men standing, each holding a Czech Model 58 assault rifle—*rank and file members. Sir Hugh's stooges.*

However, there was something vaguely familiar about the elderly man with the high forehead and the wedge-shaped face. Dressed in a navy blue suit, the man was to the right of Sir MacLean, his eyes never leaving the Death Merchant and his men.

Camellion's memory didn't desert him. The man's hair was no longer brown; now it was gray. The smoothness had left the skin around the cheeks and mouth, and there were folds of age in the neck—*but it's he. I'm positive. He's exSS General Karl Gustav Lindermanns. He commanded the SS Leibstandarte Adolf Hitler, Hitler's own personal bodyguard.*

"My friends, you are awake," Sir MacLean said. His face was serious and his voice authoritative; yet there was an underlying tone of humor and self-satisfaction. "I'm sorry that I can't make you more comfortable. Under the circumstances, I'm sure you understnad why you must remain handcuffed and kept in this dungeon. Your discomfort, however, will be short. You'll die in a matter of hours."

The man with the head of thick gray hair said, "We know that the leader of your group is named Victor Hopmeir." His tone was glacial, as were his eyes. "Which one of you is he?"

"I am, *Obergruppenfuhrer* Lindermanns," Camellion said easily. "Or should I say ex-SS General Karl Gustav Lindermanns?"

There were exclamations of surprise from Edward MacLean and John-Percy MacLean. The eyes of the four guards widened, their expressions, as well as the expressions of the two MacLeans, conveying to the Death Merchant that they had not known the identity of General Lindermanns.

Sir Hugh MacLean and the big man next to him had given a start at the mention of Lindermanns' name. Camellion, however, felt that they were only amazed that he should have recognized the Nazi butcher, who was number three on the list of wanted Nazi war criminals.

Embarrassed anger faded from General Lindermanns gray-green eyes and was replaced by an expressionless, penetrating stare. Unblinkingly, he stared at Camellion, who stared back with such unwavering intensity that Lindermanns finally blinked and looked away. Very quickly, he stared again at the Death Merchant.

"My name is Dirck Van Memling," he said in a low voice. "If I were this General Lindermanns, it wouldn't make any difference. None of you will live long enough to inform your superiors of what you have seen here."

Edward Tynes MacLean said warily, "He's not Victor Hopmeir. Hopmeir was an old man with white hair."

"Oh, I'm Hopmeir." There was a slight taunting quality to Camellion's voice. "Only I left my disguise at home. After all, I didn't expect that we'd end up down here in one of the 'guest rooms.'"

Lindermanns spoke metallically, impersonally. "We want to know what the SIS, the BND, and the CIA know about our organization."

Sir Hugh MacLean demanded, "Why did only four of you come here? What did you hope to gain? How much evidence do the British have against me?"

Added John-Percy MacLean, "What did Jackson Boyd tell the SIS?"

Melvin Kingman snarled unexpectedly, "Go to hell, you Nazi bastards. We woudn't give you the time of day in Hong Kong!"

Ex-SS General Lindermanns smiled, a smile that was half-tolerant, half-sadistic, the smirk of a man who is very sure of himself. "To the contrary, you will tell us. Before this night is over, you will either tell us everything you know or die screaming in agony."

The Death Merchant sighed resignedly. "Kingman, this is not the time to be a hero. A man can stand only so much pain. Sooner or later we'd tell them. It might as well be sooner."

*(You idiot! We'll need all our strength to do what must be done later, assuming we have a chance to do it and if they don't gun us down before they leave.)* Camellion's other worry was that Kingman, in his temper, would blurt out about the A-bomb in Greece—that would gum up the works.

Kingman made a strangled noise in his throat. "You gutless son of a bitch," he yelled at Camellion. "You're damned lucky I'm handcuffed and can't get at you."

Lynch and Shevlin glared at the Death Merchant in shock and baffled consternation, then Shevlin said slowly and distinctly, "You bloody bastard."

General Lindermanns, pleased with how events were going, leaned back in his chair, crossed his legs and relaxed. "I am waiting, Hopmeir. The first time you lie, I shall have your fingers broken, one by one."

Camellion said simply, "The SIS got onto the Brotherhood when you stole those NATO papers in Paris. It was the CIA and the BND who developed the information that led to Professor Helmut Koerber. I don't know how this was done; I wasn't part of the operation. It was all on a 'need-to-know' basis. You know how that works."

"There has to be more to it," said Sir MacLean. "Why should the British Secret Intelligence Service suspect me. And don't try to tell me it was only because of my wartime activities."

John-Percy MacLean said bitterly, glancing at his father, "That fool Boyd told them."

"Boyd didn't say a thing," Camellion replied. "What put the SIS and the BND wise was the survivor at Mayback I. He talked. His name was Archibald Douglas, and he was from Dunbeath. He was the sign that pointed at you, Sir MacLean."

And expression of total triumph flowed over the face of General Karl Lindermanns, who turned and glared at an uncomfortable Sir MacLean.

"I was right. I said at the time it had been a mistake to send any Scotsman to West Germany."

"Now we know what happened to Douglas," Edward MacLean said. A man of medium height, he seemed intense and to have a lot of energy.

"Hindsight is of no value. What matters is that there isn't any evidence against me," Sir MacLean insisted doggedly. "The SIS didn't come here in force—proof enough that

67

while the authorities suspect, they haven't any hard facts. Which means Boyd didn't talk. That leaves only the four of you."

"Why did you come to Dunbeath Hall?" Lindermanns asked. "What did you hope to accomplish?"

Camellion told him without any hesitation. "Our goal was to kidnap Sir MacLean and force him to tell all he knew about the Brotherhood. His stooges could hardly kill us once we had him." Camellion faked another sigh and tossed out another verbal probe. "It doesn't make any difference. So now we know the leader is you, Lindermanns— for all the good it will ever do us."

An angry look flashed over Sir MacLean's face, a sure signal to the Death Merchant that he had touched a sensitive nerve of pride.

"I formed and organized the Brotherhood of the Fourth Reich," the Scotsman said in a loud voice. "I have formulated all the plans and projects that will eventually rid mankind of racial trash. It was I who took the first step because I know the truth. Whites live contentedly, for the most part, in the false security that the world belongs to them. One by one their rights have been taken away. While the white man has been put to sleep, the negro and the minorities of the world have wakened. The Jews have led the way by exacting reparations from the monstrous lie that Hitler killed six million of their number during World War II. The negro, in turn, is blaming slavery solely on the white man and dishonestly pictures white slave owners as the cruelest humans that ever lived. In America, negroes and half-Indian aliens from Mexico have corrupted the nation. The whites of this world are hated because only the pure white race has been promised everlasting life. Only the Nordic Aryans are the pure white race."

He's stark, raving mad. Every bit as much of a crackpot as Hitler! He belongs in a paper doll factory!

Camellion only said in a voice filled with pseudo awe. "You've grabbed a big chunk of the impossible. To do what you want to do would take a fullscale nuclear war. Only thousands of hydrogen bombs could destroy ninety percent of the human race."

Camellion was confident that Shevlin and Lynch would not mention the atom bomb being assembled in Greece. Kingman, with his temper, was something else . . .

Sir MacLean smiled. Camellion could almost see pride

and self-satisfaction oozing out of the Scottish crackpot's skin.

"Exactly, and that final war will soon begin," Sir MacLean said. "We of the Brotherhood have seen to that. But I am not going to tell you how that war will be triggered. You can ponder the possibilities while you are waiting to die."

Kingman spit out, "Shoot us and get it over with. Personally, I'm sick of listening to your racial crap."

"Shoot you!" It was John-Percy MacLean who had spoken. "We're not going to shoot you. We're not going to take any chances of the British finding your dead bodies. You four are going to take a ride in an airplane with us. Your final resting place will be the Sea of the Hebrides."

Karl Gustav Lindermanns slowly turned his head and gave John-Percy an angry look, but did not speak.

The Death Merchant licked his dry lips and stared at Sir Hugh MacLean. "Apparently, you know very little about radioactivity, Sir MacLean. World War III would wipe out the human race, and that includes you and your Brotherhood."

Sir MacLean's laugh was pure malice. "Only if we are exposed to radioactivity. We won't be. Only two hundred kilometers from here an underground shelter is being prepared; there we will be safe for years after the end of the final war. There are dozens of other shelters throughout the world. After the bulk of humanity is destroyed, we of the Brotherhood will emerge and become rightful masters of the world. Our first step will be to return to Scotland and by force of arms subdue those who are left alive in Great Britain."

"Another impossible task!" smirked Camellion, subtly fishing for more information.

"No, it isn't!" Once more it was John-Percy MacLean whose pride got the better of him and forced him to brag. "We have enough arms and ammunition down here to start a small war right now. Furthermore, should the British authorities come here and search this house from top to bottom, they would never find them. Nor would they find anything to indicate that you four were even on the grounds of Dunbeath Hall!"

"I want to know your contingency plans, Hopmeir," Lindermanns said cuttingly, glaring at the Death Merchant. "You didn't come here without making arrangements for failure. You have failed. How soon can we expect a visit from the SIS?"

"What time were you to radio *HMS Taurus?*" demanded Sir MacLean.

Ronald Lynch and Martin Shevlin glanced bitterly at each other. Kingman stared in disgust at the Death Merchant. A glimmer of realization had managed to creep past the mighty barrier of his anger and he wondered what Camellion was planning. Whatever it was, it had better be damned good and ten times as fast.

"I don't know what British intelligence might do," Camellion said. What we tried to do was a last chance effort. There isn't one shred of evidence to connect any of you to the Brotherhood. The SIS knew it would be a waste of time to come out here to Dunbeath Hall and ask questions. You'd deny everything."

Ex-SS *Obergruppenfuhrer* ("General") Lindermanns regarded Camellion for a long moment with solemn eyes. When he finally spoke to Sir MacLean, his voice was unexpectedly gentle and courteous. "He's telling the truth. The SIS doesn't have any evidence. They took a gamble. They sent in these four fools and they failed. Luck is on our side."

"Not luck," Sir MacLean said, drawing himself up straight in the chair. "It was destiny. It was the will of God!"

For the first time, Gilbert Drummond spoke. "And when these four come up missing? What will the SIS do then?"

"The ways of Intelligence are beyond you, Drummond," Lindermanns said softly. "These four are expendable. The SIS couldn't care less about them. They will not do anything because there isn't anything legal that they can do but watch and wait, which they are doing anyway.

Richard Camellion surprised Lindermanns and everyone else by suddenly saying, "So far I've been answering all the questions. Now, I'd like an answer to a question of my own. I'd like to know——"

"How we knew you were coming!" finished Lindermanns, again twisting his thin lips into that sickening smile which seemed to be his trademark. "How that must trouble you."

"You were watched from the moment you landed on the beach," Edward Tynes MacLean said, then bit off the end of an expensive cigar. "We made it as easy for you as possible."

"All that work for nothing," Ronald Lynch said. "We should have listened to Kingman."

The Death Merchant shifted to a more comfortable position, a difficult task since he was sitting on and leaning against bare stone.

"It can't hurt to tell us," Camellion said to Lindermanns. "I don't think we'll ever be talking again to the SIS or the press. I've suspected a certain person for a long time and I'm curious as to whether I'm right. Not that I ever thought the Brotherhood was powerful enough to buy anyone in the SIS."

"We found out purely by accident." Lindermanns looked more elated than ever. "Several days ago a low level clerk in Whitehall came across the report of what you intended to do. He mentioned the matter to his wife. She told her brother. The brother told a good friend in all confidence. The good friend is a London member of the Brotherhood. Our communications are first rate. By four o'clock yesterday afternoon we were warned. It was a fortuitious chain of circumstances that worked in our favor."

"Again, the will of the Almighty!" intoned Sir Huge Mac-Lean pontifically. "The Powers of Heaven are guiding our hand.

He got to his feet, looked a moment at Richard Camellion and glanced at Kingman, Shevelin and Lynch. His two sons, Drummond and Lindermanns also stood up. One of the guards shouldered his Czech assault rifle and began to move the chairs to the outside of the dungeon.

"We will not meet again, gentlemen, until seven o'clock in the morning," Sir MacLean said, his voice heavy with sarcasm.

"I presume we'll then all go bye-bye in the Fairey Norman parked out back?" Camellion said. "And get out at 10,000 feet over the Sea of the Hebrides?"

"Death is always the penalty for those who oppose me," Sir MacLean said. Turning, he started for the doorway, saying to the four guards, "Be sure the door is bolted after we leave."

"Don't slip on any watermelon rinds, crackpot!" Kingman called out.

Sir Hugh didn't look back. Neither did any of the other

71

men as, one by one, they went out through the narrow door. The last man to leave was one of the guards. He slammed the door shut, and Camellion and the three other men could hear a heavy bolt being shoved into place. The dungeon was in darkness, except for the light that filtered through the small four-barred opening in the top of the door.

"Listen, damn you——!" Kingman started.

"Shut up, you damned fool," hissed the Death Merchant. "I have work to do and little time in which to do it . . .

# Chapter Seven

The body feeds on food. The soul feeds on impulse. And men who live always on the brink of death take nourishment by always being prepared for the impossible.

With an amazed Kingman and a confused Lynch and Shevlin watching him, the Death Merchant went to work. He stood up, wriggled his cuffed hands underneath his shirt, and squirmed them along the small of his back, his fingers searching for the zipper hidden by a flap of coverall material. Ah, there was the tab of the zipper.

"What the hell are you doing?" snarled Kingman in a hoarse whisper. "You've already ruined the worst day of my life."

"I'm going to get us out of here; that's what I'm doing."

Camellion pulled down the zipper tab and, with effort, pushed his manacled hands between his skin and shorts until they reached his buttocks. All the while he watched the small window in the cell door. With a slight grunt and a half-defecation movement of the anal sphincter muscle, Camellion forced the *Plan* from his rectum and felt it slide into his fingers. Quickly, he inched his hands and the tiny aluminum tube upward, pulling them and the *Plan* through the slit in the coveralls.

"Well, I'll be damned," Kingman whispered. "Now I've seen everything!"

The Death Merchant sat back down on the stone floor and unscrewed the *Plan* in the middle, after which he placed the top end on the floor and kept the bottom half in his hands. He tilted the bottom half slightly and, with thumb and forefinger of his right hand, took out a thin lock pick and began working on the lock of the handcuff around his left wrist. Seventy-one seconds later both wrists were free and the handcuffs lay on the floor beside him.

"All of you keep your hands behind your back and remain on the floor," Camellion whispered.

"At least we're free, thanks to you," Shevlin said.

"We still have to get out of the cell and overpower the guards," Camellion said, "and that's only the beginning."

Camellion sat down on the floor and used the lock pick to slit the rubber sole of his left combat boot, gradually prying off the bottom of the thick rubber sole. He then looked at what lay inside the hollowed out portion he had pried loose: five squares of Amatol, each square the size of a postage stamp and one-fifth of an inch thick. Twenty-five feet of thin copper wire was also included. He dropped the coiled wire and the five squares of explosive into the right breast pocket of the coveralls, then tugged at the heel of his left boot. He pulled the lower section of the heel to one side and took from the hollowed inside a tiny battery-powered combination timer and detonator, both of which he dropped into the pocket containing the Amatol and the wire.

"What next?" whispered Kingman.

"Patience is needed with everyone, but first of all with ourselves."

"Horseshit!"

The Death Merchant leaned back against the stone wall, put his hands behind his back and placed the handcuffs on his wrists, but in such a manner that each steel band was barely inside the receiver, only up to the first lock groove. A flick of his wrists and the handcuffs would fall free.

"Be prepared to act in an instant," he whispered to the men. "But don't jump them until I make the first move."

"It's your show," mumbled Kingman.

The Death Merchant called out in a loud voice, "GUARD! HEY GUARD!"

Presently a face appeared in the barred opening of the door.

"What do you want?" asked Hershel MacNab in a thick burr.

"I've got to go to the john, to the toilet," Camellion replied.

MacNab sneered.

"You do have a toilet down here, don't you?"

"We have but you're not going to use it, laddie. All of you are going to stay in the cell until it's time for you to get on the plane."

"Listen"—Camellion put a pleading note in his voice—"I'm about to crap in my pants."

74

The Scottish Nazi grinned, enjoying Camellion's supposed discomfort. "Sit in your own stink. Who cares?"

"Sir MacLean will care. What do you think he will say when his plane starts to stink like an open cesspool?"

MacNab hesitated, and by the glow of the lights outside the dungeon, Camellion could see doubt and indecision etched on the man's face.

"You'd better think twice," Camellion warned. "Not only will the interior of the plane stink to high heaven, but Sir MacLean is sure to think you're all a bunch of cowards. After all, we're handcuffed. You men are armed. Or maybe you guys are cowards and are afraid to take one handcuffed man to the toilet?"

MacNab glared at the Camellion, and his face disappeared from the door. A moment later, Camellion and the others heard the sound of a heavy bolt being slid back.

The heavy dungeon door creaked open, and MacNab, a 9-mm Sile-Bebelli autopistol in his right hand, advanced into the cell. Behind him came Robert MacHeth and David Bohanus, a Hawes/Sig-Sauer .38 super auto in MacHeth's hand, Bohanus holding a Ruger .44 Magnum revolver.

Bernard Lithglow, the fourth guard, remained in the doorway, a Czech assault rifle cradled loosely in his arms.

The Death Merchant had only one worry—*if he checks the handcuffs, the fat will hit the fan, and then some!*

Keeping their distance, MacNab, MacHeth, and Bohanus covered the Death Merchant, Kingman and the two British SIS agents.

MacNab motioned to Camellion with the Sile-Bebelli pistol.

"Get up and move to the door. Do it slow, laddie."

Camellion shrugged, got to his feet and said resignedly, "What the hell do you expect me to do, tap-dance? You have the gun."

"Keep that in mind, laddie."

Judging the distance and carefully weighing the odds, Camellion moved slowly toward Bernard Lithglow, who remained in the doorway. With each second, Camellion measured the distance and weighed the odds. He wasn't concerned about his own moves, but—*if the others don't attack at the right time, we'll all end up dead. Hell, it's not on my schedule to become a citizen of the spirit world!*

Camellion, not daring to move his wrists, afraid that the handcuffs would come loose and fall to the floor, walked

75

toward the door, MacNab only a few feet behind him. The cautious Bohanus and MacHeth began to edge back from Kingman, Shevlin, and Lynch.

The Death Merchant was less than four feet from Bernard Lithglow when he made up his mind that it was either go into action now or let the chance go by forever. As he started to twist his body to the right, he let fly a terrific *Sokuto geri* sword-foot kick that landed exactly where he had wanted it to land: right smack in the center of Lithglow's solar plexus—a grandslam dynamite kick that would have staggered a Brahma bull.

All in the same lightning-quick motion, Camellion, keeping his elbows close to the waist, spun to the right and, as the handcuffs fell from his wrists, simultaneously brought his right elbow against MacNab's right forearm, for the Sile-Bebelli automatic was in MacNab's right hand. Before MacNab could recover from the surprise attack, Camellion swung his arm, placing it on the man's elbow joint so that the Scot's right forearm rested in the crook of his right elbow.

From the corner of his eye, the Death Merchant saw that his sword-foot kick had done its job on the dummy with the Czech assault rifle. Lithglow had dropped the weapon and was curled up on the floor, just outside the door, clutching his middle and making noises like a gagged chicken being roasted slowly over a charcoal fire.

At the same instant that Camellion had struck, Kingman, Shevlin, and Lynch became alive with vicious movement. Rearing up, by pushing with the heels of his hands, Kingman became a human rocket, his legs capturing Robert MacHeth's arm, his right leg moving in the direction opposite to the direction of the left. The sudden pressure almost snapped MacHeth's arm. He yelled from the pain, opened his hand, and the Hawes/Sig-Sauer went flying across the gloomy dungeon.

Concurrently, Ronald Lynch and Martin Shelvin made a wreck of David Bohanus. Shevlin pushed himself up on his hands, forcing his body as high as it would go. Doing the same thing, Lynch propelled himself forward and kicked upward with his right foot. As Lynch's right foot crashed into Bohanus' wrist and sent the arm upward and the Ruger .44 Magnum sailing, Shevlin's left heel slammed into Bohanus' right kneecap, smashed the bone and caused intolerable agony to explode in the Scot's leg.

The Death Merchant, with MacNab's forearm resting in the crook of his right elbow, locked his right hand with his left hand and bent swiftly from the waist. MacNab had no choice but to go with the bend, or let his arm be snapped at the elbow.

MacNab was a third of the way to the stone floor when Camellion used a right foot heel stamp against the Scot's right instep and, with his left hand, twisted the Sile-Bebelli from the man's right hand and slapped him across the mouth with the side of the auto-pistol, breaking out half a dozen teeth. With a weird kind of squawk, MacNab sank to the floor, his arms flopping. Camellion kicked him in the stomach. He groaned again and fell forward on his face, his hands clutching at his belly.

Robert MacHeth and David Bohanus hardly had time to know what was happening to them. Kingman bounded up and used a very rapid, high *Pentjak-silat* kick that landed on MacHeth's chest and sent him crashing back, half-unconscious, to the opposite wall.

Bohanus, sick with pain, had dropped to his one good knee, a movement that was the final mistake of his life. In an instant, Ronald Lynch was behind him, the SIS agent's arms going around the Scot's neck in a Commando bone breaker hold. Lynch's arms tightened. There was a snap. Bohanus' head rolled to one side on his chicken-limp neck. Lynch untangled his arms from the man's neck and let the corpse sag to the floor.

"Grab the guns," ordered the Death Merchant. He rushed out the door, picked up the Czech Model 58 assault rifle. Behind him in the dank dungeon, Kingman scooped up the Sig-Sauer pistol while Shevlin grabbed the Ruger .44 Magnum and Lynch picked up the Sile-Bebelli autoloader.

On the floor, Bernard Lithglow and Hershel MacNab were in the worst kind of agony. Robert MacHeth wasn't exactly comfortable. He sat against the wall, several of his ribs pulled from his fractured breastbone, his every movement a double crucifixion of stabbing pain.

Camellion's men left the dungeon and looked around. To the north, on the other side of the low, wide arch, was the wine cellar, thousands of bottles in racks. In front of the dungeon was a table, chairs, an assortment of empty boxes, and three Czech assault rifles leaning against the wall.

To the south, at the end of the sixty-foot-long wall, were

77

the stone steps. On the other side, to the west, were five more dungeons, their doors closed.

Camellion handed Kingman the Czech A-R he had picked up from the floor. "Stand in the doorway and keep an eye on the door at th top of the stairs. We're a long way from home, buddy."

Kingman accepted the A-R and checked to make sure the weapon was loaded and ready to be fired.

"What are you"—Kingman glanced at Shevlin and Lynch who were taking two of the assault rifles from the wall—"and the two Limeys going to do?"

"You heard Sir MacLean," Camellion reminded Kingman. "He said that the British could search the house from top to bottom and not find a trace of us. That would have to include our weapons."

"Yeah, and John-Percy referred to the arms and ammo as being 'down here.' The question is, where?"

"That's what I intend to find out, starting with this idiot."

The Death Merchant looked down at Lithglow, who was groaning in pain and rolling back and forth on the floor. He motioned to Shevlin and Lynch. "Search those two in the cell; they may have second weapons."

The two British agents nodded and hurried back into the dungeon.

Camellion got down, grabbed a handful of Lithglow's hair, then released the man in disgust. The man had passed out from shock.

*Hell!* The Death Merchant went back into the dungeon and looked first at MacNab, then at MacHeth. Of the two, MacHeth was the more physically able to talk.

The Death Merchant walked over to MacHeth, who was still sitting on the floor. "What's your name, fella?"

"MacHeth," the man mumbled. "Robert MacHeth, and I'm not going to tell you anything."

Without a word, Camellion reached down, grabbed MacHeth's left hand and broke the thumb, much to the astonishment of Ronald Lynch and Martin Shevlin; and while MacHeth howled in pain, Camellion snapped his index finger.

In the meanwhile, MacNab was trying weakly to get to his feet, blood dripping from his smashed-in mouth.

Camellion walked over to him and, when MacNab tried a right cross, ducked, grabbed the man's arm, twisted it behind his back and slammed him against the north wall with such brutal force that the sound of the Scot's head hitting the stones sounded like a walnut being cracked. Camellion next grabbed the dazed, bloody-faced man by the back of the collar, kicked his legs out from under him and flung him down next to MacHeth.

Camellion held out his hand and said to Lynch, "Give me the pistol you picked up."

A disbelieving look on his sweaty face, Lynch pulled the Italian-made Sile-Bebelli from the right rear pocket of his coveralls and handed the weapon, butt-first, muzzle down, to Camellion, saying, "It's all set to fire. All you have to do is release the safety."

The Death Merchant nodded and looked toward Kingman who was standing in the doorway, looking toward the steps in the distance. "Mel go outside and close the door. I don't want the sounds of the shots to drift upstairs."

Kingman grinned, went outside and closed the door.

The Death Merchant got down on one knee and grinned crookedly at MacNab and MacHeth who stared at him in fear, hatred, and disbelief.

"One of you bagpipe boobs is going to tell me where the arsenal down here is and how we can get in," Camellion said. "I don't give a damn who talks first. I'm going to blow you apart, piece by piece, until you do talk."

"The SIS doesn't use such methods," MacNab said despairingly.

MacHeth was also in mental and emotional anguish, as well as physical agony, but before he could say anything, Camellion put the muzzle of the Sile-Bebelli against MacNab's left kneecap and pulled the trigger. There was a muffled report. MacNab screamed hoarsely and fainted.

Camellion turned the smoking muzzle of the Sile-Bebelli toward Robert MacHeth whose face was a picture of panic and black fear.

Lynch and Shevlin exchanged nervous glances, each convinced that he was watching the calculated actions of a savage, of a man whose methods bordered on the diabolical.

"Let's see how you like walking around without a right foot," Camellion said, his words a hiss, like drops of water falling on a hot stove. He started to turn the pistol in the direction of MacHeth's foot. The Scot cried out in fear, jerked both legs back and tried to squeeze himself into the wall.

"Wait! I'll tell you!" he choked out. He pulled his knees up to his chin and stared pleadingly at Camellion. "Outside, the other side of the stones. I-I'll show you."

"You have one minute." Camellion's voice was a pure warning. "Move!"

MacHeth struggled to his feet, cried out loudly from the pain of his broken ribs and sagged against the stones. "My r-ribs. They're b-broken," he muttered.

"Broken ribs are the least of your troubles," growled Camellion. "Get going. You've already wasted twenty seconds."

With effort, MacHeth straightened up and half-staggered from the dungeon. Then he pointed to the long stretch of stone wall to the left, between the last dungeon and the steps.

"I think this bagpipe boob is giving us the runaround," Kingman said through clenched teeth.

"Where's the entrance?" Camellion said coldly and jammed the muzzle of the pistol against the right side of MacHeth's neck. "All I see is a stone wall."

MacHeth stiffened. He began to tremble from fear. "I-I'll show you."

"You have ten seconds," Camellion said impatiently. "You two"—he glanced at Shevlin and Lynch who had followed him out of the cell—"keep an eye on the wine cellar. Kingman, if the door above the steps opens—shoot."

MacHeth walked twenty feet to the north, to one of the ancient torch holders—a rusted metal ring fastened to a length of iron mounted to the wall and tilted sideways. MacHeth reached up, took hold of the length of iron and pulled downward. He then went to the next torch holder and repeated the procedure.

Noiselessly, a section of the stones in the wall swung outward, a section that was six feet wide and seven feet high. A steel door was beyond, in a four feet recess. A combination lock was built into the right side of the door.

"Only Sir MacLean and his sons know the combination," MacHeth said fearfully.

The Death Merchant glared at MacHeth. "Are there automatic weapons and handguns in there?"

MacHeth quickly nodded. "Even grenades and explosives. And the weapons you laddies had, all your stuff. Sir MacLean didn't want anything found in case the British searched the house."

Kingman stared at the door, then turned to Camellion. "Think you can blow it?"

"We can try. They'll hear the big bang upstairs, but we're already skating on ice so thin we have nothing but air holding us up."

"We'll have to get in and out of there in a hurry," Kingman said. His voice was ragged with strain, his face tight and desperate. "And there's no way around it: We'll have to shoot our way out from down here."

"Which is why we need grenades." Camellion reached out and took the assault rifle from Kingman. "Put this dummy back in the dungeon and lock the door. I'll keep watch until you get back."

MacHeth, grateful to be alive, almost ran back to the dungeon. Kingman closed the door, slid the long bolt into place, and hurried back to Camellion, who handed him the assault rifle, then took the five squares of Amatol from his pocket and began forming the putty-like material into a ball.

Worry wrinkles formed on Kingman's forehead. "That steel door looks damned solid. There's enough of the stuff for the hinges and the lock?"

"We don't have to concern ourselves about the hinges," Camellion explained. "Once the lock is destroyed, we can pull open the door, or push it open, if that's the way it swings. Call Shevlin and Lynch. They can go in with me after the door blows and help me carry out our stuff and anything else we might want."

Camellion had made all the necessary preparations. He had molded the Amatol around the dial of the combination set in the steel door and had attached the timer-detonator.

"All of you get back," he called out. "The T-D has only a one minute set."

Kingman, Shevlin, and Lynch moved back from the stone doorway and took positions against the wall, rigid, expectant looks on their faces.

The Death Merchant turned the small black knob of the timer all the way to the right, backed away from the steel door, hurried through the stone entrance and moved ten feet down the wall. Standing in front of Martin Shevlin, he waited for the explosion.

*BERRRRROOOOMMMMMMMMMM!* The thunderous concussion ice-picked in their ears, punched at their skulls and shook the ancient stone wall, the deep rumbling echo bouncing back and forth without any kind of particular rhythm. A cloud of blue-gray smoke boiled from the stone opening.

"Watch those steps, Kingman," ordered Camellion, who then sprinted for the smoking opening, Shevlin and Lynch racing behind him. Each British agent carried a lantern he had removed from a hook in the low flat ceiling.

Kingman ran to the dungeon closest to the steps, opened the cell door, which swung to his left, and got behind it. As thick as the door was, it would easily stop any high velocity bullet.

Camellion and the two SIS agents saw that the Amatol had not only blown off the combination lock but had slammed the door inward on its hinges. Moving through the drifting smoke and fumes, they entered the arsenal, Shevlin and Lynch holding up the lanterns.

"I say, Sir MacLean could damn well start a bloody war!" exclaimed Lynch.

His words were not an exaggeration. Wooden racks, lining the walls, were filled with assault rifles and submachine guns of various makes and calibers. There were Soviet AKMs, Israeli UZIs, Czech Vz58s and deadly little Czech 9mm Skorpion machine pistols. An entire array of West German submachine guns—G3A4 NATO rifles; H&K 54 subs, H&K MPKs and MP5s; Haenel MKb42(H)s and Walther and Erma machine pistols; open boxes of magazines underneath the weapons. There were even submachine guns not too well known on the world market—the 9mm Argentine "MEMS," the Danish Madsen, the Swiss Rexim Fv4, and the Steyr 9mm Parabellum.

There were light machine guns—the Rumanian 7.92mm on a bipod, still in its case; the deadly German MB34 that killed so many Americans and British during World War II. It rested on a tripod next to a case of thermate grenades, the top of which Camellion was smashing in with the wooden butt of a British EM-1 rifle.

And heavy caliber machine guns. A 50 caliber Browning, with box magazine attached, sat next to a crate filled with demolition grenades. A German 7.92mm heavy machine gun, an MG-42, was mounted on a quadrupod, to one side of a crate on which lay the weapons and shoulder bags that the Brotherhood had taken from the Death Merchant and his three men. From the way the shoulder bags bulged, none of the tear gas canisters of frag grenades had been removed.

Shevlin and Lynch, sweat dripping from their faces, began grabbing shoulder bags and holsters filled with autopistols, including the Death Merchant's Auto Mags which were still in their special black shoulder holsters. Even the bags containing the Solenoid-Inductor Intensifier and the Audio Countermeasures Service System were there on top of the crate, against the sides of which were stenciled: *RIFLE NO. 3., MARK 1. (T) A—PATTERN 14 (T) A—ENFIELD. PROPERTY OF THE UNITED KINGDOM.*

"Look at that," Shevlin said bitterly, buckling on the brace of Ri-Power Brownings. "Old stuff from the last war. Either stolen or bought as surplus."

The Death Merchant walked from the crate whose top he had smashed in, carrying six thermate canisters in his hands. "Each of you take six of these babies, and put six in Kingman's shoulder bag. And strap on your Ingrams. Grab three of those H&K MP-5 subs. You'll find fifty cartridge magazines in a box below the chatterboxes. Hurry it up."

"Good idea." Lynch slipped the strap of a Gussett bag over his left shoulder. "We're going to need all the fire power we——"

An ear-splitting burst of Czech 58 assault rifle fire cut him off in mid-sentence. Lynch, Shevlin, and Camellion knew what was happening. Sir MacLean and his assortment of crazies had heard the explosion and had come down to the cellar rooms to investigate. Seeing the door at the top of the staris open, Kingman had opened fire.

"I say, chaps, we have company," Shevlin said. Surprised at the calmness in his own voice, he swung the Ingram over his back, buckled the strap to the tab-ring on his chest and rushed over to the crate of thermate grenades. Reaching into the crate, he glanced worriedly at Lynch who had already taken out six thermate canisters and was grabbing an H&K submachine gun from a rack; then he glanced at Camellion, who was coming toward him, an MP-5 sub-gun in his hands.

Camellion paused and glanced at the two bags on the crate. In one bag was the S-I-I. The other bag enclosed the A.C.S.S. device.

"We can't take them," he said, as if talking to himself. "They're too bulky to carry."

He pushed the two bags to the floor with the barrel of

the H&K MP-5, lowered the machine gun and put half a dozen 9mm bullets through each bag, turning the two expensive devices to junk.

More bursts of automatic weapons fire exploded from the outside, several bursts coming from the direction of the steps, Kingman replying with a short five-round blast of his own.

The Death Merchant hurried through the wrecked metal doorway, eased himself through the stone opening, went to the end of the stone door and sneaked a quick look around the thick edge. He pulled back in time to avoid getting his head splattered all over the door, floor, and ceiling. High energy projectiles zipped by where his head, neck and right shoulder had been. A dozen more projectiles ricocheted from the stones with high screaming whines. He had, however, seen what he had wanted to see. The door at the top of the short flight of stone steps was open. Two dead men lay sprawled out at the bottom of the steps.

*No problem with Kingman,* he thought. The CIA spook had taken all four Czech assault rifles with him. *He has more than enough ammo until we get there.*

Camellion glanced to his left and saw Shevlin and Lynch coming toward him, Lynch, carrying Kingman's bags and weapons, weighed down double.

"How does it look?" murmured Shevlin, cocking the H&K machine gun. He sniffed at the stale air thick with fumes of burnt cordite.

"Kingman's already iced two of them." Camellion cleared his throat. "There's no way they can get through that door and come down here."

"Maybe so," Ron Lynch conceded, then went on curiously, "but it's as broad as it's long. We can't get up there . . . "

"That does seem to be the heart of the problem," sighed Camellion.

# Chapter Eight

Hope is always more powerful when backed up by action—only the Death Merchant didn't like the kind of action he knew he was going to have to take. Damn it, the odds were only fifty-fifty!

Another tornado of Boat Tail bullets slammed into the other side of the stone door, the dozens of impacts setting up a crescendo of high pitched zing, zing, zings. Twenty feet ahead and to the right of Camellion, more antimony lead alloy projectiles came at Kingman, thudding into the thick wooden door whose front was already ripped and splintered.

Kingman replied by thrusting his Czech A-R around the side and triggering off a short burst. Camellion did the same—a quick blast around the end of the stone door with the Heckler and Koch.

Crouched to Camellion's left, Lynch and Shevlin looked around the area, a frantic, trapped look in their eyes; yet their jaws were set in determination.

"We can't charge the steps," Shevlin said urgently to the Death Merchant. "We'd be cut down before we got half-way."

"And the distance is too far for us to use grenades," Lynch said, all the while looking at Camellion, as if demanding that "Mr. Hopmeir" come up with an instant answer.

Camellion did!

"One man could do it if he had a lot of cover fire," Camellion said. "Frankly, I don't see any other way."

Martin Shevlin shook his head in disbelief. For the moment, speech was beyond him.

"You're out of your mind," Lynch said hoarsely. "There are three or four men firing from upstairs. You'd never get up the steps!"

"But I could get to the side of the steps. With a sprinkle of luck and a dash of fate, I could reach the wall to the left of the steps before they even knew I was there. Get the drift, old chap?"

Lynch's expression changed to one of hope and understanding.

Shevlin's incomprehension of the situation vanished and total understanding spread over his face. "Yes, that close you could use grenades," he said heartily, then glanced at Lynch who had turned and was headed back toward the arsenal room. "Where are you going? Did you forget something?"

Lynch swung around. "I'm going to move one of the empty crates out here. We can stand on it and fire over the door."

"Excellent. I'll help you," Shevlin said. "We wouldn't be able to get any kind of accuracy if two of us had to fire around the side."

The two SIS agents went into the arsenal and soon returned, carrying an empty wooden crate which they promptly turned upside down and placed against the inside of the stone door. Both then climbed up on the crate and, keeping hunched down, looked at the Death Merchant who was standing at one end of the crate, close to the edge of the door.

"Here, take this." The Death Merchant handed Shevlin the MP-5. "It will give you more fire power, and you won't have to stop to reload. But don't forget to bring it with you when you come forward."

"What happens if you stop a bullet?" Shevlin sounded puzzled.

"In that case, take three aspirin, gargle, and drink plenty of liquids. Another thing: Use short bursts and aim only at the side edges of the doorway. OK?" Camellion pulled one of the .44 Backpacker Auto Mags. "Wait until they fire another burst, then open fire during the lag time."

The two British agents, who were already of the opinion that Camellion belonged in a well-padded cell, looked even more perplexed.

"Lag time?" Shevlin asked, mystified.

"Between bursts," the Death Merchant explained, his words suddenly chopped off by another deafening blast of machine gun and automatic rifle fire from the doorway at the top of the steps, the chorus furnished by the lively rigadoon of ricochets. The seven-second blast was followed by a fearful silence filled with tumbling echoes.

"Now!" Camellion's voice was as sharp as a pistol shot. He tensed and raised himself slightly on the balls of his feet.

Shevlin and Lynch reared up on the crate and opened fire with their H&K sub-guns a fraction of a second before Kingman triggered off a long blast, his own 7.62mm slugs mingling with Lynch and Shevlin's 9mm projectiles. Scores of solid based bullets blasted the sides of the wooden doorway, sending out a cloud of splinters. Several 9mms struck one of the Brotherhood, who had been caught off guard, in that he hadn't expected anyone to fire over the stone door and had leaned out too far at the wrong time. He let out a high-pitched scream, spun, dropped the Czech automatic rifle, fell forward and pitched down the steps with all the grace of a broken tinker toy, his body jerking violently when it fell into the line of Kingman's 7.62mm projectiles.

A .44 Auto Mag in his right hand, the Death Merchant left the protective innerside of the stone door and, keeping low, streaked forward. He didn't duck. He didn't dodge. He didn't use a crisscross pattern. There wasn't time. Instead, he made a straight-in lightning dash for the side of the wall to the left of the stone steps, tapered jacketed slugs singing above him.

His heart thumping in his chest, the Death Merchant closed in on the wall. He put on the brakes, hit the wall with his left shoulder, turned to the opposite direction and did a quick analysis of his position. The doorway at the top of the steps was ten feet above him and six feet to his left. He couldn't be absolutely positive, but he was ninety-nine percent certain that none of the Brotherhood had seen him. The savage firing of Shevlin, Lynch, and Kingman had prevented them from even shoving their weapons around the edges of the doorway and returning the fire.

*Man, this is like trying to tap dance on the point of an ice pick blade!* Camellion reached into one kit bag and took out a fragmentation grenade.

Kingman and the two SIS agents were also subject to the lull of lag time. Even so, by now they had exhausted the ammo in their weapons and had to stop to reload, to shove in full clips. Taking advantage of the lull, the gunmen of the Brotherhood shoved their weapons around the sides of the splintered doorway and cut loose with everything they had, this "everything" being two Czech automatic rifles, a British 9mm B.S.A. machine gun, and a Spanish Star Model Z-45 chatter box. Now it was the turn of Camellion's men to keep down and hope that "Mr. Hopmeir" wouldn't be butched by enemy bullets.

The Death Merchant did have one thing in his favor. The four men in the doorway were also limited, in that while two of them had to kneel down and lean out, the other two had to stand behind them and lean out to fire— two men on each side, in positions that limited movement and seriously interfered with accuracy. None of the four could see the Death Merchant flattened against the wall, because he was too far to their right to be within range of their peripheral vision. He lost that safety factor after he pulled the pin of the grenade with his teeth and stepped five feet from the wall to throw the missile through the doorway.

Camellion had switched the Auto Mag to his left hand and, holding the grenade with his right, was drawing back his arm to throw when Clifton Buchanleigh, one of the gunmen on the far side of the doorway, happened to catch sight of him from the corner of his eye. Standing behind Bertram Chetwick who was on both knees, Buchanleigh choked out a strangled yell of warning and tried to swing his Spanish Star Z-45 machine gun toward the Death Merchant.

Concurrent with Buchanleigh's movement, Chetwick also saw Camellion, panicked and tried to fall back, his sudden motion knocking Buchanleigh off balance. Arthur Brudd and Brian MacMorrisy, the two neo-Nazi gunsels on the other side of the doorway, didn't know what was going on.

Even if Chetwick hadn't fallen back against Buchanleigh, Buchanleigh still would have died—Chetwick, too. Buchanleigh was not even halfway through the motion of swinging around the Z-45 when the Death Merchant's Backpacker AMP roared and a huge .44 Magnum bullet banged Buchanleigh just below the hollow of the throat. The TNT impact blew a hole in him the size of a Florida Sunkist orange, lifted him six inches off the floor, and pitched him back as though he had been shot from the mouth of a cannon.

Chetwick was next. His mouth was open and he was sitting on his butt, about to roll over, when Camellion's second .44 flat-nosed projectile struck him half an inch above the right ear and exploded his head, numerous chunks of bone, blood, skin, hair, and gray brain matter splattering all over Art Brudd and Brian MacMorrisy and four of the other men in the room next to the kitchen of the mansion, the room in which the door to the cellar was located.

"My God! What's happening?" one man cried, almost gagging as he looked down and saw part of Chetwick's brain oozing down his shirtfront.

He soon found out. Camellion tossed in the fragmentation grenade that hit the floor six feet past the doorway, rolled three feet to the left and exploded with an enormous roar and a blinding flash of fire. Three men were killed instantly. A fourth had his left arm torn off and would soon be an anemic corpse. Art Brudd had been blinded by shrapnel and his face turned into bloody strips of flesh. He kept muttering, *"Jesus save me, Jesus save me, Jesus save me."* The rest of the men had been stung by jagged pieces of shrapnel and deafened by the close-in concussion. But none were seriously injured.

Oddly enough, Brian MacMorrisy had been stung in the side by only a few pieces of shrapnel. Now, he went all to pieces and became hysterical. He jumped to his feet and in so doing exposed himself in the doorway.

Melvin Kingman, running forward, immediately stitched him from tailbone to tonsils with half a dozen 7.62mm projectiles. MacMorrisy was stone dead before he hit the floor.

The Death Merchant, having drawn his second AMP, charged up the stone steps, ready to fire the instant he detected the slightest movement beyond the doorway. Behind him came Kingman, Lynch, and Shevlin, all three running as though Satan and his legions were in hot pursuit.

The Death Merchant cannonballed himself through the doorway, saw that several dazed men were trying to pick up machine guns while two others staggered drunkenly toward the closed kitchen door.

*Dumb ding-dongs. They all have the delusion that they're human!*

Camellion's twin Auto Mags roared—four shots so fast that the explosions mingled together. The four Brotherhood gunmen, dying without a sound, fell to the floor already flowing with blood. Only then did Camellion turn his attention to Art Brudd who was crawling on the floor, walking on his knees, his hands outstretched, muttering "God save me, God save me . . ." in a strangled voice.

The Auto Mag in Camellion's left hand exploded. The big bullet tore into Brudd's left side, came out his right side and buried itself in the wooden floor. Brudd flopped on his face and lay still.

"Dummy!" Camellion said softly. "What I have split asunder let no man put together."

Without bothering to look at Kingman and the two Britishers who were staring at the bloody carnage in the room, Camellion next put four more .44 Magnum slugs through the door, just in case any of the Brotherhood, who might be in the kitchen, decided to charge. He then moved to the left side of the door, started shoving fresh clips into the AMPs, and glanced around at Kingman and the two SIS agents.

"Put on your gas masks," he said. "We're not going to linger around here for prayer meeting."

"I suppose we can scratch our plan to black-bag Mac-Lean?" Kingman said complainingly. He finished buckling the two Coonan .357 autopistols around his waist and accepted the two kit bags that Lynch handed him. "At least we won't have to take that plane ride. I always did think that flying was unsafe." He reached into one kit-bag and pulled out a British Army L-19 all-purpose gas mask.

"You have six thermate grenades in the other bag," Lynch said to Kingman. "We got them out of the arsenal."

Kingman chuckled sinisterly. "Good. We can burn this damn place to the ground."

Martin Shevlin handed the Death Merchant an H&K MP-5 submachine gun. "It's fully loaded," he said curtly. "Do you have any specific plan?"

Lynch, reloading his MP-5, said dolefully, "I hate to think about the repercussions when the 'Iron Lady' hears about this," Camellion replied, referring to Margaret Thatcher, Britain's Prime Minister. "Heads will certainly roll."

"Don't tell her," Kingman advised, his voice calm, although muffled through the gas mask he had slipped over his face and head. "Be practical and lie like hell. Why, if we told the idiots in Washington about everything we did for the good of the nation, Soviet tanks would have been clanking down Pennsylvania Avenue years ago."

Shevlin's voice was as bleak as a January wind blowing

over the moors. "By the time all this is over, I have a feeling that the whole world will know." Again, he asked Camellion, who had holstered his AMPs, put on his gas mask
and leaned the Heckler & Koch against the wall, "You
must have a plan. We should have some kind of organized
arrangement for getting back to the jeep."

"You have to crawl before you can walk," Camellion
said firmly through the gas mask. "We fight our way out,
the quickest and the most expeditiously. All of you get set."

"Christ on a camel! I'm as ready as I'll ever be," Kingman said drily and expertly pulled back the cocking knob
of the Heckler & Koch.

Lynch and Shevlin exchanged thoughtful glances, each
sensing that Camellion and Kingman were actually enjoying themselves. Shevlin looked steadily at the door for a
moment, then said somberly, "We're not going to fool them
twice with a grenade. But the tear gas should give us an
edge."

Kingman laughed slyly. "Yeah, they're not running
around in this pile of stones with gas masks in their hip
pockets." He stepped on the back of a corpse as he moved
closer to the Death Merchant. "Personally, I prefer dynamite, stick by stick. Man, with enough dynamite, you could
blow up all of Scotland."

The Death Merchant motioned for Lynch and Shevlin to
take positions by the wall to the left of the door and they
quickly complied.

"Be ready with those MP-5s," he said. "I'm going to
open the door."

The door, thick and solid, was closed by means of a
wrought iron lift bar latch. Keeping back against the wall,
he reached out with his right hand, gently lifted the latch
and pushed against the door with one finger. Then he
quickly pulled back his hand. Slowly the door swung open.

Not a single shot was fired. There was only dead silence.

"They have to be waiting," whispered Kingman sav-
agely. "They expect a grenade. So no one is in there.
They're in the room beyond the next one."

"I'm standing in blood," Lynch said in disgust, his voice
sounding metallic through the built-in amplifier of the gas
mask. "My God, it's a sticky mess."

The Death Merchant took a fragmentation grenade from
one of his shoulder bags, thinking that *this business is*

*somewhat like ranching. Every now and then you have to get your hands dirty.*

He pulled the pin and pitched the grenade forcefully through the doorway into the kitchen, the grenade exploding as he put his hand again into the bag and took out a gray canister with a single horizontal red band. He pulled the ring from the tear gas canister and flipped it into the kitchen while hundreds of pieces of shrapnel pinged all over the kitchen and pieces of torn-apart chairs and chunks of a table crashed to the floor.

The canister hit the floor toward the center of the room, rolled a few feet, stopped against the splintered leg of a chair, and began hissing clouds of white gas from holes around the bottom of the can.

Through the flat lenses of the gas mask, Kingman stared impatiently at the Death Merchant. "Are we going to do nothing but stand here and let our beards grow?"

"What time do you have?" Camellion asked.

Kingman glanced closely at his wristwatch. "Five-thirty. But what's the time have to do with it."

"It's light outside," Camellion replied, and pulled a canister of thermate from the bag, looked at it for a moment, then returned it to the bag.

Kingman, his jaw set like concrete, waited for Camellion to amplify his statement about daylight. Camellion didn't. Finally, Kingman said in exasperation, "Well, damn it?"

The Death Merchant slung the strap of the H&K MP-5 over his left shoulder, turned slightly and looked at Kingman. "You and I will go in first, You cover me. If I remember——"

"One moment, Hopmeir!" Lynch's tone was sharp. "The four of us are in this bloody business together. We don't need you and Kingman to do our jobs. The four of us will go in together."

Respecting Lynch for having pride, Camellion said patiently, "We're not trying to do your job. Kingman and I are going in first because four of us together would get in each other's way. Kingman and I are better at this sort of thing than you fellows. We want you two as backups. Once you see it's clear, you follow us." His tone became more brusque. "Do as I tell you, and let's not have any dissension at this stage of the game. Do you read me?"

Warned by the icy implication in Camellion's voice, Lynch and Shevlin nodded, Lynch saying in a curt tone,

"Very well. Just remember that this is a joint SIS CIA operation."

Giving no indication of having heard the man, Camellion said, "The diagram wasn't with our things in the arsenal. But if I remember correctly, we're in a room west of the kitchen. There's two doors to the kitchen, one on the east side, and one on the north. They both open to a hall. It's safe to say the Brotherhood will have those doors covered. We'll have to clear the whole area, although I think the gas will have done the job for us. Otherwise——"

"We use grenades," Kingman cut across him, his statement a positive assertion.

"And thermate," added Camellion. He drew one of the Auto Mags and thumbed off the safety. With his left hand, he reached across his waist, pulled a grenade from the shoulder bag resting against his right hip and, with his hand tightly gripping the safety lever, held the grenade out to Kingman. "Pull the pin; then we'll do it."

Kingman hooked a finger in the ring, pulled the pin, and dropped it on the floor. "Okay, it's your show."

The Death Merchant looked around the edge of the doorway, his eyes raking the smoky room. He had been right. The room was a kitchen, and it was a mess. The grenade had blown up a table and chairs. Shrapnel had stabbed holes in the cabinets and had peppered the walls and ceiling. The canister had exhausted its gas; however, quite a bit of the gray-white vapor hung in layers in the air and drifted slowly through both doorways.

He took a deep breath, exhaled, and hissed, "Let's go."

He charged through the doorway, the muscles of his legs straining to capacity from the effort. Behind him came Kingman. Camellion leaped over splintered pieces of wood and, when he was almost in the center of the kitchen, caught a fleeting glimpse of a gas-masked face looking around the edge of the open door to the east, the one to his right. He didn't have time to fire at the man because he had already started to throw the grenade through the doorway ahead of him, the one to the north.

Kingman had also seen the gas-masked figure, who now tried to bring his Walther MPL submachine gun around the edge of the doorway.

Kingman was a split-second faster. His MP-5 chattering, the muzzle flashed flame and a stream of 9mm slugs ripped into the gunman's chest and neck. Kingman didn't hesitate.

93

At the same time that the Death Merchant dove to the left and snuggled between the end of a large oaken cupboard and the end of the west side wall, Kingman threw himself between a refrigerator and the end of the east wall—and the grenade that Camellion had tossed exploded, several screams of pain tacking themselves onto the detonation.

*Why should they be wearing gas masks?* Looking around the side of the cupboard, Camellion saw a gas masked man leaning around the right side of the door to the east, a Beretta M-6 machine gun in his hands. Camellion snapped up the Auto Mag, aimed automatically, and fired. The .44 bullet struck Dunston Chatham in the right side of the chest, close to the shoulder bone, and, almost tearing off his arm, knocked him back against Emery Cameron who had intended to get down on his knees and fire around him. Cameron quickly changed his mind and drew back.

On the other side of the door, Dudley Belfour, his brain one big clanging bell from the concussion of the grenade, yelled "Let's get back to the stairs," at Cameron, then turned and ran toward the bottom of the stairs where other men were crouched. Cameron backed off, then turn and fled after Belfour.

The Death Merchant did some thinking. He was glad that he had removed the silencers from the barrels of the twin Backpacker Auto Mags—*too difficult to balance them with silencers*. Hmmmmm. The door to the east opens to a large foyer. He dug through the files of his memory, visualizing the diagram of Dunbeath Hall. The steps to the two upper floors were in the foyer. A hall led from the west. To the east was a short but wide hall that terminated at the main entrance to the manor. There was a large entrance to the south side of the foyer; beyond was the dining hall where Camellion and his men had been captured. To the north, the entrance to the great hall.

*They'll be waiting in the dining hall and the great hall. We'll have to clear them out of both areas before we can get outside the house.*

The Death Merchant left the northwest corner and ran to Kingman who was still in the northeast corner of the kitchen, between the refrigerator and the north side wall.

"Where in hell did they get those gas masks?" whispered Kingman incredulously. All the while he kept his H&K trained on the north door.

94

Camellion shrugged. "They had the masks up here. They searched our gear, knew we had gas and figured we'd use the stuff. What's the difference? We've come this far. Now it's the rest of the way."

He pulled back from the corner of the refrigerator, holstered his Auto Mag and took out a grenade. He pulled the pin and tossed the grenade through the north side door. He was pulling the pin from a second grenade as the first one exploded and showered the hall and three corpses on the floor with plaster and splintered wood.

"Keep that door covered," he said to Kingman. "Once I'm at the other door, I'll call the two Limeys."

"OK, I'll use this door and cover your flank."

Camellion took out another grenade, pulled the ring, and flung it through the east door. The instant he heard the big BLAMMMMMMMMMM he jerked one of the Auto Mags from its shoulder holster and tore across the kitchen to the left side of the east door, then motioned for Lynch and Shevlin to take positions to the right of the door. The two British agents raced into place, Shevlin watching the north end door, Lynch, flattened against the wall, keeping his head turned toward the east door.

It was a risk the Death Merchant had to take: He looked around the side of the doorway and saw that it would be an easy throw to the wide entrance of the dining hall. He also saw three men jerk back down behind a thick table they had overturned at the bottom of the fancy staircase. Quickly he pulled back his head to avoid three lines of high powered projectiles, fired from the entrance to the dining hall and the wide doorway to the great hall. Dozens of projectiles slammed into both edges of the doorway, the impacts sending out a shower of splinters. Then came the eventual lag pause. Lynch shoved his MP-5 around the side of the door and triggered off a short burst; then he pulled back and waited.

Camellion put his hand into one of his shoulder bags. "Save your ammo. I have something better." He turned and saw that Kingman had moved to the left side of the north door and was waiting. The CIA Q-man was also proving that he possessed a lot of experience in close-in fire-fights. He had slung the H&K over his back, had unscrewed the silencer from the Ingram submachine gun and had removed the steel frame stock. He held the Ingram in his right hand, intending to use the very short weapon

(11.5 inches without the stock) as an autopistol. His left hand was filled with a Coonan .357 autoloader.

The Death Merchant took a thermate canister from the kit-bag, his mind calculating the distance from the door of the wide entrance to the dining hall. He pulled the pin from the grenade, hesitated for a moment and thought again of the distance; then, with all the controlled ability of a master pool shark about to hit the ball that counted, he tossed the white canister around the edge through the opening. The canister hit the floor almost in the center of the wide opening, rolled a foot inside the dining area and ignited. Instead of an ordinary explosion, there was only a loud WHHHOOOOSSSHHHHHH. A microsecond later, an intense, dazzling-bright light flared and a ball of intense heat expanded until it almost filled the width of the entrance and extended seven feet into the dining area and the same amount of distance into the foyer.

Thermate (TH3), a mixture of thermite, barium nitrate and sulphur in an oil binder, burns at a temperature of over 4,500 degrees Fahrenheit, a molten hell that, at its burn-peak, eats even through steel. What it can do and does to a human being is the ultimate in horror.

Three of the Brotherhood had been standing to the right, two to the left, and drops of the burning thermate splashed on all five. The doomed men might just as well have been stark naked and have been stabbed with white-hot pokers. The liquid fire burned instantly through their clothes, ate through their skin, boiled away blood, and began to bore into bones. Screaming at the top of their lungs, the five men went insane with agony. Two fell and began rolling on the floor. A third man was lucky enough to have a low pain threshhold: He quickly passed out. The last two began leaping about and jerking like whirling dervishes out of control, much to the appalling dread of the three men behind the overturned table at the bottom of the stairs and the other gunmen of the Brotherhood waiting on each side of the entrance to the great hall. A group of reinforcements, coming in from the other end of the long hall, saw the two burning men and increased their speed in an effort to reach the other entrance.

One of the blazing men collapsed in a smoking heap close to the mouth of the hall that stretched to the front door of the manor. The other human torch, shrieking pouring from his throat, staggered toward the overturned table.

Terrified, the three men behind the table attempted to move away, afraid that they too would catch fire. Emery Cameron and Dudley Balfour jumped up in alarm. Malcolm Brechin, half-way up, lost his balance and fell back on his rearend. All three were so engrossed in staying away from the blazing man that they didn't see Camellion and the two SIS agents charging out of the east end kitchen door, or Kingman, who had raced through the north door, come up the hall, and now was storming into the foyer.

Hubert Aubigny, one of the gunmen by the left side of the opening to the great hall, was the first to see the Death Merchant and the two SIS agents. He yelled a warning and raised his NATO "FAL" rifle. By then it was too late. For only a very short time the two burning men had held the full attention of the Brotherhood, but those twenty seconds had given Camellion and his tiny attack force a slight edge.

Ducking and weaving, he and Lynch and Shevlin opened fire at the same time that the human torch collapsed over the table and Aubigny sent a stream of 7.62mm Spitzer slugs in their direction. Alerted by the firing, the other members of the Brotherhood swung their weapons to the right.

Aubigny's projectiles burned the air close to Camellion and thudded into the wall next to the east kitchen door. Camellion's first .44 AMP bullet struck Aubigny in the right wrist and tore off his hand, three fingers of which had been around the butt of the NATO FAL, the index finger inside the trigger guard against the trigger. Aubigny screamed, dropped the rifle, jumped back, and stared in awe at his hand hanging by a muscle fiber from his wrist spurting a thick jet of blood. The horror was more than he could stand. With the look of a man who had been unjustly hurt, he felt a darkness folding over his brain.

Ronald Lynch and Martin Shevlin were certainly doing their share of fighting, each man raking the sides of the rectangular entrance to the great hall. 9mm projectiles from Lynch's MP-5 chopped into several men on the left, the force of the slugs practically dissolving the fronts of the coats the "Brothers" were wearing. They fell with tiny clouds of fabric floating down gently above them.

Irwin MacTavish, the third man on the left, kept back against the wall. Terrified, he waited for the men running toward the entrance from the other end of the great hall. How could four men cause such trouble?

The Death Merchant's AMPs roared again. One .44 Magnum bullet stabbed Emery Cameron in the stomach, doubled him over, and knocked him back with the force of a mule kick. He was unconscious from shock before he had time to hit the floor.

Dudley Balfour was turned into a corpse even faster. Camellion's second bullet blew a hole in his chest and exploded his heart. The .44 slug then rocketed out his back with the speed of a Titan missile.

Malcolm Brechin, still on his butt, knew he didn't have time to reach his submachine gun. Frantically, he tried to pull a .38 Webley from his belt. His hand didn't even reach the butt of the revolver. Another distinctive roar from an AMP. Brechin's head jumped violently when a mean .44 AMP Mag slug smacked him in the throat, tore out his Adam's apple and blew apart the back of his neck. He fell with his head wobbling at an odd angle and gushes of blood spurting a foot from his neck.

Martin Shevlin, darting from side to side, his nose bleeding from concussion, sent well-placed three-round bursts at the right edge of the great hall's wide entrance. Two of the Brotherhood gunmen died without getting off a single shot. Shevlin's streams of 9mm slugs raked them perpendicularly, from knees to neck, and they died in a flurry of slug impacts that, for a few moments, made them jump like corn in a popper.

Aleck Fordun and Bennet Lindsey, the two other men to the right, were faster and braver than their two dead companions. Fordun stepped all the way out from the short protective wall and, cursing, fired a long burst with the Italian Luigi Franchi 59 assault rifle in his nervous hands, the weapon on full automatic. To his left, half-hidden by the wall, Lindsey let fly a burst from his COLT CAR-15 carbine. If the two neo-Nazis had swung their deadly chatter-boxes, they might have iced not only Shevlin, but Lynch and Camellion as well. But, being inexperienced in close-in kill-fights, both made the mistake of simply pointing the weapons, then firing, Fordun aiming at Shevlin, Lindsey at the Death Merchant.

Natural-born survivors instinctively watch all the action, and although Shevlin and Lynch were novices in the art of dispensing quick and violent death, they had detected Fordun and Lindsey's movements a mini-moment before the two men fired. So had Camellion, who had also not failed to see Irwin MacTavish who had crept along the short wall to the left and was about to open fire with a U.S. M3 grease gun. MacTavish had been in the British Army, and he was going to fire in a raking sweep.

Except that he didn't get the chance . . .

The Death Merchant ducked and snapped up both Auto Mags, his arms spread in a wide "V." Lindsey's stream of high velocity 5.56mm projectiles missed him by only a fraction of an inch, some sizzling so close that they grazed the material of the coveralls on his right side and came within a hairs-breadth of striking his right hand. Not even half a blink later, he fired at both MacTavish and Lindsey, the Auto Mags booming and jerking in his hands. Simultaneously, Shevlin and Lynch dodged to one side and fired at Fordun and Lindsey; and Kingman fired at MacTavish.

Kingman, now closing in on the entrance to the great hall, could see only MacTavish's forearms and his hands around the M3, the corner of the east wall hiding the rest of the Scot's body.

But MacTavish's arms were all that Kingman needed to see . . .

"Stupid Nazi son of a bitch!" Kingman growled and opened fire with the Ingram. The little submachine gun made a *duddle-duddle-duddle-duddle* sound, this low, malefic snarling followed by the loud clanking of ricochets as gilded, jacketed slugs slammed against the right side of MacTavish's grease gun and knocked it from his hands. At precisely the very same time, other Ingram projectiles smashed into MacTavish's right hand and right forearm, effectively "amputating" the arm at the elbow.

Yet MacTavish didn't utter a sound, not as much as a whisper or whimper of pain. He didn't, because in that microsecond, at the same instant that Kingman's finger was squeezing the trigger of the Ingram, the Death Merchant's .44 bullet hit MacTavish high in the left side of the chest and killed him without his even suspecting that he was about to die. All in one motion, the M3 grease gun went flying; MacTavish's right arm was butchered to shreds, and his corpse was jerked back as if pulled by an invisible cable.

Bennet Lindsey received a triple dose of leaden death. The Death Merchant's .44 AMP projectile stabbed him in the stomach, high up, just below the lower end of the sternum, while Lynch and Shevlin's H&K slugs poked any number of holes in his chest. The COLT CAR fell from Lindsey's dead hands. His corpse, the chest a ragged bloody mess, fell backward and landed on its back, eyes closed, mouth wide open and filling with blood that flowed down the cheeks and chin.

Aleck Fordun's line of 7.62mm L.F. assault rifle projectiles almost wasted Martin Shevlin. One nicked the lower lobe of his right ear, another jerking at the collar of his coveralls. Two single ticks of the clock, two single seconds, and a swarm of slugs from Shevlin and Lynch's MP-5s effectively blew apart the upper portion of Fordun's body. With a choked, strangled cry, he went down, so shot to pieces that two jagged rib bones protruded from the ripped skin of his chest.

"IN FRONT! IN FRONT OF US!" yelled Kingman, deep fear in his voice. He swerved to the left, almost hit the east wall, shoved the Ingram around the side and triggered off a burst, exhausting the magazine by firing at the dozen or more men who were now three-fourths of the way to the south end entrance of the great hall and raising their weapons to fire. Two of the Brotherhood, hit by Kingman's slugs, stopped as if they had collided with an invisible stone wall. The rest of the group made a dive for whatever cover they could find, some firing off short bursts as they went down.

Enemy slugs buzzing in front and in back of him, Camellion leaped over the blackened corpse lying across the overturned table and still smoldering, made a dash to the left side and stopped by the side of the wall, in back of Kingman who was several feet back from the splintered edge.

To the right, Shevlin and Lynch made a frantic effort to reach the east wall on their side of the entrance. Lynch made it to safety. Shevlin did not. One of the Brotherhood fired off a burst from a Finnish M60 assault rifle while dropping behind a massive, throne-sized chair. All but one of the 7.62mm projectiles missed. One solid base bullet struck Shevlin just above his left ear. It traveled upward at an angle, bored a tunnel through his brain and came out the right side of his head, taking with it a large chunk of skull bone and lifting the jeep cap off his head. Shevlin's arms flapped out. The H&K fell to the floor. So did he, stone dead.

"Damn it, they got Shevlin!" yelled Kingman in order to

100

make himself heard above the racket of enemy weapons that were sending dozens of slugs at the sides of the entrance to the great hall.

"Hear that chattering?" said Camellion, cocking his head to one side. "Those Hitler lovers are close enough for us to use grenades and thermate."

Kingman, shoving a fresh magazine into the Ingram, grinned within the gas mask and stepped around Camellion so that the Death Merchant was closest to the edge. "You throw better than I do. But hurry up. Any minute now, they'll decide to charge, and I'm low on ammo."

The Death Merchant pulled a fragmentation grenade from one of the shoulder bags, held it up for Lynch to see, pointed to the grenade, then at Lynch, then motioned toward the inside of the Great Hall. Lynch nodded and reached for a grenade in one of his own kit bags.

Twelve seconds later, Camellion's first grenade exploded. Some of the shrapnel was still stinging the furniture when Lynch's grenade detonated with a loud crash and a flash of fire.

A long wail of agony! Shouts and cries of fear.

Very quickly, Camellion lobbed a thermate canister around the end of the wall into the hall. He was pulling the pin from the second canister as the first 26 ounces of thermate whooshed into life, the light of the dazzling ball of molten metal flashing out into the foyer.

Lynch, taking his cue from Camellion, tossed a thermate grenade into the great hall. Camellion followed with another thermate canister, trying to throw this one farther than the two previous ones he had tossed.

Hidious howls of agony came from the great hall, of unbearable pain that the victims were being forced to bear. All the while, Kingman watched Camellion, feeling that he was the type of man who would send a bride a shroud for a wedding present.

Methodically, Camellion threw a fragmentation grenade into the great hall, and when it exploded it scattered the molten thermate. So did the second fragmentation grenade, to the extent that a dozen or more tiny blobs of the white-hot metal shot through the wide entrance and landed on the floor, several of the splashes falling on the corpse of Shevlin. Instantly, there was a sizzling sound from the corpse, and smoke rose upward from the coveralls as the thermate began to burn.

"I'm ready," Kingman said, impatient as usual. He turned from Camellion and watched the black smoke drifting out of the entrance to the hall. "Let's go in there and finish them off."

"Don't be in a hurry," warned Camellion, "or we might end up like poor Shevlin." He shoved a full clip into one of the .44 Auto Mags and proceeded to put a cartridge into the firing chamber.

"Un huh. And a zebra is a sports model jackass. So what else is new?"

The Death Merchant holstered the AMP, then reloaded the other Auto Mag, after which he pulled the other stainless steel autopistol and used the one in his right hand to signal Ronald Lynch, indicating that a charge into the great hall was in order.

"OK, get your butt in gear," he said to Kingman.

Camellion and Kingman charged in from the left, Lynch from the right, all three going in low and running in a zigzagging pattern.

Hell greeted them. Toward the south end of the hall, much of the furniture was wrecked, antique tables and chairs—priceless pieces of Chippendale, Sheraton, and Duncan Phyfe—having been turned into splinters, exposed springs, ripped covering and shredded padding. Much of the mess, having been splashed by thermate, was burning and throwing off smoke of such an intense odor that Camellion and his two companions could smell the stink ever so faintly through the respirators of their gas masks.

Eight of the Brotherhood lay in various positions on the floor, the thermate still eating into their bones. Five were blackened, crusty lumps that only faintly resembled the human form, and it was as plain as the dawn outside the high, narrow windows that some of the Brotherhood had been splashed with thermate more than others. One corpse, from the waist upward, was only a skeleton, a fire-dried framework of vertebrae, rib bones, clavicle, two scapulas, but only one humerous—the left one. Only one, because the upper right arm had not been touched by the thermate; not even the cotton of the shirt was singed. Finally there was the skull, looking blank with its empty crater eye spaces. And ridiculous with man-made dentures.

But five of the Brotherhood were alive, in good health, and in full retreat. Spread out almost the entire thirty-foot width of the great hall, all five were headed for the small door at the northeast corner of the huge room, the same door they had used to enter the hall.

Ronald Lynch stopped and, thinking of the dead Shevlin, fired the Heckler and Koch from the waist. His long bursts of 9mm projectiles chopped into the backs of Wystan Glencaire and Thurston Luther and smashed them forward with such force that their feet and legs had to do a little jig in an effort to keep up with the rest of their bodies. Glencaire crashed into an 18th Century wrought iron candle stand, taking the stand down with him. Thurston, chopped to bloody hash by the slugs, fell over a massive occasional table and hung across the top, his corpse dripping blood onto the Persian rug.

*Duddle-duddle-duddle-duddle* . . . A half dozen slugs from Kingman's Ingram hit Patrick Maitland in the small of the back. The lead expanded on contact, broke his spin, punctured his stomach, liver, gall bladder and spleen and pitched him into a gleaming suit of 10th Century armor whose left hand was holding a long pike. Maitland went down like a broken doll. The suit of armor went down with him, its palette, breastplate, helmet, brassard, and other parts of the suit making a loud ringing sound as they struck the floor. The pike made the loudest sound of all.

The Death Merchant didn't aim in the conventional sense. Experts never do. The two Lee E. Jurras Auto Mags exploded at the same time that Randal Lochabar and Owen Manchester turned to the right and started the last lap that would take them to the northeast emergency door. It was the last race of their lives and they lost.

Manchester caught a .44 Magnum slug in the right rib cage, almost lifted off his feet by the tremendous impact which pitched him against the back of one of the large easy chairs that, with others, was arranged in a semicircle in front of a giant fireplace.

Lochabar gasped, dropped the Uzi machine gun and did a fast two-step from the impact of the .44 projectile that hammered into his right hip, zipped through his intestines, came out his left hip and then glanced off the iron handle of a log roller leaning against the fireplace. Lochabar, holding the last of his life in a single reflection of uselessness, fell against the back of another easy chair, dropped to the floor and died.

The Death Merchant turned around and looked toward the south entrance. He saw nothing but drifting smoke; and only he could hear the insane laughter of the Cosmic Lord of Death.

He turned and, with Kingman and Lynch, advanced toward the north end of the hall. Kingman pulled off his gas mask, and made a face when he smelled the stink of burning wood, varnish, clothes and flesh. He looked down at the dead Maitland and the suit of armor, parts of which lay scattered around the corpse.

"Look at that man-sized drainpipe," he said with a chuckle. "How would you guys like to wear that junk to fight in?"

He dipped his left hand and the Coonan .357 Magnum pistol roared. CLANG! The bullet had easily pierced the breastplate of the armor.

Ronald Lynch hurried over to Camellion and Kingman, but he didn't raise his gas mask.

"We came for Sir MacLean," he said truculently. "What about him? And I don't like leaving Martin lying back there with those scum."

For a short moment there was a defeated silence, finally broken by the Death Merchant. "I understand how you feel about Shevlin," he said gently. "But we can't risk moving his body, not now. We——"

"Or going upstairs," cut in Kingman accusingly, looking hard at Camellion. "Only four of us coming here was dumb enough. But three of us tackling the other floors would be insanity. We didn't accomplish a damned thing. There's no telling where MacLean and his sons and that kraut-head are!"

The Death Merchant had succeeded at bigger missions with less men. He didn't, however, feel compelled to give either man a justification for his decision to attack Dunbeath Hall.

He was about to tell them that their early morning's work was over when he heard the sound, far to the west, outside of Dunbeath Hall—the noise of a taxiing aircraft preparing for takeoff.

"We know where MacLean is, don't we?" Kingman cracked. With Camellion and Lynch, he ran to the door in the northeast corner of the hall.

"Be careful," Camellion said, his hand grasping the pull-ring. "Watch the windows and stay close to the house."

Once Lynch and Camellion were outside the house, they didn't remove their gas masks. They didn't have the time. Keeping close to the north side of the manor house, the upper floors looming dangerously above them, the three men ran to the northwest corner. They arrived just in time to see the silver Fairey Norman turboprop, several thousand feet to the west, lift off the ground and begin the high climb into the early morning sky.

"Bye-bye you stupid Nazi bastard!" Kingman said, referring to Sir MacLean and looking at the plane as it grew smaller in the distant sky.

Ronald Lynch, also watching the plane, added, "Kingman, I must agree with you. We didn't succeed in doing much of anything. All we did was get Martin killed."

The Death Merchant had been inspecting the white birch woods to the north of the mansion. There weren't any members of the Brotherhood in the woods or they would have opened fire the instant he and the other two men stepped through the door.

"You're both wrong," he responded coldly to Lynch's remark and pulled off his gas mask. "We did fail to black-bag MacLean. We did terminate what was probably the cream of the crop of the Brotherhood in this area; and it won't be all that difficult to determine where Sir MacLean is going. His son did mention the Sea of the Hebrides." He thought for a moment. "That's 150 to 175 miles west of here."

"And takes in the Outer Hebrides, the Island of Skye and several other islands," Lynch said unsympathetically, taking off his own gas mask. "There is some hope. We can get back to the jeep in time to radio *HMS Taurus* and have our people contact the Navy radar station at Greenock. It's just possible that we might be able to track Sir MacLean. Frankly, I doubt it. There's always quite a bit of air traffic around the general area of the Outer Hebrides, private craft and so on."

"What's the 'so on' mean?" asked Kingman.

"Planes that carry freight, and I believe there's a few small commercial lines in that area."

The Death Merchant said in a patient tone, "I think the SIS' files on Sir MacLean will give us an idea as to his destination. Let's get back to the jeep."

Leading the way, he moved toward the east. Very soon, he and Kingman and Lynch had crossed the front of Dunbeath Hall and were running toward the woods to the south, their booted feet moving over the dew-wet grass now glistening in the early morning sunlight.

# Chapter Nine

The eight men in the Operations Room of Her Majesty's naval station at Greenock watched Charles Phegley use the pointer to tap an area of the map on the wall.

"Gentlemen, this is the Island of Skye," he said, his manner and voice making him look and sound like an Eton schoolmaster. "Let me explain that——"

The Death Merchant, sitting between Klaus Hahn and Rudolf Gertenshalger, the two West German *Bundesnachrichtendienst* agents, didn't need a history lesson on Skye. While still in the U.S., preparing for the mission, he had familiarized himself with the entire area north of Hadrian's Wall; and although he was in total command—and at the moment bored and half-intoxicated from the schnapps he was drinking—he didn't wish to hurt Phegley's professional pride by depriving him of this part of the briefing. After all, the stiff-ass was the senior British Secret Intelligence Service officer of the operation. A pragmatic paralogician, Camellion was keenly aware that life was merely one long struggle to think well of ourselves, and he prided himself on being a good leader. This meant he made it a firm rule never to set himself above his followers—except in carrying out responsibilities.

As for Skye, it was the largest and most northerly island of the Inner Hebrides, and was part of the county of Inverness, in Scotland. West of Scotland, Skye was the nearest Hebridean island to the Atlantic coast of the Scottish mainland, being separated at the Kyleakin ferry crossing by only a few hundred yards.

Skye wasn't very large either—not to Camellion's way of thinking. The island was almost fifty miles long from south-southwest to north-northwest, and was so deeply indented that no part of the interior was more than five miles from the sea.

The Cuillin Hills—the highest peak was almost 3,500 feet—dominated the landscape in south-center Skye.

Portree, the capital, lay at the head of a fine harbor on the east coast and supported the manufacture of tweeds, tartans, and other woolens. Large sheep and cattle sales were held there twice yearly.

Other occupations on Skye included whiskey distilling at Carbost, and, just north of Storr, the reworking of extensive diatomite deposits, with a processing plant at Uig.

There was also some archaeological interest on Skye, this because the island was ruled by Norsemen until the 13th century, when the Hebrides became part of Scotland. Dunvegan Castle, the home of the MacLeods, the chief clan of Skye, was built in the 9th century and was the longest continuously occupied house in Scotland, until it caught fire and the interior was burned out, in 1966.

As Kingman would probably say, "So what else is new about Skye?"

Listening to Phegley explain that the narrow body of water called the Sound of Sleat lay between part of southeast Skye and the west coast of Scotland, the Death Merchant reflected on the events of the past few days. He and Lynch and Kingman had returned to the jeep without mishap and had contacted the *HMS Taurus* by radio. The *Taurus* had carried a Kaman H-43 Huskie helicopter on a pad, and the chopper had flown twenty armed British sailors to Dunbeath Hall. With the help of the sailors, Camellion and Lynch and Kingman had explored the upper two floors of Dunbeath Hall. On the third floor they had found fourteen servants, none of whom offered any resistance. A search of the powerhouse and of the hangar had revealed nothing. Much later, under intense interrogation, not one of the servants had revealed anything of importance.

SIS agents had flown in that same afternoon to question Nigel MacLean, Sir Hugh's eldest son and the President of MacLean Fabrics, Ltd. Officially, Nigel could not be charged with any crime—not yet. Neither Camellion nor Lynch nor Kingman had seen him at Dunbeath Hall, and there wasn't any other evidence to connect him with the Brotherhood of the 4th Reich. But . . . Nigel MacLean could not be found.

It was a different matter with Sir Hugh MacLean and his two other sons, John-Percy MacLean and Edward MacLean. They were charged with illegal possession of weapons and explosives and harboring a wanted international fugitive and war criminal—ex-SS General Karl Gustav Lindermanns.

A day and a half later, the Death Merchant and the other agents of The Company and of the SIS were in Greenock, all except Catherine Griffin. She had flown back to London and would wait at the U.S. Embassy.

The SIS had gone into full swing, although it didn't require much intelligence to deduce Sir MacLean's destination. Sir Hugh's wife had been of the Mackenzie clan, the second largest clan on the Island of Skye. Before Mary Ellen MacLean had committed suicide, she had inherited the Mackenzie stronghold, Bracadale Castle on the west central coast of Skye. It was only logical that Sir MacLean should have flown to Bracadale Castle.

Or was it?

Could John-Percy MacLean have been lying about the Sea of the Hebrides? Possibly but not probably. At the time that John-Percy had made the remark to Camellion, he and the others had not dreamed that th˗ Death Merchant and his three men would escape.

The naval base at Greenock had tracked on radar a single aircraft flying on a southwest course over northern Scotland, but had lost the airplane when it had merged with other "blips" of air traffic over the Inner Sound, a strip of water between the west coast of Scotland and the Island of Raasay. West of Raasay was the Sound of Raasay. West of the Sound of Raasay was the northern part of the Island of Skye.

The really perplexing question was why Sir MacLean should have flown to Bracadale Castle, to Skye, in the first place? That he did have business there was an inevitable conclusion, since he had made plans for the trip before Camellion and his men had escaped from the dungeon in Dunbeath Hall. MacLean and his men would not have had to fly all that way to dispose of the bodies. They could have dumped Camellion & Co. in the North Sea which was a lot closer.

Camellion picked up the bottle in front of him on the table, poured a goodly portion of schnapps and impatiently waited for Charles Phegley—*he's the El Greco of the SIS*— to finish his lecture about the Island of Skye. In any phase of planning *the British are just like the Germans. They start at the very beginning and include every irrelevant detail. Never do they cut the deadwood and go straight to the heart of the matter.*

"The population of the entire island is slightly under fifteen thousand," finished Charles Phegley, "and there is no one in the vicinity of Bracadale Castle. Civilians in the area won't get in our way."

He placed the pointer on a small side table, stared for a moment at the bottle of schnapps, looked disapprovingly at Camellion and said stiffly, "At this point, Mr. Hopmeir will give us the detail of the landing and the approach—if he's able."

The implication that "Mr. Hopmeir" had imbibed too freely was unmistakable.

Phegley pulled out a chair at the end of the table and turned it around so that it faced the map on the wall, his expression severe as he waited.

Camellion got up from the table, made an intense inward effort to steady himself and then and there decided that the very proper Phegley was similar to a bad fitting suit—*it never wears out and he never ceases to be a bore.*

"I think I'm able, Mr. Phegley," he said affably. "We Americans know how to drink and how to win wars. Remember how a bunch of hard-drinking farmers beat the hell out of the British Army during the Revolutionary War?"

He moved behind Rudolf Gertenshalger, went over and picked up the pointer and turned around, pleased that his words had been effective. The faces of Phegley, Lynch, and Woofs were beet red. Kevin Woofs was the SIS agent who had replaced the dead Shevlin. Almost forty, Woofs had a narrow mustache, carefully combed brown hair, brown eyes, and large nervous hands.

Camellion looked at the two amused Germans. "Don't drink all the schnapps, *mein Kameraden.*"

"*Jawohl,* Herr Hopmeir." A smile curled at the corners of Klaus Hahn's mouth. "Don't worry, we have another bottle."

"Das ist gut," said Camellion, and proceeded to rub Phegley's nose in another insult. "Now that Mr. Phegley has completed his tourist guide's speech about Skye, we'll get down to the essentials."

Standing sideways, he used the wooden pointer to point to the diagram he had drawn and had tacked to the wall to the left of the map of Skye. He tapped a large red circle.

"This is the village of Bracadale. It's two miles east of the coast and has a population of only four hundred. Right here, thirteen miles north of Bracadale"—he moved the tip of the pointer to a large red square—"is Bracadale Castle. The castle is on the coast. It sits back a couple of thousand feet from the edge of cliffs that drop several hundred feet to the beach. By the way, there's a big cave at the bottom, about three hundred feet back from the water. It's called the Cave of Charles the Bold.

"Up here, east of the castle, is flat ground, mostly rock. It's here that MacLean's plane landed. There isn't any other place where it could put down."

Kingman, sitting across from Gertenshalger, spoke up. "If they did land there, they must have camouflaged the plane immediately, or the Navy planes would have seen the bird."

"There isn't any other answer," Camellion said. He looked from Kingman to the other men, studying their interested faces. "The attack will be based on simple tactics. Three choppers will land a fifth of a mile from the castle, one to the north, one to the east, and one to the south. We'll have the castle in the grip of a large semicircle. The circle closes. Finis to MacLean. That's it. Any questions?"

Rudolf Gertenshalger regarded Camellion with steady eyes and asked, "Why employ such a large force against MacLean? The Fairey Norman is an eight passenger aircraft, excluding pilot and copilot. Each Kaman carries twenty men."

Kingman leaned forward, put his elbows on the green felt of the table, looked at Camellion and said, "What about the castle itself? Is it a pile of ruins or what? It must be livable if MacLean's there."

The Death Merchant glanced at Phegley who had sat down at the head of the table and was looking past him at the diagram and at the map on the wall.

"Mr. Phegley can explain that better than I," he said.

Phegley turned sideways to Kingman. "Yes, one could say that the castle is a ruin," he said, his voice steady and without emotion. "However, our files show that Sir MacLean had the entire structure strengthened and part of the ground floor modernized, in 1970. For power, he had a wind generator installed on the roof and had water piped in from several deep wells." He swung around and looked at the Death Merchant who was returning the wooden pointer to the side table. "MacLean and whoever is with him should be on the ground floor. At least in theory—and if he's there."

"Thank you, Mr. Phegley," replied Camellion, who was walking back to his place at the table. "It would seem that we're all in agreement." He pulled out the chair and sat down.

There was a long pause. Phegley got up, turned his chair around toward the table and sat down again. Kevin Woofs puffed thoughtfully on his pipe. Lynch lighted a fresh cigarette from the butt of the one he had been smoking. The two BND agents retained their icy composure, Hahn sipping schnapps laced with cognac, Gertenshalger toying with a set of gold-plated brass knuckles.

Oddly enough, Kingman was cold sober. It was he who broke the silence. "When people agree on everything, one of them has to be doing all the thinking," he said thoughtfully, his calculating dark brown eyes on Camellion. "It all sounds too easy. What's the punch line?"

Kevin Woofs, not giving Camellion a chance to answer, turned and gave Kingman an odd look. "I say, you don't actually think Sir MacLean would resist, do you? How could he? It would be madness for him to even try."

"My opinion"—Ronald Lynch shot a glance at the Death Merchant—"is that we should be asking ourselves why MacLean has chosen to remain at the castle. Even though we've been able to get news of what happened at Dunbeath Hall from the press, MacLean must realize we know where he is and that we'll be coming for him. It doesn't make sense that he should sit there on the coast and wait for us."

"We've walked over that ground before," Camellion said. His hard blue eyes flicked quickly around the table and his voice and face lost half of their politeness. "We always get the same answer. OK. Either the son of a bitch is there or he isn't. We're going on the assumption that he is. Therefore, he's there because he had previously arranged to go there on some kind of business. Now, he's stuck. He's seen the planes flying over and knows that the two coast guard cutters sitting out there can block any escape by sea. What else can MacLean do?" His voice became cutting, savage.

"All of you forget, apparently, what Sir MacLean told us when we were his prisoners: that an underground radiation shelter was being prepared—and I quote his exact words—'only 200 kilometers from here.' He didn't say in which direction, but Bracadale Castle fits the bill, or some place in the village of Bracadale. We won't know until we hit the castle tomorrow morning."

"I haven't forgotten a damn thing!" Kingman's voice was loud and fierce, and he couldn't have cared less that Camellion was feeling the results of the schnapps. "I want to know where we'll be tomorrow morning, how we are going to get to the castle. You always have a gimmick in mind. You'll probably toss a sky hook on a cloud and have us slide down to the roof on a rope!"

The Death Merchant paused in raising the glass to his lips.

"Forget the cloud and the rope and substitute a Royal Navy Lynx HAS-2 egg-beater," Camellion said with a hearty laugh. "While the British commandos close in sideways, we land on the roof and go downward."

"I knew it! I just knew it!" Kingman brought his palm down hard on the table so hard that it shook the cup and saucer in front of Phegley. "I knew goddamn good and well you'd come up with something stupid that could get our butts shot off. What the hell did you do, take a vow to get us whacked out?"

Camellion restrained a belch from the equivalent of four shots of schnapps he had just swallowed, put down the glass and detected that the two krauts were in agreement with Kingman, their expressions dubious.

But it was Lynch who spoke up. "Well now, I rather like the idea of our gaining entrance from the roof of the castle." He sounded very pleased with himself. "Sir MacLean and the people with him—eight or nine at the most—shouldn't be in a position to offer much resistance."

He glanced to his left at Woofs, then to his right at Phegley. He didn't get any support from either man, both of whom remained silent and wore neutral expressions.

"Herr Hopmeir, your plan is dangerous," Hahn said cordially. "I suggest you have a very good reason for wanting the six of us to attack from the roof?"

With one side of his closed hand over his mouth, the Death Merchant restrained another belch, made another

112

concentrated effort to organize his thoughts, and hoped that his brain was still in full control of his voice box.

"When we cut through all the suppositions," he said thickly, "we really don't know what we'll find inside the castle, anymore than we can be absolutely certain why Sir MacLean is still there. My own——"

"By jove! You are smashed!" Lynch's face broke into an expression that was either joy or surprise. Camellion could not be certain. "I said the same thing a little while ago. You said MacLean didn't have a choice. I think he did. I think he still has a choice."

"Yes, indeed," agreed Woofs heartily. "With his money and influence, he could have—who knows how many elaborate hideouts he could have in Great Britain?"

"Nonetheless, it is more than reasonable to conclude that MacLean did have some urgent business at the castle," Arnold Steel said, brushing a hand against his silver-gray hair, "based strictly on the assumption that he told the truth to Mr. Hopmeir and the others. It is also logical to conclude that Sir MacLean wasn't prepared for the disaster that took place at Dunbeath Hall and, therefore, didn't have time to make preparations to go elsewhere, other than to Bracadale Castle. The truly perplexing part is why he should choose to remain there without even as much as attempting to evade capture?"

Camellion leaned back in his chair, his left hand around the almost empty glass.

"MacLean is trying to avoid capture," he said, half of his words coming out in a staggering slur, but the impact was on what he had said, not the manner in which he had said it. "He's at the castle because he's waiting for transportation."

The fox-faced Phegley blinked in surprise. The others stared uncomprehendingly at the Death Merchant.

"Well, it can't be by plane," Kingman said scornfully, crushing out his cigarette. "And a ship can't get by the two British Coast Guard cutters."

The Death Merchant didn't give a damn that his eyes were out of focus and that the faces of the men were blurry. It was all a joke. A merry-go-round of nothingness. Life was a joke!

At least I don't have to concern myself with the heartbreak of psoriasis!

"A ship couldn't get him out," he said to Kingman. "A

113

plane couldn't do it either. The Royal Air Force would force it down." A sly look crept into his eyes. "So what else is new?"

"Well now, what else is left?" Kevin Woofs said to no one in particular.

"*Unterseeboot!*" Klaus Hahn said brusquely. He nodded his head slowly and turned and looked at Camellion "*Ya, das ist der antworten!*"

"A submarine!" The words jumped out of Kingman's mouth. For a moment, he looked astonished; then it appeared that he might laugh. Off to one corner of his mind, he wondered how Camellion could consume so much booze and yet remain clear-eyed. And his hands and movements were quick. It was only when he spoke that one could detect a lack of control. It's more than odd, thought Kingman. It's goddamn weird! A submarine?

"I don't buy it," he said. "I wouldn't even consider it in one of my books, and man, they are crazy!"

"A submarine has to surface," Lynch said tersely, trying to act casual. "I suppose, Hopmeir, you're going to tell us next that a U-boat is going to come along, torpedo the two patrol boats, then pick up Sir MacLean and his party?"

"You tell me who or what could stop a sub from putting a couple of fish into those coast guard boats? The Death Merchant never ceased to be amazed at the lack of imagination exhibited by professional intelligence agents— *especially Kingman. It must have taken some creative inventiveness to write those screwball paperback books of his! It's like a musician who can't read notes sitting down to play a piano concerto!*

Lynch didn't answer. All he did was fumble with a button on his blue sports shirt and squirmed a bit in his chair.

"This submarine concept," Steel said slowly. "It would be incredible, should your theory prove valid." He suddenly fastened his eyes on Phegley. "Do those two cutters have modern detection gear and carry antisubmarine underwater missiles?"

Phegley first looked confused, then embarrassed. "I'll— I'll find out," he said in a nervous voice. "Excuse me, gentlemen." He got up from the table and hurried from the room, every man at the table knowing that he was going to confer with Captain Warren Merriweather, the commander of the Royal Navy base at Greenock.

"Another fumble," complained Kingman. "Captain Mer-

114

riweather and Major Simpson should have been at this briefing." He stared accusingly at the Death Merchant. "You're in charge. Why didn't you put your foot down?"

"Don't be an arse, Kingman," Camellion snorted. "There are certain rules in the SIS that even Whitehall doesn't bend or break until the proper time. The 'need-to-know' rule is one of them. I have a feeling that Phegley has decided that now is the time to let Merriweather and Simpson know what's going on."

"Mr. Phegley does go strictly by the book," Kevin Woofs offered conversationally. He knocked the bowl of his pipe against his palm, put the ashes in an ashtray on the table, and looked at Camellion, his eyes speculative. "Tell me, what is your rationale for a submarine?"

Lynch gave his opinion. "We can't discount completely the possibility of a submarine. Sir MacLean and his organization have a lot of power, but you don't park a sub in any old cove that comes along. And building one! Considering the technical help and what-not, it would be almost impossible to keep that kind of secret. Another thing: Where would he get the crew?"

*I need a steak and a lot of Alka-Seltzer!* thought Camellion, but he said, "Hahn, tell him."

The good-looking West German smiled mysteriously. "In reference to Sir MacLean, let's call it the 'Lindermanns Connection.'"

Speaking rapidly, and with only a slight accent, Hahn explained that Lindermanns, as *Obergruppenfuhrer* of the *SS Leibstandarte Adolf Hitler,* had been a willing helper of *Reichleiter* Martin Bormann. Both men had been in Hitler's bunker at the end, but had successfully escaped to South America, where, for over thirty years, they had made fools of Sheruth Modiin, the military intelligence department of the Mossad, the Israeli intelligence service, and of the BND, the West German intelligence apparatus.

"Lindermanns is Bormann's front man," Hahn said. "We can't prove it, but we are almost positive it was Lindermanns and his agents who made the arrangements to have a skull and other bones found, with the intention of 'proving' they were Bormann's."

Startled, Lynch and Woofs sat up and stared at Hahn.

"But didn't dental records prove that the skull was Bormann's?" Lynch asked.

"That is what we told the press. Lindermanns and his

agents found a man about Bormann's size, a man with very good teeth. We'll never know how they did it. A dentist then 'doctored' the man's teeth to conform with Bormann's dental chart. The dentist made one mistake, only one, but that mistake was enough. I'm not at liberty to tell you what it was."

Hahn then said that Bormann was hiding out in Brazil, at the southernmost tip of its border with Paraguay, his precise location a mile inland from the West Bank of the Paraná River. In effect, Bormann had positioned himself in one of the world's greatest natural fortresses. His estate stretched in a rectangle forty miles along the river by a hundred miles—all of it jungle and savannah, so treacherous that it was all but impassable, certainly impassable without alerting the local Indians, most of whom were on Bormann's payroll.

The name of the estate was *Kolonie Waldner 555*.

The roads to the west—from Asuncion to Paraguay, or down the Brazilian border from Bella Vista—passed through territory combed by militia hostile to any stranger. And there were hostile German settlers. Between Bella Vista and *Kolonie Waldner* were 16 German settlements, most of them containing a large number of ex-SS men.

To the north lay the only international airport, at Campo Grande. The final avenue of attack, an assault up the Paraná River, would be just as suicidal: The river shoals were treacherous, and almost to a man the Paraná pilots were Germans from the River Elbe.

"*Kolonie Waldner 555* is a very secure place," Hahn said "Its ——"

. . . layout was basically the barrack square, dozens of huts facing a central courtyard. Bormann's house, the only solidly constructed bungalow, was at the far left of the square from the entrance. It was, not surprisingly, the nearest house to the colony's escape route—seven Piper Cub light aircraft standing on a runway.

It was Bormann's vast wealth that insured both the colony's protection and its freedom from the grinding toil of the self-supporting settlements further inland; and that wealth was over ONE BILLION—Hitler's private wealth, plus hundreds of millions in Nazi Party and SS funds, all of which Bormann expropriated.

Hahn paused long enough to light a cigarette, then continued.

"To us in the BND, it is obvious that Bormann and Lindermanns are not only backing Sir MacLean but using him for their own ends—a resurgence of Nazism throughout the world. Bormann is a past master at manipulating people. For example, he made Himmler look like an idiot. Himmler was a child in the hands of an expert wet nurse like Bormann, who kept him comfortably in his place without Himmler's even knowing it."

"The Brotherhood of the 4th Reich," mused Kingman. "I think it should have been called the 'Bormann Brotherhood.' Yet how does this fit in with the submarine?"

"I'm coming to that," Hahn said. "I'll call the operation *Aktion Adlerflug*, since that's what the Nazis called it— 'Operation Eagle's Flight.' Several years before the end of the war, Bormann realized that Nazi Germany could not win. He then used his immense power as the Fuhrer's central authority to move documents and gold through intelligence routes to South America. He had full authority to utilize Lufthansa and cargo-carrying U-boats. By the end of 1945, everything was ready. We estimate that as much as two and a half billion, in dollar value, had been scattered throughout the world, in secret bank accounts. Now we come to the submarines.

"After the war ended, there were nine German submarines that could not be accounted for. Four of these were the newer S-type that were much larger than the ordinary U-boat. Not a trace of any of these nine submarines has ever been found—and *ya*, we know some of them were taken to South America. We know because we had an agent within *Die Deutsche Gemeinschaft*, The German Brotherhood. One of the S-types was even spotted a few years ago not far from the Marquesas Islands in French Polynesia, in the South Pacific."

"Balderdash!" Woofs exclaimed, chuckling slightly. "Nine U-boats 35 years ago is understandable. Today it is more than slightly ridiculous—no insult intended, old man."

"There's the matter of crews," Lynch said. "The original crews would be in their late fifties and early sixties. Many of them would be dead by now. You just don't go out and pick out anybody to be a submariner."

His tone clearly indicated that he expected an answer. Neither Hahn nor Gertenshalger spoke, and not because they were insulted. Both BND agents considered the British

117

SIS to be composed of well-mannered but pompous fools.

"None of you SIS boys understand the Nazi mentality," the Death Merchant said, "or Nazism, for that matter. Nazism is more than an ideology for fanatics. It's similar to Moslemism and Judaism: it's a way of life. Its members live it, 24 hours a day, 7 days a week, 365 days a year, year in and year out. I'll tell you jokers where the crews come from—the children of SS men and other Nazis who fled the Third Reich after the war. That's where the sub crews come from."

Hahn and Gertenshalger nodded in firm agreement, Gertenshalger saying in heavily accented English, "It's *Die Deutsche Gemeinschaft* that controls such matters. It's the 'Vatican' of Nazism throughout the world, with offices all over the world, even in America; and as Herr Hopmeir has said, it is a way of life. Its members have a fanaticism that makes a missionary seem lazy in comparison. Also, it is a system that breeds hatred. The hatred breeds fear. The fear creates iron obedience."

The precise, careful Arnold Steel folded his bony hands on the table while his eyes carefully measured the two Germans and the Death Merchant.

He said in a casual way, "I find it incompatible that Sir MacLean should fly to Bracadale Castle and radio whomever he might radio and expect a submarine to rescue him and his party. It isn't likely that a *Die Deutsche Gemeinschaft* submarine would be in the vicinity. It could be a month or more before one of the subs could reach the Island of Skye. Surely, MacLean doesn't expect us to sit around for weeks and not come after him. Somewhere, there has to be a missing piece to this confusing puzzle."

Wearing puzzled expressions, Lynch and Kingman shifted uncomfortably, the quandary of the situation irking at their sense of order. A further paradox was that they sensed "Mr. Hopmeir" was not a man to make statements lightly. How could he be right and yet wrong?

They were both surprised when Camellion drained the glass, picked up the bottle, poured more schnapps into the glass and started to supply the answer.

"We've been approaching the problem from the wrong angle," he said lazily, as though it were a great effort for him to talk (which it was). "We've been talking about MacLean going to the castle on business. Very well. What kind of business? What could he and his sons and Lindermanns do while up there on the west coast of Skye? I'll tell you: They went to the castle to meet a submarine. They made arrangements weeks ago, maybe months ago. That explains why Sir MacLean hasn't tried to fly out. He's waiting for the U-boat."

"By God! You might have something," Kingman said resolutely. He took off the dark glasses that had been perched on his forehead above his eyebrows. "If you are right, it's going to be a toss-up who gets there first—us or the sub."

"Have you forgotten the two cutters?" Lynch interposed. "I hardly——"

He stopped talking and glanced to his right when the door opened and Charles Phegley hurried into the room, came back to the table and sat down.

"I talked to Captain Merriweather," he said, slightly out of breath, his eyes going around the table. "He informed me that the two cutters are strictly for surface patrol. Neither vessel carries submarine detection gear or any antisubmarine weapons."

The Death Merchant shook his head, much to the annoyance of Phegley, who looked quickly from Cemellion to Steel. "I informed Captain Merriweather of the possibility of an enemy submarine in the area. He is going to dispatch a subchaser to reinforce the two cutters." He cleared his throat and glanced down at the table. "It will, however, take time. The nearest subchaser is at the Royal Navy base at Blackpool."

Camellion interjected, "And from Blackpool to the west central coast of Skye is more than four hundred miles." His short laugh was sinister. "You had better pray to whatever gods you pray to that the U-boat doesn't arrive before the subchaser gets there."

Phegley looked trapped. "We can't be positive that there will be a submarine," he insisted, sounding unsure of himself.

"No, and we can't be positive that the sun will not explode into a nova next week, or tomorrow!" laughed Camellion. "In case you jaspers don't know what I'm saying, I'm telling you that we can't afford to take a chance that a sub won't show up. I still can't understand how you British ever won any wars!"

Phegley stiffened, mounting anger making his thin cheeks twitch. Lynch and Woofs stared angrily at Camellion while Rudolf Gertenshalger whispered to Hahn in German, asking him what a "jasper" was.

Grinning, Kingman lighted a cigarette.

Camellion leaned back and took another drink.

"Mr. Hopmeir," Lynch said bitterly, "rumor has it that you fight strictly for monetary gain. We don't consider it proper that a mercenary should criticize the British. We are fighting for moral principles; you, apparently, are concerned only with money."

"I'm not all that fond of money," Camellion said with a half-laugh, "although I do admit it quiets my nerves. And by the way, I'm not a mercenary. I don't enjoy killing anymore than I sit around and concentrate on the enjoyment of breathing—or talking to unrealistic fools who apparently can't see what must be done."

"Suppose you tell us, damn it!" Woofs said angrily, stabbing at Camellion with the stem of his pipe. "All we can do is leave tomorrow morning as planned."

"We can leave early enough so that we can attack the castle at dawn," Camellion said. He leaned forward with amazing speed. "Even then we might be too late."

Charles Phegley was so shocked that he almost knocked over his chair as he stood up.

"Damn it, man!" He stared at the Death Merchant. "You're so drunk right now, I doubt if you'll be in shape by tomorrow afternoon!"

"Suppose you let me worry about my condition," Camellion said sharply. "Tell me why the commandoes can't be ready to assemble by midnight. They're here and Major Simpson is here."

"By jove! You are serious!" exclaimed Phegley indignantly. He sat down again. "You actually mean it."

"I mean it," Camellion said. "We lift off in time to land at Bracadale Castle at dawn. So start figuring out when the sun rises."

He stood up, steadied himself, and looked at Kingman.

"Let's go get a steak."

# Chapter Ten

In the past, Bracadale Castle had been a gleaming fortification, its white limestone walls and keep glistening in the sunshine. Built on a tremendous slab of rock, it dominated much of the coastal plain of west-central Skye and could be seen for miles by vessels in the Sea of the Hebrides.

Time, however, had taken its toll. Over the centuries the limestone had turned from white to gray-black. Vines, some as thick as a man's wrist, had crept steadily up the rusticated walls that were thirty-five feet high and eighteen feet thick. At each corner of the wall was an eighty-foot high rounded tower, strengthened with machicolations. A third of the way up each tower was a series of crenels, narrow openings through which Mackenzie defenders had rained down arrows on MacLeans. There was another series of crenels at the halfway mark. On top of the towers were the battlements with their embrasures, the same kind of battlements prevailing on the top of the outer walls. Other protective measures were bartizans, small overhanging turrets, spaced out at the top of the walls.

In the center of the courtyard was the square keep, 125 feet on each side, its height the equivalent of a six-story building.

A total anachronism in the 20th Century, Bracadale Castle was now only a useless relic of dead days, of years forgotten by the modern world. Man didn't need it. Man—"God's most noble creation"—no longer slaughtered his fellows with swords and pikes, bows and arrows and battleaxes. Man had progressed. Man could now wipe out millions with one bomb.

A thoughtful observer would have noticed two features about the castle that were totally out of place. The first was the very modern wind generator which rested toward the northwest corner of the roof of the keep. The four-legged silver tower was fifty feet tall, the propeller that turned the electric generator almost fifteen feet long.

The other modern feature was the hi-gain shortwave antenna that stretched from the bottom of the wind tower to the top of the stone tower at the northeast corner of the defensive walls.

Sir MacLean had put the four towers to good use. He had strengthened the inside walls and the floors with steel girders and had made it possible to reach the top embattlements by means of steel ladders placed on each four.

Sir Hugh MacLean, Dirck Van Memling, and Gilbert Drummond were on the roof of the keep, standing toward the west edge, all three using binoculars to stare through a six-foot wide crenel at the two coast guard cutters five miles to the west.

For half a day and an entire night and today, the cutters had been at anchor in the Sea of the Hebrides. But since four o'clock in the afternoon, the two cutters had been on the move, their screws churning the water at full knottage. The cutters would move from north to south, then back again, but always in a crisscross pattern, as if expecting trouble.

As if expecting a submarine . . .

Sir MacLean lowered the binoculars and shoved them into the case hanging on a strap around his neck.

"They know," he said in a low, final undertone. "Somehow they have guessed that we are here to rendezvous with a submarine."

"It doesn't matter what the swine know," Van Memling said acidly. He stepped back slightly and put away his own pair of binoculars. "The two submarines will arrive at five tomorrow morning. It will take no longer than three hours to load the gold. By eight-thirty, nine o'clock at the latest, we should be on board and on our way to Greece."

He raised the fur-lined collar of his windbreaker, for although it was summer, the wind was always chilly in these latitudes and at these heights, especially after the sun went down.

Sir MacLean's face, the grayish pallor of parchment, reflected worry, an infinite melancholy in his deep-set eyes. So much had happened in so very short a time. Dunbeath Hall, his ancestral home for almost 450 years, was gone. Never again would he be able to set foot in the offices of

MacLean Fabrics, Ltd. Nigel. Was he safe? Sir Hugh doubted if Nigel would manage to get to Greece on his own. Nigel had always been the weak one, like his mother. A good head for business, but without any talent whatsoever for intrigue. Thank God that John-Percy and Edward had more spirit and drive, and a willingness to make the world safe for the master race.

He looked toward the west. Already the sun was close to the horizon, its slanted rays filling the water with ripples of red, orange, and yellow.

"They could attack tonight," Sir MacLean said to Van Memling. "It's common knowledge that I inherited this castle from my wife. They know we're here. The two cutters out there prove as much."

"It's only been several days," Van Memling said, his voice without emotion. He shoved his hands deep into the side pockets of his jacket. "They will check and double-check. The British, and the Americans, operate methodically; never do they rush headlong into anything."

"The British are very good at night operations," said Gilbert Drummond, who had stepped back from the wide opening at the top of the battlement wall. "There is no guarantee that they won't pay us a visit before we are ready to leave. We eight would be defenseless against such a force. Have you an answer for such a possible catastrophe, Mr. Van Memling?"

"An answer?" repeated Van Memling, stressing the last word. "Yes, I have an answer. The British would find our dead bodies, unless you gentlemen prefer capture to suicide. I do not."

Unlike the fanatical Van Memling, neither Sir MacLean nor Gilbert Drummond wanted to die. Come what may, this was the only life they had, and they wanted to hang onto this existence as long as possible.

"Come, let's get downstairs," Van Memling said, his tone sounding like a direct order. "The wind is getting stronger."

Without glancing at Sir MacLean or the mammoth Drummond, he turned and walked to the wedge-shaped housing in the southwest corner of the huge roof, opened the metal door in front and waited impatiently for Sir MacLean and Drummond to catch up with him. Moments later, the three men started down the steel stairs.

When Bracadale Castle had functioned as a fortress, the

four upper floors had served as a warehouse and living quarters for the Mackenzie special guard. The second had been the living quarters of the lord of the castle and his family and close kinsmen. The great hall, kitchen, stables and armory had been on the first floor. Below were the dungeons. Now all the rooms, except those on the ground floor, were empty, filled only with the dust of centuries, bitter memories, and unfulfilled dreams.

Shields, broadswords, battle-axes, and pikes, all coated with centuries of rust, hung on the walls. There was some ancient furniture in some of the upper rooms and tumbled masses of stone that, over the years, had been replaced by other stones. It had been a matter of pride with the Mackenzie clan. Every year the keep was inspected. Crumbling stones were replaced. Loose stones were remortared.

Sir MacLean and his two companions didn't have any trouble descending the stairs, which were brightly lit with electric lights.

"I hope you're right about the British," Sir MacLean said. His hand on the railing, he glanced at Van Memling. "I don't like it at all, when I stop to realize that I and my sons and close friends will not be able to return and use the radiation shelter in the dungeon section at the proper time. It cost almost a million pounds to build the shelter and stock it with food and water. At least we have the consolation of knowing that the bomb will be assembled and exploded, even if the British do attack before we're able to leave."

The three men rounded a bend in the stairs and came to the fourth floor landing.

"You can use one of our shelters in South America," Van Memling remarked. "One bomb shelter is as good as another."

"You don't understand. This shelter here is mine. The others are not mine; they're yours.

"It's your fault," Van Memling said with a slight sneer. "Your own lack of security that caused the mess at Dunbeath Hall. I wanted those four killed immediately. But no! You had to keep them alive. You wanted to rub their noses in what we were doing. You wanted them to suffer emotional torture by knowing what was going to happen to them. Your stupid pride accomplished nothing but disaster."

"They were handcuffed and in a dungeon!" Sir MacLean

snapped. "There were guards outside. The door was bolted securely. Who would have thought they could escape?"

"You're talking nonsense." Van Memling's tone was curt. "We'll never know how those four did it. I couldn't care less. That mistake—and it was yours—is in the past. It's the present with which we must concern ourselves—the present and the future."

Sir MacLean tried to act nonchalant. "There isn't anything we can do but wait." He added with a bitter smirk. "Should the British pay us a visit, we'll know it."

Gilbert Drummond, walking behind the other two men, spoke up.

"We could save as much as an hour by not carrying the gold through the tunnel."

Van Memling frowned only briefly. "The gold will be transported through the tunnel," he said. "We transported that gold from Spain for safekeeping. To risk its discovery by carrying it outside of the castle, out in the open, would be madness. And how would we get it down to the beach and the boats. Lower it, bar by bar, on a rope, down the face of the cliff?"

Drummond did not reply. His eyes on the back of the German's neck, he thought how nice it would be to put his hands around the chicken-sized neck and strangle the Nazi son of a bitch . . .

# Chapter Eleven

Up front, on the port side of the Lynx HAS-2 helicopter, the Death Merchant looked out the window, his head pounding like an oversized voodoo drum, and the roaring of the chopper's two Rolls-Royce Gem 10001 three-shaft turbines didn't add anything but more misery.

In the twilight of the brand new dawn, he could see two of the KAMAN Huskies, to port. By leaning down slightly and looking out of the first window on the starboard side, he could see the third KAMAN H-43. Each K-H-43 carried twenty British Commandoes, every man a battle-hardened vet of Northern Ireland.

Next to the Death Merchant sat Melvin Kingman and Klaus Hahn. On the other fuselage bench, on the starboard side, were Rudolf Gertenshalger, Kevin Woofs, and Ronald Lynch. The faces of Woofs and Lynch were tense and strained, in contrast to the two Germans who appeared as unconcerned as a moon rock. Kingman, leaning back, his legs crossed at the ankles, was dozing, his Klamath cap pulled down over his face to keep out the light.

There was no partition between the passenger section and the cockpit, and by looking between the pilot and the copilot, Camellion could see the area ahead—half-dark cloudless sky, then haze.

He consulted his watch: 04.41 hours. They should be at Bracadale Castle by 05.00 hours.

*The worst hangover of my life, but we're on the nose, right on schedule!*

The chopper dropped sharply when it hit an air pocket, then rose again to its proper 7,500 foot height, the unexpected motion sufficient to awaken Kingman, who would have fallen off the bench if his safety strap had not restrained him. Kingman sat up straight, yawned, pushed back his cap, reached for his cigarettes and blinked at the Death Merchant.

"Listen, if you ever do this again and I'm around, count me out," Kingman said. "I'm a night person. These dumb dawn raids aren't my style. I'm apt to be half-asleep when I get myself killed. Hell, I'd never know I was dead! How's the schedule?"

"On the mark," answered Camellion. "Fifteen minutes at the most, we should be on the roof of the castle. That includes the time for the swing around and the line up."

Kingman finished lighting his cigarette, inhaling deeply. "We shouldn't have any trouble." He blew out smoke and laughed. "It's not as though we had to eat crackers and whistle Yankee Doodle at the same time."

Ronald Lynch called over, "I estimate another nine minutes."

He and Kevin Woofs eyed Camellion closely, amazed that "Mr. Hopmeir" had such a rapid recovery on only four hours of sleep.

"I'm going up front and check," Camellion said. He got up from the end of the bench, his shoulder bags of grenades and ammo bulging, moved the short distance to the cockpit and leaned over the right shoulder of the pilot, a young dude not over 24. The man had a full beard and hair almost to his shoulders. The copilot also resembled one of the patriarchs out of the Old Testament.

The pilot turned and grinned at Camellion.

"How's the target time?" Camellion inquired.

"Seven and a half minutes, sir," the man said cheerfully. "I'm dropping down now to two thousand."

"Don't worry, sir," the copilot said, turning around. "Landing on the roof of that castle will be a snapper."

"No, not on the roof," Camellion said in a loud voice to make himself heard, emphasizing the "on." "We don't know how firm the roof is. A few feet above the roof will be fine. Did you get that? A few feet above the roof."

"Righto," the pilot said. "A few feet it is. Take a look. You can see the coast—better with binocs."

Camellion looked through the wide rectangular windshield. Ahead, but mostly to port, was the dim whiteness that was the Sea of the Hebrides; to starboard the deeper tinges of the land, various shaped patterns, some square, some triangular. The hilly high ground was a zigzag scar running north—to the left.

"Give me the green when you're within three miles, then

drop to five hundred feet," Camellion said, feeling for the first time a tiny tingle of excitement.

"As good as done, sir," the pilot replied. "I'm going to rev down now." He pushed down on the collective pitch stick and moved the cyclic control stick to port. The helicopter started to descend and to swing to port.

The Death Merchant, bracing himself by holding onto overhead handholds, started to move back to the passenger section, thinking that the Westland/Aerospatiale Lynx was one damn fine piece of machinery. Not only was it the world's most maneuverable helo, but it could also be rolled at over 100 degrees per second and flown backward at 80 mph.

This particular Lynx did not have the usual tricycle landing gear. Instead, it was equipped with high skids, to make room on the belly for the electrically fired .30 caliber machine gun mounted on what resembled an enormous ball bearing. The machine gun could be fired straight ahead through the skids, or moved to the bottom of the ball and rotated. On the side of each set of skid braces was a rocket pod, each container filled with an SS-11 anti-tank missile.

Moving against the forward tilt of the Lynx, the Death Merchant reached the end of the bench and eased himself down. He didn't strap in. The men turned from the windows, and he saw that their faces were anxious. Even Kingman and the two Germans exhibited tenseness.

"We're almost there," Camellion said, "but stay buckled. We have to size up the situation. The pilot might have to do a lot of tricky maneuvering."

"Oh shit! Let's land and get it over with," Kingman grumbled.

Camellion looked out of one of the starboard windows and saw that the single KAMAN Huskie had cut altitude and was keeping even with the Lynx. He turned, looked out the first port window and was pleased to see that the other two H-43s had also dropped, although they were still higher than the Lynx and the other KAMAN to starboard.

At 500 feet the Island of Skye was no longer a checkerboard of various colored patterns. Masses of trees, individual farms, and roads were visible, all rushing past, as if it were they that were moving while the Lynx hung suspended.

Fastened to a ceiling mount, a green light began to flash. A buzzer next to it sounded loudly.

With six tiny devils drilling in his skull, Camellion got up and, going from handhold to handhold, moved again to the cockpit.

"There's the castle, sir," the pilot said. "Dead ahead."

Camellion stared through the windshield. Through the fog rolling along the top of the cliffs, he could see the castle, built on a gigantic shelf of rock and looking like a giant toy that needed a good scrubbing.

"Don't go straight to the keep," the Death Merchant ordered the pilot. "Drop to 200 and swing out to port. I want to move over the beach and have a look at the cave and the water."

"Yes, sir," the pilot acknowledged with a slight nod, his hands working the pitch stick and the cyclic control stick.

BANG! God closed the last shutter of night, and the sun popped up over the horizon, its rays splashing over the entire countryside.

Rapidly the Lynx closed in on the cliffs. The terrain below became more uneven and rocky, the trees becoming more and more sparse. Scattered among the rocks were patches of brittlebushes, carpets of golden evening primroses, and tiny meadows of lavender beardtongue.

The Death Merchant turned and saw that the other five men in back were watching the ground through the port and starboard windows. They had removed the submachine guns from the clip-on racks above their heads and had strapped the chatter boxes to the cartridge belts around their waists. Camellion swung back to the front.

In places, the beach was filled with granite boulders, perfectly rounded like bowling balls, and huge arrowhead shaped rocks, over which the breakers crashed, the water turning to spray and foam.

Moments later, Camellion, the pilot, the copilot, and the five intelligence agents got the first big surprise of the day.

*The two Royal Navy coast guard cutters were gone!*

In their places were two submarines, the bow of one pointed north, the bow of the other pointed west. Both U-boats were moving.

"I'll be damned!" the pilot exclaimed. "Two bloomin' submarines!"

"World War II U-boats!" the copilot said in awe. "I've

seen photographs of World War II subs, and we still have half a dozen of that old junk for training purposes.

In the next instant, water broke over the sharp prows of the two German U-boats and started flowing over the wooden slat boards of the forward decks. The conning towers tilted forward. The two U-boats were diving.

"We might be able to get one with the rockets," the pilot said. "I doubt it. By the time we'd make the approach, they'd be gone."

"Don't bother; it would only be a waste of rockets," Camellion said. "You might need them when you reach the keep. Stay on course."

He became aware that Kingman was standing next to him, hanging onto a hand-hold next to the buzzer and the flasher.

Surprise number two! In front of the tallest cliffs was a long expanse of sandy beach not separated from the water by large rocks. Three modern longboats, powered by large outboard motors, had been pulled up on the shore, their engines tilted forward, to protect the propellers which were out of the water. The beach was not deserted. Several dozen men were racing over the wet sand toward the dark mouth of the Cave of Charles the Bold. Above the cave towered the limestone face of the cliff, seamed in shades of blue, the sun-burnished summit a ragged sawtooth in whose pockets of rock mist still clung.

"We didn't arrive too early or too late," Kingman shouted, "We got here right in the middle of breakfast."

"Yeah, and we can expect trouble," Camellion said. Looking through the windshield to starboard, he saw the three KAMAN H-43s headed northeast.

He tapped the pilot on the shoulder and, when the man turned, pointed to the headset and the attached loop mike the man wore. The pilot nodded, had the copilot take the controls, took off the set and handed it to Camellion. Since the channels between the four choppers had been set on the radios of the four helos, Camellion had only to press the button on the loop-wire mike.

"Major Simpson, this is Hopmeir," the Death Merchant said loudly, his tone urgent. "Did you see those two U-boats?"

Major Claud Simpson's bass voice came over the earphones.

"Indeed we did. You must be congratulated, Mr. Hopmeir. Your theory was correct."

"Did you see the longboats and the men running into the Cave of Charles the Bold?"

"Negative. Our course wasn't over the beach. We wondered why you chaps were flying so close to water."

"Major, give the order and have one of the KAMANS put down on the beach, say 500 feet south of the cave. They can bottle up those Nazis. With us going into the castle through the roof, forty of your boys should be enough to get the job done."

"Negative, Mr. Hopmeir. My chaps and I will proceed with the original plan. I am not going to have twenty of my group land on the beach."

With great effort, Camellion controlled his temper. "Will you tell me why not?"

"Now see here! I don't know how many of the enemy are in the castle. The enemy in the cave isn't going anywhere. The submarines have submerged. We can clean out the cave after we've completed the sweep in the castle. Any other requests, Mr. Hopmeir."

"NO!" The Death Merchant bit off the word, then shut off the mike in the middle of Major Simpson's "Good luck to you and your chaps."

"Why didn't you remind the son of a bitch that you're the boss?" demanded an angry Kingman, who had gleaned Simpson's refusal from listening to Camellion's half of the conversation.

"We don't have time to argue with an idiot," Camellion said. "And it's not all that important. It isn't likely that the U-boats will surface with the choppers around."

The Death Merchant put together what had happened. Hearing the helicopters approaching, the *Kapitans* of the two U-boats had made the instant decision to submerge, thinking of the safety of their vessels. The Germans still ashore had been marooned. *Damn it! It's a toss up! If Sir MacLean and his close people are aboard one of the subs, we'll never get any information about the nuclear bomb!*

He handed the headphones and mike back to the pilot. "Swing to the roof, but only for a looksee. There's no need to get overanxious."

"Hang on!" the pilot said and started to turn the Lynx to starboard. By this time the helicopter was a mile to the northwest of the castle. Its heading changed within seconds, to a course that was due south, one that would take it right over the roof of the castle keep.

At a distance, Camellion, Kingman, and the pilot and copilot saw the tiny figures crouched by the battlements to the north and to the east, weapons in their hands.

"This is going to be one of those days," Kingman said, "all bad." His head was bent, his eyes riveted on the figures on the roof.

"Take us up," Camellion said to the pilot. "At this low height we could catch slugs in a vital spot."

Instantly the pilot made the adjustments, and the Lynx jumped into the early morning air, its four-bladed main rotor chopping the air furiously. At a height of 450 feet from the ground, or 300 feet above the castle keep, the Lynx shot over the roof. Below, 14 submachine guns roared, the Germans making an all out effort to bring down the Lynx.

But the height of the craft, coupled with the terrific downdraft of the four blades, made hitting the craft virtually impossible. There were a few loud pinging sounds, but the high velocity slugs had struck only the bottom of the skids.

By leaning down and looking through the port windows, Camellion could see that one of the KAMAN Huskies was setting down to the east of the castle, behind a line of low hills. Ahead, to the south, another KAMAN had already touched down and was discharging its cargo of commandoes.

The pilot glanced around at the Death Merchant. "Your orders, sir? The roof's not a problem. We can use the machine gun below. We can sweep them off the roof like bugs."

"Son, what's your name?" asked Camellion.

"I'm Lieutenant Leslie Champion, Sir."

"Well, Lieutenant Leslie Champion, I want you to head out to where we saw the U-boats. Skim at fifty feet. I want to see if we can see any wreckage floating from the cutters."

The pilot nodded. Kingman frowned.

"Why waste time poking around over the water?" Kingman demanded, his big face twisting with resentment. "Let's attack the damned roof and get it over with. Major Simpson is counting on us to do damage inside while he gives them hell on the outside."

Camellion explained. "If there's any flotsam floating

around, it means that the subs sank the cutters only a short time before we arrived, in which case Sir MacLean and his sickies wouldn't have had time to get aboard. The lack of any wreckage will indicate that the water has had time to disperse it and that the U-boats have been around for an hour or more. In that case, MacLean might have had time to get aboard."

"Well I think the subs just arrived," Kingman said. "We saw those guys running into the cave. Those were the krauts that had just come ashore. There were only a dozen of the bastards. Stop and think. Each of those long boats will hold twenty men. No one got aboard. MacLean's still in the castle. And those guys on the roof had to be krauts unless MacLean had some men at the village of Bracadale."

"You could be right," Camellion said. "We'll soon get some idea."

He felt his body sway from the momentum of the Lynx's turning to starboard.

The pilot called out, "Sir, we carry a Plessey 195 sonar on a 200 foot line. If you want to see if the subs are still hanging around, we could hover and lower the sounder into the water."

Unfamiliar with the Plessey type sonar, Camellion asked, "What's its range?"

"Ten miles maximum."

"Don't bother. We don't have the time. Make several low passes over the area, then head back for the roof."

"As good as done, sir."

The Lynx headed west, moving lower and lower. Once more the cliffs passed underneath, this time at less than a hundred feet below the chopper, the massifs glaring up at the helicopter.

In many places along the cutup, rocky coast spray exploded almost fifty feet into the air as waves crashed over rocky points. But 200 feet off the shore in front of the Cave of Charles the Bold was calm, the surf normal. How Norsemen and pirates must have loved that stretch of calm beach . . .

The longboats were still there.

There was no sign of the Germans.

"Too bad one of the U-boats isn't on the surface," Kingman said, nudging Camellion. "Heaven help them if one of them comes up."

The Death Merchant, his gaze fixed on the water, did not reply.

*No, my friend. Heaven won't help them. God uses only the good ones. The bad ones use God. Fools like us use ourselves* . . .

The Lynx, so low that now Camellion could see that the water was very calm, with a speed from one to three knots, made the first pass over the general area where the two submarines had been seen, Camellion and Kingman closely scanning the water. Everything was normal. There was not a trace of any wreckage.

Five miles to the west, the pilot turned to port, swung the craft around and took it several miles east. Once more he swung to port. Again the Lynx skimmed the water at 50 feet, flying this time to the north. Again, not a trace of wreckage. Not a single life preserver. Nothing . . .

"Head for the roof," Camellion said to Lieutenant Champion.

Kingman wore a puzzled expression. He leaned closer to the Death Merchant, his right hand still gripping the overhead handhold. "It doesn't make sense. There's not any wreckage floating on the water. The U-boats must have been around at least an hour, and, considering the large area we covered, maybe longer. That was more than enough time for MacLean and his crumbs to get aboard. Yet the subs were still around when we showed up."

Camellion, giving no indication that he had heard Kingman, suddenly said to Lieutenant Champion. "Forget the keep for now. Put us on a course that will let us lob a missile at those four boats on the beach. Think you can hit them?"

Champion glanced around and gave Camellion a quick grin. "Take a look at this, sir." He turned back toward the instrument panel and tapped a big dial marked LRMTS. Above the dial was a square 3" screen with crosshairs, a small circle in the center of the crosshairs. "That's the Laser Ranger and Marked Target Seeker. All we do is lock the target on the screen. When the target is centered, the LRMTS does the rest, fires the missile automatically."

"I'll take your word for it," Camellion said heartily. "OK, do it. Blow up the boats; then we'll head for the roof." He turned to Kingman. "Go back and tell the others what's going on. I'll have Champion use the buzzer when it's time to unbuckle."

"Before then, we'll be able to see the approach from the windows," Kingman said, turning to go, "and hear the thirty caliber."

"You're right. There's no need for the buzzer."

Several minutes later, Champion turned to starboard, turned the Lynx around and headed south. The copilot turned on the LRMTS. Steadily, as Champion made the approach, he lowered the Lynx, revving down the rotors by turning the throttle on the collective stick and at the same time pushing the stick forward. All the while he watched the LRMTS screen. With each second the distance between the Lynx and the boats on the beach decreased.

Methods of dispensing death had become so modern, so easy.

Camellion chuckled, in spite of the situation. *If the safety pin were invented today, it would have a regulator, two transistors, an off and on switch and require a once-a-year check up!*

Very suddenly the four boats appeared on the green lighted screen. Lieutenant Champion worked the controls, moving the chopper so that the boats would be centered in the screen. A bit to port. Down a degree. Now up. Slightly to starboard.

And then the four boats were centered.

There was a short whooshing sound from the left skid pod, and the SS-11 anti-tank missile was on its way, leaving a trail of white vapor behind it.

*BLLLAAAMMMMMMMMM!* A big, brief ball of yellow fire, tinged with red and edged with black, and the task was completed. What was left of the four boats came tumbling back down, some of the twisted and torn metal hitting the surf, other pieces stabbing into the sand.

The copilot laughed. "That's tough titty for those boats. If those two U-boats come to the surface, the men in the cave can swim!"

"Good shot!" commented Camellion. "Now let's go shoot the tails off the dirt-bags on the roof."

"Coming right up, sir." Lieutenant Champion turned to starboard, swung around and headed the Lynx north. Four miles to the north of the castle, he again turned to starboard, skidded the craft around on air and sent the chopper south, the nose pointed at the target.

The Death Merchant watched the copilot shut off the pod-firing switch and change the firing mechanism of the

.30 machine gun to the LRMTS. The Browning could be fired either by the LRMTS or manually. If the latter, the shooter would use the LRMTS' screen as the sight.

His hands on the lever, one finger touching the firing button, the copilot watched the screen. There was the castle. Lieutenant Champion glanced at the screen, moved the controls, and swung the 'copter slightly to port.

Dead center on the screen. Range: 300 yards. The copilot pressed the firing button. The Browning machine gun, mounted to the underside of the Lynx, roared. Working the lever, the copilot moved the weapon from left to right. With high velocity projectiles popping all around them, the frantic Nazis rushed for the metal wedge-shaped housing covering the steps to the uppermost floor inside the castle. Most of the Germans reached the door. Two didn't. The Browning's slugs chopped into them and kicked them back a dozen feet before knocking them to the floor.

The Lynx was flying over the north-side battlements when the copilot pushed the "Rotate" button and the "Full Automatic" of the LRMTS device. The weapon dropped to the bottom of the "ball" and began to revolve, all the while spitting out .30 slugs. Hundreds of the steel-cored missiles stabbed into every section of the roof, the impacts kicking up tiny geysers of stone chips. Nothing could live in such a vicious cloud of steel. Nothing did, including the two Nazis trying to reach the door of the housing. One died "gloriously" for the "greater glory" of the Brotherhood of the 4th Reich. Five slugs exploded his chest. Two more blew up his head and scattered his brain to the stiff wind. The corpse crashed to the floor amid a cloud of tattered clothing, bloody pieces of flesh and tiny slivers of bone. The second man went down, and skidded several feet across the roof on his face, his right leg hanging by only several bloody strands of muscle, his whole body dripping blood.

Several dozen loud pings, the sounds all rolled into one, and the metal housing was riddled, as well as the two Nazis who had been waiting at the top of the stairs. They tumbled down the steps, their corpses almost falling on several wild-eyed Germans who jumped back at the bottom of the stairs.

The copilot switched off the Browning, saying, "Those bloody bastards bring out the best in me! I hope we shot off their dockers."

The Lynx chopper hung suspended, fifty feet above the roof of the castle keep.

The Death Merchant said to the copilot, "Put the Browning on manual and keep it trained on the housing in the southwest corner. If you see as much as a flea, fire." Then, to the pilot, "Don't set us down until I give you the word . . ."

"Righto, sir. I'll make it several feet from the roof."

"Fine." Camellion turned around in time to see that Kingman was tilting a pint bottle of brandy to his lips. Camellion wanted to laugh and laugh and laugh when he thought of how he had gotten drunk the previous day. The misery of the hangover was worth it. The intelligence services of the world knew quite a bit about the Death Merchant, even if they didn't have a clue to his true identity. Among the things they did know was that he was a man who gave no quarter and asked for none. They also knew that the faceless Merchant of total destruction was a nondrinker.

It isn't likely that Kingman or Steel or any of the SIS agents will suspect me of being the Death Merchant, not after my performance yesterday. Hahn suspects, ever since we were together in West Germany. But he can't be sure. Even if he were, he's not the type to say anything and invite disaster.

He saw that the men had unbuckled and were all set to step out of the helicopter.

"Hahn, Kingman!" he shouted, "open the starboard door and keep your Mausers trained on the housing over the steps. After the rest of us are out, we'll take over."

"Right." Kingman shoved the bottle into one of his kit bags, swung the Mauser M-60 submachine gun from his shoulder and, with Klaus Hahn, moved to the sliding door on the right side of the Lynx. The rest of the men stood up and prepared to jump to the roof.

The Death Merchant turned, yelled "TAKE HER DOWN!" to Lieutenant Champion, then walked to the end of the left side bench and pulled the Mauser from the cliprack on the wall.

The Mauser Model-60 submachine gun was ideal for this kind of invasion, quick-kill operation. Only sixteen inches with the stock retracted, the weapon, the M-60 had a double-box magazine, 32 nine-millimeter cartridges in each section of the box. Next to the rate of fire switch was another lever marked *LINK* on the left side and *RECHT* on the right side. When the lever was to the left, the Mauser ate cartridges from the left box; from the right when the lever was pushed on *RECHT*.

Down went the Lynx, until the bottom of the two skids were almost touching the gray stones of the roof. Out jumped the men, first Woofs and Lynch, then Gertenshalger, while Hahn and Kingman, on either side of the doorway, kept the hooded barleycorn sights of their Mauser machine guns trained on the housing, and Camellion yelled at Lieutenant Champion, "As soon as you lift off, contact Major Simpson and land by his chopper. But keep on the walkie-talkie frequency. I might need the Lynx later."

Doubt flashed in Champion's eyes. "Sir, whose orders do we follow, yours or Major Simpson's?"

"You follow my orders. If I tell you to lift off and fly to the moon, you lift off and fly to the moon."

"And if Major Simpson refuses to let us go?" asked the copilot whose name was Charles Orbis.

"In that case, you ignore his orders and follow mine—period. When it's all over with, I'll see to it that he's busted to a noncom. And if you don't follow my orders, I'll make sure you end up as common seamen, so far below decks you'll have to look up to see the bilges. You got it?"

"Yes, sir!" both men said, a bit in awe of "Mr. Hopmeir."

The Death Merchant turned and motioned to Hahn and Kingman, who jumped from the Lynx to the roof. The Death Merchant followed them. His feet were still feeling the sting from the jump as Lieutenant Champion revved up and the Lynx lifted upward.

The Death Merchant and his squad of five were on their own.

# Chapter Twelve

Blue sky above! Death below! Death waiting on all six floors of Bracadale Castle. Far to the east, Camellion and his force could hear the chattering of British Sterling submachine guns, along with the cracks of EM2s, the standard British Army automatic rifle, which fired a 7mm (0.275-inch) bullet. From the first floor of the castle, the Nazis were answering the fire with automatic weapons of their own.

The Death Merchant began barking orders. "Kingman, you and Hahn go to the front of the housing, drop flat and keep your Mausers trained on the door." He stopped talking and stared disbelievingly at Kevin Woofs, who, in a low crouch, was moving toward the east battlement.

"Woofs, where in hell do you think you're going? Get back here!"

The British SIS agent stopped, turned, and looked at Camellion.

"I was going to see if I could spot Major Simpson and some of his chaps," he said haltingly.

"You bloody pinhead!" he thundered. "Stick your head up and look through one of those openings and you'll get it blown off. Simpson and his men are too far away to see who you are. Get your bald butt over here and take a prone position with Lynch to the south of the housing. Gertenshalger, go to the north. Woofs—MOVE!"

An angry look on his florid face, Woofs went about moving into his assigned position with the other men. Camellion scurried toward the northeast corner of the roof, moving so low that the tip of his nose was less than 30″ from the stones. He stopped, reached into one of his canvas-duck Gussett bags, took out a half pound block of Pentolite, placed it on the floor 15 feet from the corner and attached a remote-control detonator to the block, pushing the twin ice-pick pointed prongs through the oiled brown paper into the soft, putty-like material, and thinking that Pento-lite had been an excellent choice on his part. Pentolite was a 50/50 mixture of penta-erythritol-tetranitrate (commonly referred to as P.E.T.N.) and T.N.T. A very violent high explosive, Pentolite was very stable with a desensitizer, such as wax—*just what I need for a job like this.*

He hurried back to the men, got down on his knees beside Rudy Gertenshalger and took out a small black box from his gray coveralls. He flipped open the cover and pushed the toggle switch to the ON position. A tiny red light came on.

"Here we go, guys." He lay down beside Gertenshalger, turned his head and pushed the black button.

For a shave of a second it seemed that the tremendous explosion might bring down the entire roof, judging from the thunder of the blast. Because their heads were down, no one saw the actual burst, or the chunks of rock, some the size of washtubs, that flew upward. But after the rocks had crashed back to the roof and the smoke and dust had cleared, Camellion and his men saw that a six foot hole had been blown in the 4-feet thick roof.

Camellion and Gertenshalger stood up. Camellion spoke to the broad-faced BND agent in German. "Go over to the hole. Stay far enough back so that no one down below can fire up at you. I'm going to have Kingman toss a grenade down the steps. The instant it explodes, you toss a grenade down the hole, then get down the steps with the rest of the men—*verstehen?*

Gertenshalger nodded, his pale gray eyes almost sinister. *"Ya, tun nicht qualen,"* he said, and moved off toward the cavity in the roof.

Camellion turned, motioned to Hahn to join Lynch and Woofs and beckoned to Kingman to come to the north side of the housing and join him. Hahn went to the other side of the housing; Kingman hurried over to the Death Merchant, who stepped to the center of the housing.

"The door opens outward," Camellion whispered. "Stand in front of me. I want you to open the door, push it back, and toss in a grenade. Then get the hell out of the way."

Kingman glanced at Gertenshalger who was perched on one knee, ten feet from the edge of the hole, watching them, a grenade in his hand. Kingman turned to Camellion. "Not bad. And the kraut tosses one down the hole to distract them. You should have three to five seconds on the lag."

The Death Merchant pulled the two .44 Backpacker Auto Mags from their shoulder holsters. "That's all the time I need. Once I'm in, you and the others follow."

Kingman made a sad face. "We're going to have to take one of the higher ups alive, if we're going to get any information about the bomb. I guess you know that."

"I know. Get on with it."

Kingman moved to the corner of the housing and took a grenade from one of his shoulder bags, a grenade that did not resemble the conventional MK2 fragmentation grenade. It didn't because it was a MK4 Special Purpose Offensive Grenade. Within the red-colored canister were ten ounces of T.N.T. and thousands of steel slivers, each of which could pierce flesh with the force of needle propelled by a shotgun charge. Range: 30 meters, or 100 feet.

Kingman pulled the safety-pin ring from the grenade, his right hand clamped down tightly on the lever.

"You ready, Hopmeir?"

"Do it. Be sure to toss it far enough so that it goes beyond the steps."

"You don't have to tell me that," Kingman said crossly. "I'm not one of the Limeys. You'd better watch those tea-drinking dunkle-heads."

Using his left hand, he reached out, slowly turned the knob, pulled open the door and jerked it back, with just enough force to make it open all the way. He then turned to the side of the housing and tossed in the grenade.

1-2-3-4! The 5th second came and the grenade exploded, the pings of tiny slivers of steel lost within the volume of the detonation. There were several high-pitched screams, a prelude to Gertenshalger's pitching the secone grenade through the hole in the stone roof. Another brain-jarring BLLLAAAMMMMMM!

*"Glueck auf,"* said Kingman and stepped away from the housing.

"Thanks, but I don't need 'good luck,'" Camellion said. "It's all a matter of Fate." *Death has a precise appointment with everyone. Today is not my day . . .*

A cyclone of speed, Camellion tore around the corner, stormed through the doorway and started streaking down the steps. Halfway down, he spun to the left and got down

141

in a low crouch. From his position in the southwest corner, he could survey the entire floor, and he liked what he saw.

Through the still drifting smoke from the two grenades, he saw several bodies on the floor. They didn't move. Corpses never do—until rigor mortis starts to set in and causes the muscles to contract. The grenade that Gertenshalger had dropped had wasted the two Nazis. To the right of the two dead men, several more men were staggering around; like the two corpses on the floor, they too were dressed in slacks and summer-wear sports shirts. The latter two men had been partially shielded from the blast by a wall of ancient stones; yet the proximity of the blast had left them dazed and disoriented.

Three of the other Nazis—forty feet in front of the Death Merchant and slightly to his right—were very much aware of what was going on. Apparently submariners, since they were dressed in gray-green coveralls, they, too, had been behind a pile of stones and were untouched by the minuscule slivers of shrapnel. They had also been far enough away from the two grenades to escape the full force of the double concussion.

Seeing the Death Merchant, the three neo-Nazis swung into action. One attempted to level down on Camellion with an MP40/II, the German machine pistol commonly referred to, incorrectly, as a "Schmeisser." The two other Nazis tried to target Camellion with more modern Walther MP-L-SMGs. To the side and above Camellion, Kingman and Hahn started down the steps.

Camellion lifted the two Auto Mags and first wasted the two men closest to capturing him in their own sights. The AMPs roared. One .44 Jurras Magnum slug hit the man with the "Schmeisser" in the chest; the second .44 projectile popped the second man high in the stomach. The two could just as well have been in the center of an exploding barrel of black powder. They both died that quickly.

The third man squeezed the trigger of the Walther chatter box at the same time that Camellion jerked to the right and snapped off a round from the AMP in his left hand. A dozen flat-nosed 9mm projectiles zipped past him and struck the south wall, ten feet away. Three hit the north side girder supporting the steps and screamed off in howling ricochets. A third and a fourth bullet struck rivet heads on top of a step and, with shrieks, glanced off. One buried itself in the sole of Kingman's left boot. The other struck the barrel of Camellion's M-60 Mauser which was strapped across his back. The flattened-out slug, its power gone, glanced a few inches and fell through one of the holes in one of the flat sections of the steps.

The Death Merchant's .44 bullet slammed into the Nazi's left shoulder bone and sent him flying backward in two parts. He went one way. His left arm, trailing blood like a comet from hell, went another.

Hahn and Kingman raced past Camellion and started to swing around their Mausers to fire. They were too slow. The Death Merchant's AMPs roared two more times, and the two jokers, dressed in sport shirts and slacks, found out what it feels like to be dead.

Camellion got to his feet, glanced briefly at Lynch, Gertenshalger, and Woofs coming down the steps, and moved on down to the dust-covered floor. Frowning he motioned for the other men to keep back from the opening that led to the steps on the 5th floor of Bracadale Castle.

"Ach, ve need *aufgedonnert bombes*," Gertenshalger said, looking around the enormous 100 foot square room. At one time, in the long dead past, the floor had been partitioned into rooms. But the wood had long since rotted away, and much of the interior stone walls had been torn down, the stones used periodically to reinforce the foundation of the castle. What looked odd and totally out of place were the steel I-beams against the interior of the walls and stretched out across the ceiling, supporting the floor above.

"We didn't have time to fly flash bombs from London," Camellion answered Gertenshalger in German. "As it was, we were lucky that the Royal Navy base at Greenock had special offensive grenades."

For a moment he studied Kingman who had just taken another long slug of giggle-water and was capping the bottle. Noticing Camellion watching him, Kingman held out the pint bottle of blackberry brandy.

"Have a snort, Hopmeir. You can kill better when you're relaxed."

"No thanks. I'm still fighting yesterday's mistake with a bottle." The Death Merchant didn't smile. "Today isn't one of my better days."

Kingman carefully returned the bottle to the right breast pocket of his coveralls and, with a half-laugh muttered, "*When I am dead and nervous hands have thrust, My body*

143

*downward into careless dust; I think the grave cannot suf-
fice to hold, My spirit 'prisoned in the sunless mould."*

Camellion said in a chilling voice, *"And if you continue
to drink, From that bottle filled with booze, Your body to
the stones will sink, And from the bullet holes the blood
will ooze.* So—watch it!"

Woofs spoke up, his voice nervous and uncertain. "Do
we use the same methods to get to the fifth floor?"

"We don't have that kind of time and enough Pentolite,"
Camellion grunted and waved one of the Auto Mags to-
ward the opening in the southeast corner of the giant area.
"We'll toss down a couple of grenades and charge."

"Have you considered the risk?" asked Ronald Lynch.
He hadn't removed the cigarette in the left side of his
mouth, although it had gone out. "We don't know how
many Germans are down there on the next floor."

"We've come this far," Kingman interposed, his words
half-slurred. "There were seven on this floor, and it wasn't
any big deal getting here. Hell, MacLean doesn't have that
many men. There had to be enough of the crew to take
down those two U-boats.

"You might have something there," Lynch said. He
scratched his cheek, thick with three days growth of beard.

"He has a lot there," said Camellion, who had shoved
the AMPS into holsters and was unbuckling the Mauser
machine gun from his back. "Listen to all that firing from
below. Most of the Nazis who came ashore have to on the
ground floor fighting Major Simpson and his boys."

"Maybe so," Woofs said, "but it takes only one man to
kill us with a machine gun."

"It could happen," Camellion said acidly. "Let's get over
there."

He and the others hurried to the opening that contained
the steps to the 5th floor of the castle keep. In theory, the
top of the steps should be at the end of the opening closest
to Camellion & Co., since the rectangularly shaped slot was
in the southeast corner of the floor.

The Death Merchant edged closer and soon saw that he
was wrong. The top of the steps was on the east side of the
opening.

*Perfect. We can throw under the west and the north
ends of the floor and saturate the area.*

A few minutes later, everything was ready. The Mauser
music box in his hands, Camellion stood by the northeast

corner of the opening, Hahn and Gertenshalger lying flat at the north edge, Woofs and Lynch by the west edge, Kingman standing guard.

The Death Merchant switched off the safety of the Mauser and nodded.

As fast as they could pull the pins, the four men by the sides of the slot pitched in a grenade each, throwing them inward so that they would sail far to the west and the north sides of the 5th floor. One after another the grenades exploded, each explosion showering the area with thousands of lilliputian slivers of steel.

The echoes slowly died within the stones; yet Camellion didn't move. Slowly he counted . . . 16, 17, 18, 19 . . . He reached 20 and nodded again. This time, only Lynch and Gertenshalger tossed grenades down into the floor below.

*BBLLLAMMMMMM–BBBBLLAAAMMMMMMM!*

With the detonations still bouncing around in his brain, the Death Merchant charged through the opening down the steps. The men by the two sides of the opening jumped to their feet and, with Kingman, waited.

The Death Merchant was at the bottom of the steps when the three Nazis, behind a low wall that was almost to the northwest corner of the 5th floor, decided that it was safe enough to rear up and take a look around. It was the biggest mistake of Helmut Kalauer's 27 years! A short burst from Camellion's Mauser erased his face, exploding his brain and splatterd chunks of it and bone and blood all over Max Halmer and Joseph Brunner. Like Kalaeur, Halmer and Brunner had grown up in Argentina where their SS fathers had found refuge after the war. Now, Brunner and Halmer wished they were back in Bahía Grande.

Gagging from the blood and gore dribbling down their coveralls, They dropped down while Camellion dove for cover behind a length of square blocks that had once been the wall of a room. Now the wall was less than six feet high and only eight feet long, its top a mass of broken and cracked stones.

No sooner had he dived behind the wall than Halmer and Brunner leaned around each end of their wall and cut loose with Argentine Halcon submachine guns, several dozen .45 caliber projectiles chopping into the top and the edges of the wall between Camellion and eternity.

*They can't get to me and I can't get to them—and time's a' wastin'!*

From his not too secure position, Camellion could look up to his right and see Klaus Hahn looking down at him from the northeast corner of the opening at the top of the stairs. Hahn pointed to himself, then at the steps, indicating that he could come down and help him. The Death Merchant shook his head to the negative and pushed his right hand upward. He then took a half pound block of Pentolite from one of his bags, pointed to it, made a throwing motion and grinned. Hahn nodded and grinned back.

On his knees, Camellion shoved the Mauser machine gun around the right end of the wall and triggered off a burst to let the two Hitlerheads know he was alive and well. Halmer and Brunner replied with two more bursts; again .45 slugs threw up chips and dust.

*I have to give it weight!* He took out a grenade and, from his "emergency" pocket, a roll of copper wire. He twisted off a 4′ length of wire and wired the grenade and the half pound block of Pentolite together. The remote control box and the remote control detonator were next. He shoved the prongs of the detonator into the package of explosive, opened the lid of the box, picked up the makeshift bomb and hefted it in his hand—*a bit more than a pound*. He stood up and, in a crouch, stepped six feet back from the side of the wall.

Another dozen .45 slugs slammed into the other side of the wall.

*I'm going to give you Nazi halfwits a big surprise.* He threw the bomb with his right hand, sensing from its arc and momentum that it would land very close to the enemy's wall. He dropped to the side of his protective wall, picked up the remote control box, turned it on and pushed the button.

BBBEEERRRRROOOOOMMMMMMMMMMMMM!
The concussion from the giant blast was terrific, for a moment jarring even his very consciousness. As he picked up the Mauser submachine gun, he felt blood trickling from his nose onto his upper lip. Then, carefully, he looked around the left end of the wall.

His eyes glowed with pleasure at the sight—*on dit que Dieu est toujours pour les gros bataillons!* Voltaire was right about God being on the big battalions' side.

Nothing remained of the enemy wall, and in the vicinity where it had stood, there was only a large hole. Halmer lay at the north edge of the hole, a mess of battered and torn flesh within shredded clothing, the corpse covered with gray-white dust and stone debris.

Brunner lay a few feet from the east end of the cavity. His right arm and right leg were missing. The rest of the corpse was covered with a layer of dust that was slowly turning into a bloody paste. Smoke and dust were so thick, hanging in layers, that the grayness seemed solid. The bomb had exploded close to the wall and had tossed the two Nazis high in the air. Only by a stroke of Fate had they fallen to the floor instead of dropping through the hole.

The Death Merchant switched off the remote control device, closed its cover, and returned the instrument to its proper place in the bag. He picked up the Mauser, stood up, and called up the steps, "Come on down. Those Nazis were a day late and two bucks short and they paid for their mistake."

The Death Merchant and his men tossed several grenades through the hole in the floor, and two more down the steps, in the center of the room, onto the 4th floor level.

Down they charged, the Death Merchant in the lead, which prompted Woofs to mutter to Lynch, "I swear, that chap seems bent on suicide."

"You had better be wrong," Lynch said. "We're with him."

The 4th level was empty . . .

Camellion & Co. didn't count the rusty broad swords and other ancient weapons of combat hanging on the walls, nor the scattered pieces of broken furniture gray with age and filled with worm holes. Above the racket of gunfire—now louder since they were closer to the ground level—they could hear the wind moaning through the narrow window openings.

On this level the architecture was more elaborate than on the other two upper floors. There was corbeling where the ceiling met the walls—an overlapping of stones, each course projecting above the one below, faces carved in the stones. Here, too, the cressets—those round containers used to burn pitch for illumination—were of a better quality. On the 5th and the 6th floors, they had been stone bowls mounted to the walls. On the 4th floor they were of iron and fastened to the walls by means of iron braces. Other cressets stood secure in high iron stands.

Lynch, his hands on his hips, looked around the huge area, a fresh cigarette dangling from one side of his mouth. "The inhabitants of the castle were the better class of their day; yet their lives were very harsh compared to what we have today. No modern lighting, primitive plumbing. All those things we take for granted were beyond their imagination."

"Maybe so, but right now they're better off than we are," remarked Kingman. He stared at the opening to the steps, in the northeast corner of the room. "The dead don't have any troubles. They can't. They don't exist."

"I wouldn't be too sure about that," mused the Death Merchant. "You could be in for a surprise . . ."

The 3rd level was empty.

While the men watched the stair opening in the center of the 3rd floor level, the Death Merchant took a walkie-talkie from its case on his belt, contacted Major Simpson and asked about his progress.

"We're pinned down," Simpson reported, his voice coming in angry through the walkie-talkie. "My group can't move in from the east, and neither can the men from the south and the north. The enemy has heavy machine guns in the north and the south towers. Where are you?"

The Death Merchant hesitated, fighting a battle to control his temper.

"Are you there, Hopmeir?" Simpson asked.

*You idiot! Is the Pope Italian? Come to think of it, he's Polish.*

"Major, have you thought of using one of the KAMANS to knock out those towers? Each KAMAN carries four S-13 HE missiles. It would take only one to blow each tower. I strongly suggest you employ one of the choppers to do the job."

"I was about to give the order when you called," Simpson replied, annoyance in his husky voice. "Please give me your position."

"We're on the third level and about to storm the second. We are not going to attempt an invasion of the first floor until you're ready to storm in. There's too many of them on the first floor."

"Wouldn't it be possible for you and your laddies to use explosives and bring down the ceiling on them?"

*The man's an idiot!*

"Sure we could!" Camellion said with false innocence. "And in the process we might bring down the whole keep and bury ourselves!"

*And we'd never learn where the A-bomb is being assembled and how it's going to be smuggled into Egypt.*

"We'll wait until you explode the towers and make the charge," Camellion finished. "Out."

With an angry motion he switched off the walkie-talkie, pushed down the antenna and shoved the walkie-talkie into its leather case.

He detected the thought struggling in his mind, some kind of revelation simmering in the stew-pot of his subconscious. But he couldn't bring it to a boil. Disgusted, he went over to the men and gave them the report on Major Simpson's progress.

Lynch and Woofs and the two Germans didn't comment. Being British, Lynch and Woofs didn't want to speak disparagingly about a fellow countryman. Being foreigners, Hahn and Gertenshalger felt it would be improper for them to do so.

The blunt spoken Kingman was not bound by any kind of protocol.

"Well, that's cut the cat's tail," he sneered. "I doubt if that damn fool Simpson could successfully attack a doll house. But he's there and we're here." He looked squarely at the Death Merchant. "By ourselves, we'd have as much chance on the first floor as worm-eaten apples hanging in a high-wind. I don't see any sense in going to the second floor. Why don't we wait right here?"

Camellion thought for a moment. "I want all the floors above the ground level cleared. Let's go do it."

Four grenades were used against the second floor; then Camellion and his men rushed down the steps. Too late they realized that they had thrown the grenades in the wrong direction. Instead of lying prone on the floor and tossing the grenades to all points of the compass, they should have tossed all four to the southwest.

It was toward the southwest that the Nazis had together put a three-sided wall of stones and had roofed it over with sheets of corrugated iron. The wall was five feet high, with only a five inch space between the top of the stones and the roof of iron. None of the steel slivers of shrapnel had reached the Nazis, the arrangement of stones and iron protecting them. To make matters worse for the Death Merchant, the wall was only twenty feet from the bottom of the steps, to the right. Twenty feet due south of the wall was the stair opening to the first floor.

It was Camellion's ultra-fast thinking that saved him and his men from instant annihilation. The concussion had dazed the eight Nazis, but not to the extent that they were disoriented and couldn't fight. To the contrary: They were in full possession of their faculties. An instant before they could poke their sub-guns through the five inch gun port, the Death Merchant raked the entire horizontal opening with a long burst of Mauser slugs and yelled, "GET IN BEHIND THEM OR WE'RE DEAD!"

Desperation increasing their speed, the men sprinted to the left and the right, Camellion again raking the opening with a burst of 9mm projectiles, all of which missed the Nazis who, guessing the intention of the attackers, turned to meet the attack from each flank. The Death Merchant darted to the left, dropped the Mauser, and pulled both Auto Mags on the run.

So quickly did both sides react to the situation that within ten seconds the Germans were face-to-face with Camellion and his men, every man ducking and dodging in an attempt to get in a burst and yet not get hit by enemy slugs. All except Keven Woofs and Oscar Leidke.

The SIS agent and the Nazi miscalculated simultaneously. Each should have ducked and tried to maneuver. They didn't. Both fired, Leidke triggering a U.S. M3 submachine gun, Woofs using the Mauser M-60. Half a dozen 9mm Parabellum slugs cut into Leidke's midriff, as ten .45 caliber projectiles blew out Woofs stomach, leaving a hole big enough to stuff in a football!

Just as dead as Woofs, Leidke also collapsed, a large part of his bloody insides showing.

Kingman tried to swing the barrel of his Mauser to Alfred Schultz. He tried but failed because Franz Kitner, too close to Kingman to use the long barrelled StG assault rifle, reached out with his right hand, grabbed the barrel of Kingman's Mauser and pushed it upward.

"Kill him! Kill him!" Kitner snarled in German at Schultz as Fritz Stangl, almost nose to nose and toe to toe with Klaus Hahn made a desperate attempt to poke the muzzle of his Bergmann machine gun underneath Hahn's chin.

Coinciding with this action by the desperate Germans, Karl Orlendorf and Adolf Hundhammer, only five feet from Rudolf Gertenshalger, tried to get the big BND agent in a crossfire. Left of the three men, Frederich Schwiend raised his Czech 58-P assault rifle at Ronald Lynch and a terrified Herbert Lubke made an effort to poke holes in the Death Merchant with .223 caliber slugs from his Beretta M-70 assault rifle.

Camellion could have terminated Lubke with one quick shot. He couldn't because the powerful .44 Magnum slug would have gone all the way through Lubke and then have struck Gertenshalger in the right side. Camellion did the only thing he could do, hoping to all the gods in the universe that he could do it in time. He did. He threw himself to the north a micro-second before the Beretta roared and vomited out a deadly stream of sharp-nosed .223 projectiles that hit the west wall.

During those few seconds, the Death Merchant had moved eight feet, to a position that gave him a clear shot at Lubke. The Nazi was making the swing to the right when the AMP in Camellion's hand roared and the big bullet smacked Lubke in the right side of the chest. The Nazi let out short, cut-off "OHHHHHH!" dropped the Beretta and started to die.

Camellion moved in like an extra fast whirlwind on Orlendorf and Hundhammer, neither of whom was making any progress against Gertenshalger. The big BND agent, knowing he had time to kill only one of the men—then the other Nazi would waste him—had done the unexpected. He had jumped forward, dropped the Mauser machine gun, reached out with both hands and grabbed the barrel of Hundhammer's Swedish 9mm chatter-box and the barrel of Orlendorf's Heckler and Koch 33Ka-1 assault rifle. In a rage, and having the leverage, he had then pushed the weapons away from his body.

Now he went to work with lightning speed. He delivered a tip-of-the-toe kick that landed on the target: right between Orlendorf's legs. The young Nazi gurgled a scream that died in his throat from shock. Helpless, he let go of the H & K assault rifle and began to double over.

Hundhammer didn't have time to do anything. Now that

151

Gertenshalger's right hand was free, he used it to crack Hundhammer across the bridge of the nose with a sword-ridge hand strike. Almost in the same instant, the Death Merchant brought the barrel of an AMP down on the back of Hundhammer's head. The Nazi fell with the speed of an anvil dropped into the swimming pool.

Fredrich Schwiend was the next Nazi to lose all his luck. Lynch, using his Mauser sub-gun, first knocked Schwiend's Czech A-R to one side. But instead of trying to swing the barrel around to blow the Nazi away, he now used the rear end of the Mauser to smash in Schwiend's face. Teeth and blood flew. There was a crunch as the nose bone broke. Staggered and in agony, Schwiend wilted and his hands relaxed on the A-R. Lynch knocked the weapon from his feeble hands by breaking his left wrist with the underside of the Mauser's barrel. Another instant and Lynch shoved the muzzle of the Mauser against the agonized man's stomach and barely touched the trigger. There was a short snarling sound and Schwiend's eyes opened as wide as possible. Then they closed forever, and he sagged to the floor, only six feet from where Klaus Hahn had managed to push aside Fritz Stangl's Bergmann machine pistol and was on the verge of killing the desperate Nazi by slowly pushing the muzzle of the Mauser in Stangl's direction. It was a simple battle of strength and Stangl was losing.

A short distance away, the half-drunk Kingman wasn't about to let two Nazis terminate his life. Alfred Schultz did his best to line up his 9mm Steyr SMG on Kingman, who instantly wrecked the German's ambition by employing a powerful left-legged Pentjak-silat Bukiti kick that knocked the Steyr from the astonished Schultz's hands and sent the machine gun flying upward. As the Steyr struck the ceiling, there was a deafening roar to the right and the diddle-diddle-diddle sound of a Mauser SMG that was half-silenced, muffled.

The Death Merchant's .44 AMP bullet hit Schultz low in the left side of the neck and slammed him to the right. His head wobbling, he fell with blood spurting from the enormous wound.

Fritz Stangl fell also. Hahn's blast of 9mm projectiles had gone into his stomach at an upward angle and had torn out the inside of his torso, five of the projectiles coming out through his back, just below the neck.

Kingman, turning his full attention to Franz Kitner,

snarled, "You want the Mauser, you Nazi son of a bitch! Take it!"

He let go of the Mauser to have both hands free. With the same speed, his hands shot to the wrists of the surprised Kitner, who was now holding the StG A-R in his left hand and the Mauser, by its barrel, in his right. The Nazi felt stupid, but only for a second. That's all the time it took for Kingman to stab him in the throat with a spear-hand and crush the upper portion of his windpipe; and during that second, when Kingman had released his right hand from the German's left wrist, Kitner had not even seen the karate thrust coming at him. The Nazi dropped both weapons and started to sag on melting legs, hideous gagging sounds pouring from his throat, that certain special expression on his face, one that can be worn only by the doomed and the damned.

The Death Merchant and his four men were surveying their work and looking regretfully at the riddled corpse of Kevin Woofs when the explosion came, a terrific *BLAMMMMMMMMMM*. Chunks of ripped and twisted steel shot up through the stair opening to the first floor. The metal struck the ceiling, then fell back, some of it onto the floor, most of it dropping back through the opening.

The Nazis had blown up the stairs to the first floor level.

Breathing heavily, Kingman's voice was a half-croak. "We sure as hell can't jump! And I can't fly!" He stooped and picked up the Mauser.

"This is a disaster," Lynch said fearfully. "When Major——"

He stopped at the sound of an even greater explosion, this one from outside the castle. With the others, he glanced to the northeast.

One of the KAMAN Huskies had destroyed one of the towers with an S-13 HE missile.

"Pick up your weapons," Camellion said harshly, a hint of urgency in his voice.

"The roof?" Lynch frowned.

Kingman stared at Camellion in disbelief. 'Why the roof?"

"I'll tell you when we get there."

# Chapter Thirteen

In many fanatics, hatred is often stronger than fear, a violent, all-consuming hostility more potent than even the will for self preservation. It was this type of self-destructive emotion that controlled Sir Hugh MacLean, John-Percy MacLean, and ex-SS General Karl Gustav Lindermanns. It was different with Edward MacLean. All he wanted to do was live. Yet he didn't entertain any false hopes. There would be no miracles. There was no future, and the present was becoming more and more limited.

Sir Hugh MacLean's eyes blazed with hellish fury. The damned gold was the cause of it all. The two cargo submarines had arrived an hour and a half ahead of schedule. They had sunk the two patrol boats without any difficulty and had machine gunned those of the British crews who had survived the torpedoes. But the gold bars, all nine tons, had to be loaded first. Not even a third of the gold had been loaded on one of the submarines when the British had arrived. Yes, it was the gold's fault—and what good was gold if one wasn't alive to spend it?

Sir MacLean thought of all the money he had spent on remodeling the first floor level of the castle. There were bedrooms, a kitchen, a dining area and a small great hall. Now—all useless . . . about to be destroyed.

Sitting at the head of the large walnut table, Sir Hugh looked around his pride and joy. The haze, from weapons that had been fired, was so thick that the shafts of sunlight, slanting inward from the high, narrow embrasures, seemed to be solid.

Two hundred and thirty-one Germans—all new generation men of the Brotherhood of the 4th Reich—had come ashore from the two U-boats. The majority of them were outside the keep, some were on the castle walls, some in the towers that faced the east, the others spread out along the battlements.

154

Twenty-seven Germans had been below, loading the gold, when the helicopter had landed on the roof. Another fourteen had been in the castle, a few already on the floors above. Other Nazis had raced upstairs, and the Nazis in the dungeons had come to the surface to protect the great hall. At least for the time being, the enemy could not reach the first floor. Lindermanns had made sure by having men blow up the steps, the evidence of the blast very evident. Concussion from the explosion that had demolished the first floor steps had shaken huge paintings from the walls and no one had bothered to replace them.

Sir Hugh's fierce eyes went to Lindermanns, who sat to his right. The German was smoking a cigarette and listening to the firing from the walls and from outside of the battlements.

"I refuse to concede that the situation is hopeless," MacLean said with a grimace. "Surely there must be some way we can get aboard one of those submarines. There has to be!"

"There isn't," Lindermanns said grimly. "The submarines are not equipped with modern weapons. By now the British have sent a destroyer that will have anti-submarine missiles. In case of trouble, the captains are to submerge and retreat. They did just that. The submarines are gone. They will never return."

John-Percy MacLean, sitting to Lindermanns' left, sucked in his breath. "We can't sit and do nothing but wait!" he almost shouted. "I don't intend to spend the rest of my life in prison. I refuse to do so!"

"You have a pistol," Lindermanns intoned. "At the proper time, use it. As a member of the Brotherhood, you should realize that we Nazis control our own destinies."

John-Percy, his eyes wild-looking, clamped his mouth shut. Helplessly, he had to admit he was trapped, the hopelessness of the situation numbing his thoughts. The thought of imprisonment was a horror. But killing himself was the ultimate of all terror.

Gilbert Drummond, who was across the table from John-Percy and Lindermanns, joined forces with John-Percy. "We could make a dash for the plane," he suggested. "But I suppose the British have found the plane by now."

General Lindermanns smiled, then drained the glass of port. "We'd be cut to pieces before we got five feet from

155

the walls," he said, putting down the glass. He tapped ashes from his cigarette onto the rug, a portion of the Old Days sliding up from the storehouse of memory. He thought of the potholed road that had climbed between large slabs of rock to huge bronze doors. Behind the doors was a long tunnel struck into the flank of the mountain. At the end of the tunnel, guarded by the elite of the SS *Leibstandarte Adolf Hitler*, was the copper-plated elevator that lifted upward, through several hundred feet of solid rock, to the Eagle's Nest, the impressive retreat of Adolf Hitler. The top of the vertical shaft opened into a great gallery of Roman columns, part of a circular hall with windows all around, giving one the sense of floating in the golden glow of an alpine twilight. Ya, those had been happy days.

In contrast, the very last days of the war flashed vividly in Lindermanns' mind. The Fuhrer Bunker, a miserable concrete warren fifty feet below the bombed, burned-out Chancellery, had not been a happy place.

*Donnerwetter!* From ruling all of Europe, the Nazis had been reduced to a damned hole in the ground! Even so, thought Lindermanns bitterly, he and Bormann had escaped—all the way to South America.

Ya, the *Reichsleiter* was slowly dying of cancer of the stomach. But others were alive and well. SS General Richard Glucks, who in happier times had been responsible for the concentration camps and the property taken from the Jews gassed in them, was living in style on a ranch on Lake Ranco, in Chile. There was Heinrich Muller, who had been head of the Gestapo. He and his Italian wife were operating a hardware store in a suburb of Natal in northeastern Brazil. Hundreds, even thousands of SS men, were well submerged, many of them *die grossen Bonzen* ("the big bosses") from Hitler's Third Reich.

Yet every single one of them was a faithful member of the Brotherhood . . .

Lindermanns glanced in amusement at Edward MacLean, who was sitting in an easy chair, not far from the table, leaning over and holding his head in his hands. The *dumkopf!* Almost as stupid as his father . . .

Behind Edward MacLean, close to the wall, sat the others who had flown from Dunbeath Hall to Bracadale Castle—Bernard McHale, the MacLean butler, a trembling old fool who worshiped the MacLean clan; and Cecil Jimwickie, the pilot, and Colin Seldom, the copilot, of the airplane. All three had a trapped, frantic look about them. Lindermanns couldn't blame them. The castle did have the air of a mortuary between funerals.

The tremendous explosion to the southeast made every man in the room give a start, including Lindermanns. Half a dozen Nazis, weapons in their hands, ran into the room.

"*Herr Obergruppenfuhrer* Lindermanns," one of them began "Der——"

"Ya, I know, Rolf," Lindermanns cut the man off angrily and stood up. "The swine have blown up the southeast tower."

Sir MacLean pushed back his chair and got to his feet. "Next they'll use a shell against the walls and storm the keep," he said aggressively.

The other non-Germans stood up and stared imploringly at Lindermanns, who picked up a Walther submachine gun from the table. Whenever there is hatred among people, there is always a bond of brotherhood of some kind, and instinct told each person that safety, if only for an hour, lay with Lindermanns. He had, after all, been a general.

Lindermanns looked for a moment at Rolf Koutinger, the Nazi in command of the second generation Germans from South America.

"Bring all the men in the castle to the radiation shelter below," he said. "We'll make our last stand there."

He turned and started across the big room, a twisted expression on his face, a mask of remembrance. It had been like this at the end, years and years ago—retreat to a hole in the ground while the last battle was fought.

Today, however, would be far different.

There would be no *Ausbruchsversuch*—no breakout attempt.

The radiation shelter would become their tomb . . .

# Chapter Fourteen

The explosion that had demolished the first floor steps had also jarred the Death Merchant's subconscious. The stew-pot of logic overflowed. A lot of pieces of the puzzle were suddenly in place. Now he knew—at least he suspected—why they hadn't seen any of the enemy between the cliffs and the castle when the Lynx had flown over the area. The British force hadn't caught any of the Nazis in the open because the Germans had never been in the open, with the exception of the Germans who had retreated into the cave.

*The Nazis are using a tunnel, one that connects the castle to the Cave of Charles the Bold.*

His feet pounding on the stones and the steps as he raced to the roof with the other men, Camellion recalled the maps and the diagrams he had seen at the Royal Navy base in Greenock. Bracadale Castle was several thousand feet *east* of the cliffs, but only 1,000 feet *north* of the Cave of Charles the Bold, that is, from the mouth of the cave. The direction of the cave itself was 100 feet to the *east,* after which it turned and moved *north* for another 800 feet.

*Give or take a couple of dozen yards, there should be only 200 feet of rock between the end of the cave and the foundation rock on which the castle sits.*

In this day of modern technology, it would be a matter of simple engineering to use explosives to blast through the rock and explode a 200 foot-long tunnel to connect the rear of the cave with the dungeons in the castle—*Maybe! We'll soon find out.*

Camellion and his men were moving up the steps to the fifth floor when they heard the second S-13 HE missile blow up the tower to the southeast.

"Simpson's finally showing some sense," panted King-

158

man. He lagged behind slightly because of the pain in his left foot.

They reached the 5th floor, glanced briefly at the seven dead Nazis, rushed to the steps and hurried upward. A minute later they were coming out of the bullet-riddled housing on the roof, sniffing the fresh air.

"Suppose you tell us what we're doing here on the roof?" Kingman asked, giving the Death Merchant the eye. He immediately sat down on the roof, pulled a Quicksilver knife from a sheath on his belt and began to probe for the 9mm slug that had buried itself in the thick leather sole of his left boot and for the last twenty minutes had made him feel that he was walking on a marble, a broken marble with rough edges.

The Death Merchant, taking the walkie-talkie from its case, explained that they were going to use the Lynx to ferry them to the beach. He told them why: because he was almost certain that a tunnel connected the back of the cave with the castle.

"And if the tunnel doesn't exist?" said Lynch, wiping sweat from his dirty face. "We could be wasting our time."

Camellion gave the British SIS officer a long reproachful look and extended the telescoping antenna of the walkie-talkie. "In that case we'll have made the trip for nothing, and we can go swimming in the sea, or practice hearing the light of the stars and smelling the fragrance of the sunlight."

"Or count the drops of water in a wave!" snickered Kingman.

"Herr Lynch, we won't be wasting our time down there anymore than we are here, on the roof," Klaus Hahn said evenly. He proceeded to shove a full double-box magazine into the feed opening of the Mauser and say to Camellion who was about to turn on the walkie-talkie.

"Herr Hopmeir, have you considered the time required to haul heavy machine guns to the top of the towers? In my opinion the *Unterseeboots* had been there for sometime."

Camellion nodded. "I've been thinking along the same lines. Speed would be essential. The only reason for any delay that I can think of is that they were engaged in something important, something that was time-consuming, perhaps loading something valuable aboard."

"We might find evidence of what it was in the cave," Hahn said.

"Only if I'm right about the tunnel," Camellion said. He switched on the walkie-talkie and held the set close to his mouth.

"Lieutenant Champion."

"Champion here, sir."

"Bring the Lynx back to the roof. You can put her all the way down; the roof is firm enough."

"Sir, should I ask Major Simpson for permission?"

"Do it, and do it *NOW!*"

"We're on our way, sir."

No sooner had the copter lifted off than Major Simpson contacted the Death Merchant on the walkie-talkie, his voice shaking with anger.

"See here, Hopmeir. I did not authorize that craft to lift off. I demand an explanation."

Camellion smiled at the man's supercilious attitude. "I see that you've destroyed the towers holding up your advance. I presume you're about to move in—hopefully before the third Thursday of next month?"

"Yes, quite. As soon as several KAMANS blow up sections of the east wall. Now be a good fellow and tell me why you ordered the Lynx helicopter to the roof?"

"Major—go to hell."

Kingman who had just cut the 9mm slug from the sole of his boot, laughed. "That's telling him proper, 'old chap!'"

"I believe in humility," Camellion said with a straight face.

With the others he watched the Westland/Aerospatiale Lynx coming in at 500 feet from the northwest, its rotor making thap, thap, thap sounds.

The men were ready to board by the time Lieutenant Champion set the Lynx down gently on the center of the roof.

Ten minutes later, the Lynx was hovering 700 feet over the beach, and Lieutenant Champion was protesting to Camellion, telling him it was impossible to sit down closer to the cave.

"We're about 500 feet south of the cave," Champion said, "and the only place is right below us. I'm not about to put down on the beach in front of the cave. Those lads inside could blow us right out of the air. You know that."

"And there isn't anything else but waves crashing over the rocks," added Charles Orbis, the copilot.

The Death Merchant, standing in back of the cockpit, studied the terrain below through binoculars. At length he found what he was looking for. He lowered the binoculars and tapped both Champion and Orbis on the shoulders.

"See that little clearing about 250 feet south of the cave and several hundred feet back from the surf? You can put down there. The larger rocks will shield us while we're jumping to the ground, in case the Nazis are waiting in the cave."

Champion and Orbis took a long look before Champion finally said, "Yes, we can set down there. You and your people get out fast. I'll want to lift off as quickly as possible." He turned and looked at Camellion. "Sir, when we get back to base, we'd appreciate your keeping Major Simpson off our backs. He's a stickler for the book, that one."

"You have my word," Camellion said, "and we'll get out fast once you put down. Get us over there."

Champion worked the controls, and the Lynx was soon revving down over the area the Death Merchant had indicated, down until the bottom of the skids were only a foot from the sand and rocks and Camellion and his men were jumping out. Champion lifted up and away, the two Rolls-Royce turbines screaming with increased power.

The pounding of the surf, a short distance to the west, was very loud, the force of the water was such that, at times, Camellion and the others could feel a few drops of fine spray hitting their faces.

They left the tiny clearing, headed north and began to pick their way through the cemetery of rocks, of boulders and granite monoliths eroded by wind and water, kissed by time and age. As Camellion and Co. neared the cave the route curved northeast and the wilderness of rock became a natural garden of exquisite beauty, the stones mingling with moss cushions, lichen beds, and blueberry edgings heavily laden.

Finally, they were fifty feet south of the cave, at a slanting angle that placed them thirty feet in front of the mouth.

Protected by man-tall rocks, the Death Merchant and the four men studied the mouth of the Cave of Charles the Bold.

161

"They could be playing opossum in there," Kingman warned.

"I doubt if they're even in there," Camellion said, "unless I'm wrong and there isn't a tunnel."

"What's the difference," Lynch said drily. "The Nazis on the walls saw the helo putting down. They've guessed what we're doing. If a tunnel exists, MacLean and his bloody swine will be expecting us to use it."

"Good thinking," Camellion said. "Here's how we'll do it."

While Lynch and Kingman covered the north edge of the cave's mouth and Hahn and Gertenshalger watched the south side, Camellion crept toward the south side of the entrance, darting from rock to rock whenever possible, then moving flush against the wall of the cliff itself. The mouth of the cave was between twenty-five and thirty feet wide, the height, at the tallest point, not more than 10 feet.

In another ten minutes, Camellion was at the south edge of the mouth, an AMP in each hand. He didn't dare stick his head around the ragged stone edge and take a look. There was too much of a chance that it could have been the last look of his life.

From where he stood, however, he could see past the north edge for a distance of fifteen to twenty feet; then the twilight became darkness. He turned and looked to the northeast. Three men were there, on either side of the monolith, covering him.

He holstered the Auto Mags, took out an offensive grenade, pulled the pin, tossed it around the south edge, pulled one of the Auto Mags, and stepped back.

The grenade exploded hollowly, the echo of the blast rolling back into the bowels of the cave. There were no screams. The Death Merchant pulled the other Auto Mag and waited a few more minutes. The final echo died. He holstered the AMPs and tossed in a second offensive grenade. There was another muffled explosion followed by sepulchral-like reverberations. That was all. No howls of pain. No one fired. Camellion waved the men forward, and watched and waited until they were standing beside him against the face of the towering cliff.

"The cave goes back a hundred feet to the east. Then it turns to the north," Camellion said. 'We have to go along the north side wall, or we'll be exposed when we make the turn. We'll—" He stopped and drew back in slight surprise when Kingman left the group, raced across the entrance and took a position by the north wall, ten feet inside the mouth.

"That's one way to find out," Lynch said in a clipped voice.

"The only way," Camellion said.

Kingman being first in line, they moved single file along the north wall of the cave. With each step the light filtering in from the outside grew dimmer, changing first to deep twilight, then to total darkness; yet once their eyes were adjusted to the blackness, it became evident that there was a very obscure glow in the distance, one that could not be a natural illumination.

They moved slowly, feeling their way in the darkness along the wall wet with moisture. The walls of the cave were almost smooth, and as far as Camellion and his men could detect, there weren't any stalactites nor stalagmites.

Reaching the end of the hundred foot section, they saw that the blush of light was cast by lights far to the north of the cavern. Lights indicated a tunnel, at least some kind of complex.

It had to be done. Kingman stuck his head around the edge, stared toward the north, then pulled back and said, "It's a light, far ahead. It's so far back it must be at the end of the north end. There's a wall in back of the light and carts of some kind in front of the wall. And there isn't any kind of protection for us either."

"Let me have a look," Camellion said impatiently.

Kingman stepped to the right and the Death Merchant stepped forward and stared around the edge for a full minute.

"The light is at the end of the natural cave," he said, drawing back. "I'm not sure, but I think the wall is the beginning of the tunnel. I believe I saw a door."

"Mein Herr, you are talking about a distance of eight hundred feet," Hahn pointed out in a low voice that carried a warning.

The Death Merchant considered all the possibilities. "We'll run for it," he said, "with our sub-guns ready. I'll go first." He turned and looked at Hahn, and the German felt grim determination in the calm insistence in his voice. *Ya*, thought Hahn. Camellion was *eine saubere, gediegene Per-*

*sönlichkeit"*—a clean-cut, splendid individual. He was always ready to take the first risk.

"Bullshit!" snapped Kingman. "We're not Boy Scouts. We'll do it together or not at all. Whether we die now, or next week, or twenty years from now—what's the difference?"

*"Ya, zusammen,"* (together) agreed Gertenshalger.

"Let's do it and get it over with," Lynch said tersely.

They did it. They rounded the corner and sprinted toward the light in the distance, desperation a trigger for extra adrenalin, for extra speed. Time stretched out into a double eternity, but finally they reached the two carts that were twenty feet in front of the metal wall, lungs gasping, hearts pounding. The light bulb was screwed into a socket mounted to a conduit, the rounded pipe mounted to the ceiling and running through the wall.

The two dollies, four wheels on each one, were loaded with gold bars.

"There must be millions here!" gasped Kingman, staring at the neatly stacked gold. "They didn't have time to move the gold, so they left it sitting here."

"Keep your eyes on the door in the wall." Camellion's voice was drawn and heavy. "We're in one hell of a dangerous position."

He went to the steel wall and inspected the seven-foot-wide, six-foot-high door, the edges of which fit so snugly into the wall that he couldn't have inserted a piece of paper into the hairline crack. He looked up at the top of the cave—solid rock. If the explosive was too powerful it could bring down rock and clog the entrance.

He glanced around to make sure the others were covering the door with their weapons. He then took a Jakal from his belt, a half pound block of Pentolite from his bag, and a roll of surgical tape from his emergency pocket. He used the Jakal to cut the block in half and a length of the surgical tape to fasten the Pentolite to the left-side crack, halfway up the door. He returned the Jakal and the other one-fourth block of Pentolite to their proper places, fastened a detonator to the explosive taped to the door, and hurried back to the men.

"Let's move these dollies another thirty feet from the door," he said, his voice hard. "Turn the carts and the gold sideways. We'll use them for protection against the blast."

Kingman said, "Did you guys notice the lever on the

164

right side of the push bar? It controls the brakes for all four wheels. I never heard of such a thing."

"Push," Lynch grunted. He and Kingman pushed one dolly and Hahn and Gertenshalger the other, a task that required a great deal of strength, since the gold bars were dead weight and the wheels, although rubber-tired, did not roll easily over the uneven rock floor.

"Now we know why the subs were hanging around," Camellion said, watching the door with the two AMPs in his hands. "They were waiting for this gold."

Presently the two dollies were end-to-end, placed horizontally across the cave. Camellion got down behind the gold with the rest of the men, took out the remote control box, flipped the ON switch and pressed the firing button.

The explosion made Camellion and the other four feel that they were locked in a metal drum while a dozen midgets pounded on the sides and each end with sledge hammers. Coming at the end of the detonation was a loud crashing sound, made by the metal door that blew inward, tumbled ten feet through the air and slammed down on the rock floor with a loud ringing sound.

The fumes and smoke gradually cleared and the Death Merchant, looking around one end of the dolly, had to use a reinforced stare to see what had taken place. The blast had blown out the single light in front of the wall, and the only illumination was from the end of what appeared to be a man-made tunnel, one that was several hundred feet long and slanted sharply upward. The Death Merchant and his men rushed to the wall, one end of which, blown from its supports on the right side, was leaning inward.

"Well, Kingman, now you know why the trucks had brakes," Lynch said, staring at the incline with fearful eyes. His face had a queasy look.

"Ve are not seeing der end of the tunnel," Gertenshalger said in his heavy accent. "It makes a turn at der end."

For a change, Kingman was not impatient. "We don't know how many Nazis are waiting around that bend."

"Why worry?" laughed the Death Merchant. "We're an army of five!" In a serious tone, then. "I don't think that any of the enemy are down here. MacLean and Lindermanns don't have that many men to spare, and the end of the tunnel is no doubt sealed off and well guarded. Let's go see."

They entered the tunnel and in short order came to the

turn. The others strung out behind him, Camellion looked around the corner and saw a short thirty-foot tunnel that, on an angle upward, opened to a larger area which was brilliantly lighted. He motioned the men forward.

When they came to the end of the short tunnel, Camellion stuck out his head and surveyed the larger area. Hollowed out of solid bedrock—granite—the section was a forty-foot square with a nine-foot ceiling. Across the room, in the north wall, was another metal door. Beyond that door had to be the "basement" section of Bracadale Castle.

"I feel stupid," Lynch said flatly. "In another half hour we could all be dead. I guess you never feel it when it happens all at once."

"The wind blows, the sea flows, God knows," Camellion said in amusement. "Wait here."

It didn't take him five minutes to make the necessary preparations, to fasten the other one-fourth-pound of Pentolite to the door and attach the remote control detonator. Back at the end of the thirty-foot tunnel, he took out the R-C box, his eyes going from face to face.

"Make certain your weapons—sidearms, too—are fully loaded. "I'm going——"

"Of course they're loaded!" Kingman asserted righteously. "We know what to do. The door blows and we charge through."

"Like hell we do!" Camellion snarled, the raw violence in his voice making even the tough-skinned Hahn stare strangely at him. "Use your head, Kingman. The door is in the center of a forty-foot long wall. For all we know, it might open to another tunnel. We'll charge to the side of the door and lob in grenades. Only then will we storm the entrance. You got it?"

Kingman and the others nodded.

The Death Merchant's finger pushed the button.

*BBBEEERRRROOOOOMMMMMMM!*

The explosion stabbed in their ears and rattled their brains, the rolling echo not even off to a good start when Camellion and his force of four tore from the end of the tunnel and rushed to the sides of the opening still filled with acrid blue fumes and a gray cloud of smoke.

The Death Merchant, on the right side of the opening where the door had been, tossed the first offensive grenade.

*BBBLLAAAMMMMMMM!* Screams and shouts! Camellion felt as though it were Christmas. There wasn't any doubt in his mind. *We've reached the dungeon section of Bracadale Castle.*

Klaus Hahn tossed the second grenade through the opening.

Another *BBLLLAMMMMMMMMMMMM*. More howls and shouts.

An Auto Mag in each hand, the Death Merchant charged through the splintered doorway.

# Chapter Fifteen

Neither the flying door nor the two offensive grenades had harmed Sir Hugh MacLean and the five persons who had flown with him from Dunbeath Hall to Bracadale Castle. He and they and a group of South American Germans were in the bomb shelter that had been built into the north end of the dungeon space beneath the castle. The door to the chamber was securely locked.

Amazingly, the iron door had not struck any of the Nazis in front of the shelter, those who were in the larger portion, the section that had once been a torture chamber; and because five more dollies of gold were near the door and had absorbed much of the steel slivers of shrapnel, the two grenades had killed only four and wounded three. Concussion had stunned the rest of the Nazis.

It was during this brief lag period that the Death Merchant and his four men stormed into the chamber and found themselves face to face with dozens of Nazis whose expressions showed that they were both terrified but furious, afraid but still filled with a maniacal hatred that made them desperate.

*It's a crap-shoot!* During those few compacted moments, the Death Merchant perceived an enormous vaulted chamber, the arches decorated with trefoils, quatrefoils, and crenelated molding. He could hear gunfire from above the chamber, and assumed that Major Simpson and his commandoes had broken through the defenses of the east wall and were storming the first floor of the castle keep. To his right, sixty feet to the south, was the flight of wide wooden steps, and double doors above the steps, the doors secured by a long, thick iron bar. Major Simpson would have to blow those doors to get into the torture chamber.

There wasn't anymore time. The Death Merchant had found the last refuge of the Brotherhood of the 4th Reich, and now it was kill or be killed, win or lose, live or die.

Camellion raced to the left. The four others rushed in behind him, their Mausers roaring in unison with his two Backpacker Auto Mags. The first .44 Magnum bullet hit a German in the stomach, doubled him over and kicked him back into several others who had been trying to line up Lynch with Walther MP-K machine pistols. The second flat-nosed .44 smashed into Willy Krause who was doing his best to rake Camellion and the rest of the group with a Belgian 9mm Vigneron M2 SMG. A big hole in his chest and in his back, Krause uttered a long *"Ahhhhhh,"* dropped the SMG, crashed backward against a stone pillar and slid slowly to the floor.

The two Nazis who had been trying to scratch Lynch were trying to struggle to their feet when Rudolf Gertenshalger stitched them with a long burst, his 9mm × 19 Parabellum slugs slicing off small pieces of clothing and chunks of flesh as they stabbed into the doomed men.

Other Brotherhood crackpots opened fire, but they had hesitated a bit too long after the second offensive grenade had exploded. The Death Merchant and his force were safe behind ancient columns that supported the arches of the numerous bays. The staccato roaring of automatic weapons became deafening, the thudding of high powered slugs hitting stone, a steady tattoo.

A dozen 7.65mm projectiles, fired from a Vz61 Skorpion machine pistol struck the edge of a pillar protecting Hahn, throwing dust and chips into his face. Two more Nazis opened fire from the right with Spanish Largo SMGs and two dozen more projectiles hit the other side of the column, three of the projectiles tearing through the cloth of his right arm. Kingman and Gertenshalger caught all three Nazis in a devastating crossfire and made them dance and jump with streams of Mauser slugs. The corpses fell to the floor, little more than bloody bundles of ripped apart flesh.

Nonetheless, Camellion & Company were right on the brink of eternity. The Death Merchant killed two more Brotherhood gunmen with his AMPs, then had to jerk back behind a column and stand sideways to avoid dozens of projectiles thudding into each side of the stones.

Kingman riddled three more of the Brotherhood with a sweeping burst of submachine gunfire. His Mauser empty, he jumped behind a column, pulled the two Coonan .357 Magnum pistols and waited, enemy bullets sizzling by him on both sides.

Lynch, Hahn, and Gertenshalger were facing the same kind of deadly danger; so was the Death Merchant, all pinned down by the savage firing from a dozen Nazis, who continued to trigger their weapons as they charged. Several minutes after Camellion and his men had stormed into the chamber, they found themselves swimming in a sea of new age Nazis.

A slight lag time. Camellion ducked and moved to the left. From the corner of his eye, he spotted a man raising a machine pistol and ducked to the right, the stream of 9mm slugs that buzzed by his body striking a metal shield on the wall and riddling it. Camellion killed the man with one quick shot to the chest. He was, however, running out of ammo and didn't have time to reload. Neither did the Germans. With the AMP in his left hand, he shot another of the enemy in the face at point blank range, at a distance of less than six feet, and saw the Nazi's face and head explode in a cloud of skin, bone, brain, and blood. Jacob Roth grabbed his right wrist and swung the barrel of an empty Mauser machine pistol at his head. Ludwig Reitsch—so ugly that his face must have been exposed to an exploding land mine—came in from the left, holding an empty Star SMG like a baseball bat.

The Death Merchant's four men were also under personal attack. Peter Muller knocked the Magnum autopistol from Kingman's left hand. Joseph Schrubers twisted the Coonan .357 from his right hand. Then, as Muller grabbed Kingman in a choke hold from the front, Schrubers pulled a knife and rushed him from the rear. Schrubers didn't half-way succeed. Klaus Hahn, using a Heckler & Koch autoloader, put a .45 bullet into Schrubers left side, the slug knocking the dying Nazi against Otto Seubert, who was rushing at Ronald Lynch with a 10th Century pike. Hahn then had his own problems, when Julius Stumpfegger grabbed him in a rear overarm body hold, and Kurt Thayer came at him from the front, an upraised spiked mace in his right hand.

Rudolf Gertenshalger's situation was not quite so desperate. He had killed several Nazis with the last cartridges in his Mauser sub-gun, but before he could pull his pistols, two more came at him, one from the left, one from the right, both armed with bayonets.

Amid smoke and sweat, grunts and snarls of anger, the battle raged.

On the first level of the castle, the great hall resembled a battlefield. Furniture had been shattered by grenades, and bodies lay strewn like cordwood, corpses of both the Nazis, who had retreated from the walls into the keep, and the British commandoes. But the fierce desperation of the Brotherhood could not compete with the training and the discipline of the British commandoes. Steadily, the Germans were being driven back toward the steps that led to the underground level.

Jacob Roth and Ludwig Reitsch found that they had grabbed a tiger by the tail. The Death Merchant easily ducked the Mauser barrel and, with his right leg let Roth have a *Sokuto Geri* sword-foot kick, the flat of his foot shattering the Nazi's nose, teeth, and jaws. Half-choking on his own blood, Roth released his hold on Camellion's wrist and felt his face explode in excruciating pain; then the velvet blackness began creeping in, shock protecting him by pushing him into unconsciousness.

Roth's mistake didn't deter Ludwig Reitsch, who was positive he could smash in the side of Camellion's head with the Star machine gun. He swung. Camellion ducked, muttered, "Your father passed out blindfolds when you were born!" and took out the German with a left legged *Mae Geri Kekomi,* a karate front thrust kick that landed in the middle of Reitsch's solar plexus. The kick was a TNT smash that Reitsch's nervous system could not withstand. Dead from the worst kind of shock possible, he melted to the floor.

During those few seconds, the Death Merchant saw that the other four men were in trouble—*but I can't help them by getting myself wasted.* He jumped behind a column and started to reload his Backpacker Auto Mags.

Ronald Lynch, not far from Gertenshalger, didn't relish the idea of being skewered on the point of a pike. Seubert attacked with a powerful thrust, his hands in the middle of the shaft. Lynch twisted his body to the left, and four feet of the shaft streaked by him. Instantly, he struck the rusty iron shaft with the palm of his right hand to deflect the shaft from his body. The momentum of Seubert's thrust had carried him very close to Lynch, who now grabbed the Nazi's left hand with his right hand. Lynch also took a long step with his left foot toward Seubert's right, after which he reached under the shaft with his left hand and pressed his left shoulder against the upper portion of the Nazi's body. With his left hand, he grabbed Seubert's right hand where it was wrapped around the shaft, pulled the man's fingers loose and pushed with his right hand. Keeping his weight on his left foot, he used the heel of his right boot to stamp on Seubert's left instep. Seubert howled in pain. His grip relaxed on the pike. Lynch twisted the weapon from his feeble grip and kneed him viciously in the groin. A quick spin around of the pike. He thrust the point of the pike into Seubert's belly, then quickly pulled backward. As the dying Nazi started to fall, Lynch threw the pike at one of the Germans attacking Gertenshalger. A foot of the shaft buried itself in Wilhelm Zeitzler's right side. Zeitzler let out a scream, dropped the bayonet and started to wobble, the shaft bobbing up and down and from side to side with him. He fell as Christian Holtz, the other German with the bayonet, charged Gertenshalger, the long blade in his right hand raised for a downward stroke.

Gertenshalger snarled. *"Hurensohn!"* (son-of-a-bitch) and met the attack by catching Holtz's right wrist in the pocket formed by bending his own right fist forward at the wrist. He stepped forward with his right foot to protect his groin area, then struck Holtz sharply in the crook of his right elbow with his right forearm. Holtz cursed loudly when his right arm bent.

Gertenshalger brought his left hand behind the German's right forearm and underneath his own right wrist. Swiftly, he grabbed his own right forearm, brought his elbows close to his body and bent quickly from the waist, putting intense pressure on Holtz's arm. The German let out a yell, fell backward, and the bayonet slipped from his right hand. Gertenshalger kicked him squarely in the scrotum, the kill-kick eliciting a high pitched scream from Holtz, one that was quickly reduced to a pathetic blubbering. He was sinking to his knees when the BND operative kicked him in the left temple, crushed his skull and killed him.

Peter Muller, the son of an SS *Standartenfuhrer,* or Colonel, had made a lot of mistakes in his 31 years. But now he made the biggest one. He tried to choke Melvin Kingman to death. Before his fingers could begin digging into Kingman's neck, Kingman clasped his hands together, gripping the knife edge of his left hand with the fingers of his right hand and tightly wrapping the left thumb around the right thumb. He did not interlock the fingers. Kingman then drove his hands up between Müller's arms, forcing the surprised man to release his hands from the American's throat. Instantly, Kingman struck with the knife edges of his hands. He brought them down like two hammers on each side of Muller's neck, breaking the man's collarbone. Muller was as helpless as a newborn calf. Kingman— almost as fast with his feet as the Death Merchant was with his hands—executed a high, twisting *Pentjak-Silat* kick that smashed Muller in the throat. Another deadly kick went to the Nazi's solar plexus. A hidiously frozen look on his face, Muller pitched to the left and fell.

Kingman, wishing he could take time out to take a drink, stooped, picked up the two Coonan Magnum autoloaders and, with Camellion who was firing his Auto Mags, put a .357 Magnum slug into a grinning Kurt Thayer who was swinging a mace at Klaus Hahn. The powerful projectile hit Thayer in the right side, above the hip. The good-as-dead Nazi dropped the mace, quit grinning, and fell to the left.

Kingman then began triggering off shots at other Nazis across the large chamber.

Klaus Hahn made short work of Julius Stumpfegger, who held him in a rear overarm stranglehold. Hahn first loosened Stumpfegger's grip by stomping on the Nazi's left instep, the German yelling in agony as the bone shattered. Hahn raised his elbows shoulder high and at the same time lowered his body by bending his knees. He turned his body slightly to the right, and drove his right elbow into Stumpfegger's midsection. He followed through with the movement by reaching up with his right hand and grabbing Stumpfegger's right upper arm just above the elbow. Hahn gripped the agonized German's right wrist with his own left hand, then jerked, bent over, and tossed the man over his head. Stumpfegger struck the stone floor on his back, landing on the mace that Thayer had dropped, the lower part of his spine coming in contact with the two inch long studs of the weapon. There was a loud cracking sound. Stumpfegger twitched and lay still, his mouth and eyes open wide.

Hahn picked up the Mauser submachine gun, darted behind a column and thrust a full double-box magazine into the weapon. He pushed the lever on the side marked LINK and pulled back the cocking bolt. In another moment, he was firing at the Germans coming in from the west, triggering off short bursts with the Death Merchant and the three other men.

The slaughter lasted less than 120 seconds, and when the guns were finally silent, the area was strewn with dead Nazis.

The Death Merchant quickly assembled the men and pointed to the stainless steel wall to the north of the chamber. The wall, built entirely across the wide area, had only one door, one that resembled the door of a bank vault.

"What the hell is it?" Kingman was so intrigued by the wall and the door that he forgot to pull the pint from his breast pocket and finish off the blackberry brandy.

"It's a shelter of some kind," offered Lynch. "A bomb shelter."

"It's a radiation fallout shelter," Camellion said, a thin smile curling on the corners of his mouth. "MacLean and the Brotherhood are supposed to start World War III—or have you forgotten the bomb. The damn fool thought he could ride out the holocaust in that radiation shelter. If he and his sons and Lindermanns are still alive, that's where we'll find them—in that shelter."

Klaus Hahn looked south, at the barred double doors at the head of the flight of steps. "The swine upstairs can't get in," he said heavily. "If Major Simpson and his commandoes don't corner them . . ." He let his voice trail off and looked at Camellion.

"First things first," Camellion told him. "We'll worry about that problem when we come to it." He continued to study the wall, then said to Kingman, "Take out two grenades and remove the main bursting charge."

Kingman blinked. "Why?"

"You'll see."

The Death Merchant ran to the wall, removed two one-half-pound blocks of Pentolite from one of his bags and went to work, his thoughts jumped to the radio message he had received from Courtland Grojean while aboard the *HMS Taurus.*

*Is it even possible? Could a destroyer be made invisible?*

Ten minutes later he had returned to the men, all of whom were behind large stone columns. Kingman had given one of the doctored grenades to Hahn and had kept the second one for himself.

Camellion called out in a businesslike voice, "Everyone ready."

"No, but let's do it anyhow," Kingman responded.

The Death Merchant did. He pushed down on the firing button of the remote control box.

*BBBLLLAAAAMMMMMMMMMMMMMM!*

There was a blinding flash of fire, and a ten foot long section of the wall vanished. Plates of stainless steel flew inward, upward, and outward, some of them hitting the forward pillars with the force of guillotine blades. One of the columns collapsed in a cloud of dust, chunks of ancient masonry tumbling to the floor.

The Death Merchant and his four men tore across the smoky, dusty room, Kingman, Lynch, and Gertenshalger spraying the jagged metal opening with steady bursts of Mauser submachine gunfire. They reached the wall, Hahn and the Death Merchant going to the left, Kingman, Lynch, and Gertenshalger to the right. Kingman and Hahn, who were closest to the smoking edges, tossed in the doctored offensive grenades and just as quickly charged in behind them, the Death Merchant, Lynch and Gertenshalger following.

The ruse worked. Everyone in the fallout chamber had been stunned by the explosion that had destroyed part of the wall. Flying metal had killed six of the Nazis, but Sir Hugh MacLean and the others toward the rear of the chamber had not been harmed. Everyone had gotten down behind boxes, and Lindermanns, waving a Walther MPL submachine gun, had screamed; "Kill as many of them as you can. Die for the honor of the Fourth Reich and for the memory of *Der Fuhrer!*"

The two grenades had sailed through the opening into the chamber, and Rolf Koutinger had shouted, *"GRENATES!"* With everyone else he had made himself small and had gotten down behind behind a crate of canned food.

In two more seconds the grenades exploded, each one no louder than a large firecracker. With the burster (or filler) charges gone, all that had exploded were the primer and the igniter charges. By the time the Brotherhood realized how it had been cleverly tricked, it was too late: The Death Merchant and his tiny force were in the chamber, darting, weaving, and firing.

Outside the chamber there was a giant *BLAMMMM-MMMMM,* to the south, but none of the Nazis could see what had taken place. The Death Merchant and his men didn't dare turn around and look.

"KILL THEM! KILL THEM!" screamed Sir Hugh MacLean hysterically. He looked around wildly for his sons and saw John-Percy rear up, a U.S. M3 .45 caliber submachine gun in his hands. But where was Edward? Sir Hugh reached for the Heckler and Koch SMG lying on the crate in front of him, a crate of medical supplies.

Advancing and running in a zigzagging pattern, the Death Merchant and his men raked the thunderstruck Brotherhood with deadly streams of 9mm fire, all five wondering about the explosion to the south. It was either the work of Major Simpson or the Nazis.

The Death Merchant, racing up the side of the chamber to the west, spotted Sir Hugh MacLean reaching for the H & K SMG in front of him on the crate. Of all the men the Death Merchant didn't want to terminate, Sir MacLean was that man. Camellion snapped off a shot with the right Auto Mag, desperately hoping that he wouldn't miss. He didn't. The .44 JFP bullet struck the magazine of the Heckler and Koch machine gun and exploded several of the cartridges. Although he wasn't harmed, Sir MacLean yelled in fear and jumped back down behind the crate.

Both Auto Mags roared and two more Nazis went down, large holes in their chest. Spotting another man about to cut him down with a Mauser 7.63mm selective fire machine pistol, Camellion ducked to the left and fired the right AMP, his bullet catching the man in the mouth and exploding his head a second after the Nazi pulled the trigger of the Mauser, which he had set on full automatic. A stream of 7.63mm passed to the Death Merchant's left. Two were very, very close. The first one ripped through the top of the left shoulder bag and tore one of the straps. Another zipped through the left holster on his hip. A third bullet was even closer. The slug stabbed through his coveralls and cut a deep ditch in his left side before speeding on its way. Camellion felt the hot wetness flowing down his sides, past his belt and onto his hip. *DAMN!* Plus the burning pain, there was a severe stabbing agony. He knew from experience that the bullet had broken a rib.

Kingman, racing to the right, cut Rolf Koutinger in two

with a blast of slugs, the Argentine PAM SMG in the dead Nazi's hands continuing to vomit slugs as he pitched to the floor.

Kingman then barely managed to avoid a shower of projectiles from Gilbert Drummond, doing so by jerking himself back as Drummond, to his left, opened fire. One bullet tore through his Klamath cap, ripping it from his head. Another 9mm slug from Drummond's H&K MP-K burned only inches from his chest, hitting and breaking the pint bottle of brandy in Kingman's breast pocket. It was the next slug that did all the damage. The 9mm bullet struck Kingman in the left side and knocked him to the right. Pain burst in his side and spread to his chest. There was a loud roaring in his head and he felt himself falling, thinking that it was weird that he was totally unable to do anything about it. This was dying? Hell, how easy it was . . .

No sooner had Kingman hit the floor than Gilbert Drummond was a corpse, his chest ripped open by a burst of 9mm fire from Rudolf Gertenshalger.

Cecil Jimwickie and Colin Seldom didn't even get a chance to fire. Lynch, to the right and in a rage over seeing Kingman go down, killed the pilot and the copilot with one long burst of Mauser slugs. Out of ammo, Lynch then dropped down beside a crate and shoved the last Mauser magazine into the weapon. Something had better happen damned soon or they'd all be dead.

Camellion didn't have a choice when he found himself only fifteen feet from John-Percy MacLean. "God damn you!" screamed John-Percy, and started to spin to his right and swing the .45 M3 grease gun. The Auto Mag in the Death Merchant's right hand roared. The big .44 Magnum projectile stabbed John-Percy in the center of the chest, killed him instantly and knocked him back against a crate. The M3 fell from his hands, and he fell into eternity.

Other members of the Brotherhood reared up from behind crates, the Death Merchant recognizing one of them as ex-SS General Karl Gustav Lindermanns. Camellion snapped up both AMPs. He was about to pull the trigger of the right AMP when a Nazi with dark glasses—six feet in front of Lindermanns and seven feet to the SS General's right—stood up bold as winter to fire at a group of commandoes storming through the long rent in the stainless steel wall. A shave of a second before Camellion fired at Dark Glasses, Lindermanns triggered off a chain of hot

9mm projectiles that Klaus Hahn was not able to duck. The swarm of 9mm Parabellum missiles stabbed into Hahn's throat and chest, the tremendous impact spinning him around. The windmills of his mind turned to a billion splinters. Life and all reality became plastic models and the delusion ended. Stone dead, but still on his feet, Hahn began to wilt toward the floor.

*"Hoc est corpus meum!"* snarled Camellion and fired the last two cartridges from the left and the right Auto Mags. One .44 Magnum stung the Nazi with the dark glasses in the right side and flung him against a crate in back of him. General Lindermanns was ducking down, but the projectile from the left AMP still caught him, hit him in the right temple and sent the top of his skull and a goodly portion of his brain splattering all over crates, cartons, and corpses.

The Death Merchant skidded to a stop behind a crate and with hatred in his heart and speed in his hands reloaded the AMPs. He waited, listening to the sudden silence which was like steel jaws clamped around his mind. From somewhere toward the rear of the large fallout chamber, he heard a dood-dood-dood, and recognized the sound as an air pump. Cautiously, with a great deal of pain in his left side, he turned his body around and looked around the corner of the crate. Toward the front of the fallout shelter were Major Simpson and a group of commandoes. Ha! So it was Simpson and his boys who blew the doors above the steps. Thank God.

"Hold your fire!" Camellion yelled in a loud voice. "I'm Hopmeir."

"Lynch! Over here."—To Camellion's right.

"Rudolf Herman Gertenshalger!"—Farther to Camellion's right.

Major Simpson called out in his clipped voice. "Stand up. Arms above your head, laddies, until we see who you are."

Thirty-one commandoes had been killed, Simpson explained. On the first floor, all but a dozen members of the Brotherhood had been killed. They had rushed to the underground level, only to find the doors locked from the inside.

"We dropped grenades on those fellows," Simpson said lightheartedly. "We then came down here and blew the doors. Sorry we didn't get here sooner. We might have

178

been able to save that German chap. What was his name? Oh yes. Hahn."

"We did what we came to do," Camellion said evenly. The blood on his left side had trickled down his left leg and into his boot. He felt weak in his stomach.

Major Simpson glanced toward the steps. Several commandoes were carrying an unconscious Kingman to the first floor.

"At least the American is still alive," Simpson said. "We'll fly him out to the base at Greenock. They might be able to save his life."

Camellion studied Claude Simpson, who was a florid-faced man with a mustache upturned at the ends and a habit that annoyed the Death Merchant no end: His mouth was always in motion. Even when he wasn't talking, his mouth was moving, as if he were chewing on something with only his front teeth.

In spite of his misery, Camellion had the feeling of a job well done when he saw two British commandoes holding onto Sir MacLean's arms and leading the Scottish nobleman from the bomb shelter. Sir MacLean didn't blink, the expression on his face wooden, mask-like, his eyes lusterless. That is how the commandoes had found him. He had been sitting on the floor, his back against a crate, the same defunct and inanimate expression on his face. Sir MacLean's mind had snapped and he was in a catatonic trance.

Camellion and Simpson, as well as Lynch and Gertenshalger who were standing by, gave a start of pleasant surprise at the sight of four commandoes prodding two men along with EM2 automatic rifles. The two captives had their hands on their heads and were trembling so violently that they wobbled when they walked.

*The younger man was Edward MacLean.*

The scarecrow with the bald head was Bernard McHale, the MacLean retainer.

"We found these two blokes 'iding in the rear, sir," one of the commandoes reported to Major Simpson. "They was down behind a lot of oxygen cylinders."

"That's the lot of the boogers, sir," another commando said. "We searched all three rooms."

Ronald Lynch walked over and stared furiously at Edward MacLean who avoided the SIS officer's eyes. "This one is Edward MacLean," Lynch told Major Simpson. "Put him and the other man on the helicopter with Sir

MacLean. Tie their hands securely behind their backs, and that includes Sir MacLean. I don't care if he has turned into a loony."

Lynch's gaze turned to Camellion, and he held out his right hand, a smile on his grimy face. The two men shook hands.

"I'm going in the craft that carries the MacLeans," Lynch said. "I don't intend to let those two out of my sight."

"They'll be flown to London?" The Death Merchant's voice was tense.

"First to Greenock, then on to London." Lynch rubbed a hand across his jaw. "This one here"—he poked a finger at Edward MacLean—"will be only too happy to tell us where the 'item' is. We'll know before midnight." He paused. "We'll be in touch, Hopmeir."

The Death Merchant, Rudolf Gertenshalger, and Major Simpson watched Lynch move off with the commandoes and the two captives.

"Today we were lucky, Herr Hopmeir." Gertenshalger spoke to Camellion in German. "And so was Herr Lynch. Not so with Klaus and the American. Let us pray that Herr Kingman lives."

"Each day we learn a lesson, or should," Camellion replied in German. "Today we learned again what the human race has known since recorded history, that every battle must have its dead."

*And that only the Cosmic Lord of Death is always the real winner!*

Major Simpson cleared his throat and glanced from Gertenshalger to Camellion. "I'd appreciate you chaps speaking English," he said irritably. "What were the two of you discussing?"

"He asked me to give him the limits on the defining integral of the Laplace transform," Camellion said without cracking a smile. "I explained that the lower limit is zero, and that the upper limit is infinity."

Simpson frowned and shifted from his right foot to his left.

"I see. Quite." He blinked and gave Camellion his most professional look. "Now then, there is a matter I wish to discuss with you: your ordering Lieutenant Champion to use the Lynx helicopter without my authorization. I should like an explanation."

Major Simpson got what he asked for—and what he deserved. The Death Merchant's right fist came up in a lightning fast uppercut and connected solidly with the Major's jaw—much to the astonishment of Gertenshalger and the commandoes.

Out cold, Simpson sank on rubber legs to the floor.

The Death Merchant's left side exploded with excruciating pain, the sudden surge of agony generated by the sudden movement of his body. A blue-hot poked knifed stabbed across his ribs and through his chest, a torment that raced up to his brain and started drawing the curtains of darkness across his consciousness.

Sinking into unconsciousness from the pain, Camellion would have fallen if Gertenshalger hadn't caught him . . .

# Aftermath

Three days later.
The hospital at Her Majesty's Royal Naval Base,
Greenock, Scotland, United Kingdom.
15.00 hours.

For a change, Arnold Steel did not have a yellow legal pad in front of him, nor was he taking notes. Even his usual gloomy expression was gone. At times he even smiled. Then again, he had a lot to smile about.

"We received the report yesterday," he said to Richard Camellion, who was sitting up in bed, his torso bound tightly with a bandage. "The Greeks lost quite a few men, but the invasion of the island was successful. The assembled bomb was deactivated on the spot, then the cave was blown up."

Camellion nodded approvingly. "And the files found in the fallout chamber? Of course, The Company and SIS are having a field day."

Steel shifted uncomfortably on the chair. "It's all on a need-to-know basis. I don't have any information on the findings. I couldn't divulge such information anyhow. You understand, I'm sure?"

There was a moment of uneasy silence. The Death Merchant watched Steel's Adam's apple move slowly up his throat and bounce back again. "Kingman is coming along nicely," Steel said, with a burst of confidence. "I talked to Dr. Cracross before I came to your room. He said Kingman was even yawning." He paused for a moment and tapped the front of his chin with a finger. "I don't know what yawning has to do with recovery, but Dr. Cracross seems to attach some importance to it."

"Yawning can signal anything from hunger to empathy," Camellion explained. "In an audience people yawn from boredom. Sick or injured people close to death never yawn.

182

Dr. Cracross was actually saying that Kingman has passed the critical stage. Come to think of it, I doubt if Sir Mac-Lean will ever yawn."

"He won't?" Steel adjusted his glasses.

"Psychotics seldom yawn. It's an encouraging sign when they do. It indicates to psychiatrists that the nuts are in an accessible mood and haven't lost all contact with reality."

"I see."

"Did you take care of the other matter for me, in regard to Lieutenant Champion and Lieutenant Orbis?"

A resentful expression crossed Steel's face. "Yes, I attended to the matter. I talked to an official in SIS in London and he talked to Captain Merriweather. Champion and Orbis are under Merriweather's jurisdiction. He assured me no action is contemplated against them. In fact, he's going to recommend them for action above and beyond the call of duty. I can't say that the SIS or Captain Merriweather were happy about Major Simpson. I don't blame them. You did break his jaw. They feel very strongly that you should apologize to him. The SIS insisted that I report the matter to the Center back home."

The Death Merchant smiled slightly and glanced out the window. The afternoon sun was warm and bright. Birds were singing.

"Mr. G. couldn't care less," he said, "but I understand that you must make the report—no hard feelings."

Camellion himself was not the least bit interested in how Simpson or the rest of the British felt about his hitting the major. He had another matter to worry about.

*Grojean calls it Blueprint: Invisibility* . . .